The JOSLIN de LAY MYSTERIES

A PACT
WITH
DEATH

DENNIS HAMLEY

WITHDRAWN
FOR SALE

**■SCHOLASTIC**

Scholastic Children's Books,
Commonwealth House, 1–19 New Oxford Street,
London WC1A 1NU, UK
a division of Scholastic Ltd
London ~ New York ~ Toronto ~ Sydney ~ Auckland

First published in the UK by Scholastic Ltd, 1998

Copyright © Dennis Hamley, 1998

ISBN 0 590 19394 5

Typeset by Falcon Oast Graphic Art
Printed by Cox and Wyman Ltd, Reading, Berks.

10 9 8 7 6 5 4 3 2 1

All rights reserved

The right of Dennis Hamley to be identified
as the author of this work has been asserted
by him in accordance with the Copyright,
Designs and Patents Act, 1988.

This book is sold subject to the condition that it
shall not, by way of trade or otherwise, be lent,
resold, hired out, or otherwise circulated without
the publisher's prior consent in any form of
binding or cover other than that in which it is
published and without a similar condition, including
this condition, being imposed upon the
subsequent purchaser.

The Joslin de Lay Mysteries
are written in memory of
Tony Gibbs (1938–1966)
of Falmouth, Jesus College, Cambridge
and Langwith College, York,
who loved the Middle Ages
and would have been one of the greatest of
scholars and writers about them.

| WEST SUSSEX LIBRARIES | | | |
|---|---|---|---|
| Copy No. 6701928 | | Class No. | |
| Supplier PETERS | | Date Invoiced 14.1.99 | |
| 1st Loc HN | Initials JPH | 2nd Loc | Initials |
| 3rd Loc | Initials | 4th Loc | Initials |

My grateful thanks for his help on many of the
details of life in fourteenth-century London
go to John Clark, medieval curator of the
Museum of London.
The inaccuracies and misapprehensions
which remain are all down to me.

The JOURNEY of JOSLIN de LAY

**England**

King's Lynn • Norwich
Bury St. Edmunds
Cambridge • Stovenham
Cry Ashbourne
Ipswich
Oxford • Colchester
Stoke Poges • Chelmsford
Windsor • London
River Thames

Bristol

Dover

The Voyage of The Merchant of Orwell

**Wales**

**France**

Cherbourg
The Castle at Treauville
Le Cotentin

# PROLOGUE

The two great unfinished towers of Cologne Cathedral brooded over the city. Busy life teemed in the narrow streets which twisted in their shadow. Nearby, the River Rhine flowed wide and placid towards the sea many miles away. And through these streets trudged a traveller, weary and dust-stained, dreaming of that sea and wishing away those miles so he could leave this hot, noisy continent and return home at last.

But return home to what? Well, he'd lived on his wits for so long now and he was sure those wits would see him in good stead. Yes, he'd manage. Just as he always had so far. It might not take many strokes of fortune to give him an estate and riches beyond his dreams in England. Perhaps at last his luck would change. It was about time Providence remembered that once he'd helped in a great service to his King which had gone unrewarded. Besides, he'd not done badly in these years of wandering. The bundle on his back alone contained more than many men would see in a lifetime. All he had to do tonight was to find good lodging and then on the morrow seek a boat going down the Rhine to take him to the Low Countries, the North Sea and then, at long last, home. Ah, yes, life could be good after all.

Suddenly, without warning, every plan he ever had nearly went for nothing. Rough, strong hands gripped him. A foot thrust between his legs sprawled him on the ground. Everything went chokingly black; a coarse cloth closed his mouth and blanked out his eyes. He fought hopelessly for breath. *After so long, this is my end,* he thought. *Done to death by thieves.* He heard their harsh, guttural German voices. He muttered desperate prayers to a God who seemed very far away.

And then those prayers were answered. The voices stopped in mid-oath, with breathy gasps, then were silent. The gripping fingers slackened, the pressure on his back was gone. The cloth was loose; wonderingly, he pulled it from his face. Two assailants lay on the cobbles. From one, blood flowed from a rent in his tunic between his shoulders. The throat of the other was cut from ear to ear. They had died in an instant, never knowing what had happened. Over them stood a man, smiling, wiping his knife on the clothes of one of his victims.

The traveller stood dumbfounded, speechless with relief and gratitude. The new arrival spoke. "Quick," he said. "Run. Follow me. I know where we'll get good lodging."

Without question, the traveller followed. His rescuer moved with an easy lope through tortuous streets until they came to a small, timbered house by the edge of the city. All the while, the traveller's stunned brain was wrestling with a strange problem. When they stopped, he finally voiced it. "But you speak the language of someone who lives as I did, near the Thames, not the Rhine," he said.

"And why shouldn't I?" said his rescuer. "Seeing as

that's where I come from." He laughed as he ran. "I could tell you were English. That's why I helped you."

They entered the house. The hausfrau welcomed her new guest with pleasure. Soon they were sharing a meal of sausage, dark rye bread and pale wheat beer of incredible strength. They talked far into the night – until the strong wheat beer (and who could tell what else?) overcame the traveller and he passed right out. But before this oblivion he had a strange, unlooked for feeling of power. Together, thought the rescued traveller, we can do anything.

But his rescuer was thinking something different. Has my salvation been delivered into my hands? I must play with cunning to make it happen and not count the cost at the end.

Next morning dawned and the traveller struggled awake with a splitting headache. He refused food and took only a little water, half drunk, half splashed over his face. His rescuer waited patiently. The traveller's reeling mind remembered yesterday's events with difficulty. Yes, his life had so very nearly ended. He would give his rescuer anything in his gratitude. Yes, anything.

The rescuer seemed to sense his thoughts. "Perhaps you already have," he said.

What had happened last night? With a shock, the traveller realized he could not recall a thing. He remembered the sausage, the rye bread, his first full stein of that head-bursting wheaten beer. But after that – nothing. But he'd drunk his fill before – yes, and more – and never gone spark out like that. Was there a strange substance made by some apothecary in that beer? What had he and his rescuer talked about? How long had he stayed there before he had struggled – or been taken – to his bed?

The rescuer smiled. "You'll come with me on the little errand I mentioned last night – and then I'll take you to the river and help you find a boat to take you down the Rhine," he said.

"Errand? What errand?"

"It's nothing. Don't you remember? I have a document of law that I need witnessing. I just want you to come with me to a public notary. I'll sign, you'll sign, he'll fix his seal. It will be legal all over Christendom."

"What is it?"

"Nothing. Here, you can see it if you like."

From inside his grey tunic he took a roll of parchment and spread it open. It was freshly written in a fair hand – but in Latin.

"I don't understand it. Apart from the Mass, I have no Latin," said the traveller.

"It's no matter," said his rescuer. "Latin is the language of the law and it's understood in Germany as much as in England."

"But I don't know what it says."

"It's merely my claim to what I'm owed when I go home. I did you good service – you wouldn't refuse to write your name on it, would you?"

The traveller felt ashamed. "Of course not," he said.

Soon he was ready to go. They paid the hausfrau and left.

First, the rescuer led the traveller to a tall, narrow, timbered building. They struggled up a steep staircase to the dark room of the public notary. The rescuer handed him the paper. The old man in a dusty black cloak read it gravely, looked at both men and spoke in German.

"What is he saying?" asked the traveller.

"He wants to be sure you understand what is written there."

"Tell him I do."

The rescuer spoke in German himself. The notary nodded, then watched them as they signed before signing himself and sealing it with his own seal and that of the city of Cologne. Then he bowed stiffly and the transaction was over. The rescuer placed the paper inside his cloak and they left the high, rickety building.

Outside, the traveller breathed the open air deeply. "Now you said you would go with me to the river and find a boat which will take me nearer the sea," he said. "Will you be sailing with me?"

"Not I," said the rescuer. "There are more places for me to go before I touch England's shores again."

It was not long before the traveller found a place on a barge headed for the Low Countries. Before it cast off, the rescuer spoke.

"I wish you good fortune," he said. "By the way, I have one last transaction. Last night you spoke of a brother and his new wife who you looked forward so much to seeing again."

"Did I?"

"You did indeed. I have a gift for them. For them, mind you, and nobody else. If it goes to another, then our friendship is broken."

In his bundle of possessions was a package wrapped in cloth. The rescuer handed it over. "Take it. They will enjoy it. And as they do, remember me, our night spent talking and our hopes and fears for our new lives."

The traveller took it, felt it, weighed it in his hand. Was it a flagon? Was it full of liquid?

"Is this wine?" he asked. "Good Rhenish, perhaps?"

"It is for them to find out." The rescuer smiled. "We say farewell here. But we'll meet again, never fear."

So the traveller clasped hands with his rescuer and went on his way, rejoicing that the world still contained men of such honour and bravery as he who had saved him from miserable death on a foreign street corner miles from home.

And the rescuer watched the barge edging its way down the river and laughed inwardly. Perhaps it would have been better for you if the robbers had ended your life last night. You don't know that I recognized you weeks ago and followed you for many days and many miles. We were near neighbours once, but you've forgotten. If you once did me the worst turn of my life, Providence has made it so you'll do me the best. You've just met someone who's become a true child of Satan, who's been made *immortal* by the wonderful agency of the Devil himself, who's been assured that he can never die of the ills ordinary men fall victim to. We'll soon see what you make of that.

The traveller stood on the deck of the boat as it forged down the Rhine through Germany and towards the Low Countries. He was so happy. Not too long now and he'd be treading on English soil, ready to make a new life for himself among his own people. And he had survived only because of his new friend. What a stroke of Providence that meeting was! Perhaps at last his luck was changing. Should he have offered some greater reward than gratitude and a mere signature? No, his rescuer seemed quite content with what he'd got. And he'd even found a little gift to offer the traveller's only family left alive in England. He shook the leather bag with a flagon inside. Wine. What thoughtfulness. No, he wouldn't drink it himself.

He'd make sure he saw his brother and wife as soon as maybe.

He thought affectionately about his rescuer, this man to whom he owed everything. But already his face had grown dim. The traveller could not remember a single detail; with a shock he realized he wouldn't recognize him if he were to meet him in the street. Here was a mystery. And as for a name. . .

The deep, dark water of the ever-widening Rhine, sparkling in the hot sun of high summer, thrummed and foamed under the boat's prow. The traveller, even though his unknown rescuer's face had faded from his mind, hugged himself with excitement as the sea came nearer, and across it England and fortune.

The tight square mile of London city was bounded by the Tower in the east and the River Fleet in the west. The Romans had been and gone a thousand years before, but the city wall they had left still curled round it, though nothing could stop the hot and noisy life inside from bursting through the gates and spreading into the fields beyond.

On a dark night in late September, 1368, three months after the traveller was saved from murder in the streets of Cologne, it looked as though a couple were trying to add to this escape beyond. The curfew had long gone; it was two hours after midnight when a watchman on Ludgate saw a tiny light approaching along Bowyer's Row towards him. Only he was on duty. Though the watch was twelve strong, the others were inside, playing games of hazard. And why not? England was as much at peace as was ever likely. The French would not come knocking at the gates with an invading army demanding reparation for their prisoner-King, Jean, captured at Poitiers and dead before he saw his homeland again. The Scots would not have left their wild borders to stream through England and set up siege outside the city. No dissident baron would have raised a rebellion to push his doubtful claim to the throne. Oppressed peasants, would not have decided enough was enough and risen in revolt – at least, not yet. So there was no need for twelve – or twenty-four or forty-eight – to keep a look-out from the gate which watched over Fleet Street and the road along the Thames from the King's city of Westminster. Alfred of Ware, veteran soldier who'd volunteered for the watch because old habits died hard, was used to being on his own in the dark.

At least whoever approached him carried a light. Alfred now had a problem – should he unlock the little door set in the great gate and let him through on his way westwards across the Fleet bridge?

He shone his own lantern out. There were not one but two people coming near. They wore cloaks. Afterwards, Alfred could not say what made him so sure that these people in long cloaks like monks were *staggering*. Just as he could never say why he was so sure they were not monks.

He ran down the steps to the street. London's night noises were quieter now. This was too late for anyone to pass under Ludgate. If he couldn't recognize them or if they carried weapons, they'd be in the lock-up and there was a good force of men at hand to call to stop them causing trouble. He waved his lantern and called out.

"Who are you? Where are you going?"

Afterwards he was asked to describe what he saw. He never could – not so his questioner was any nearer knowing who it was. Underneath the hood of the taller figure with the lantern was a face with nose, eyes and mouth like many another but – how could he say? –

forgettable, anonymous, never to be remembered. Yet it made him shiver with an obscure fright. It was almost as if God said, "You are never to recall this face." But God would never say such a thing of one of His creatures, surely? No, but another, whose name he would not speak so late at night, might. Alfred was brave, survivor of many battles, well used to facing those who willed his death, but this bland, level gaze somehow scared him more than Frenchman or Scot ever had.

"It's nothing, friend," said this person in a low voice which could have been a man's or a woman's. "My cousin is visiting the city. He comes from Barnet, deep in the country, so the city's ways are a shock to him. He drank too much, however hard I tried to stop him. So I'm guiding him back to his lodgings in a tavern in Fleet Street."

"How do I know that's true?" asked Alfred suspiciously.

"Because in an hour I'll be back here without him," was the reply.

"Why doesn't he speak for himself?"

"London ale's too strong and the gin's too fiery. He's dead drunk. I have to prop him up to make him move at all."

Alfred shone his lantern in the cousin's face. Younger, finer features, this time a face he would never forget – why, if the stranger had not said "he" and "him" Alfred might have thought this was a female face. Well, if there was a bit of you-know-what going on, who was he to interfere? But those *eyes* – so big, open in a fixed, unblinking stare. That gaping mouth, lolling tongue. The way the head dropped forward. Even by his weak lanternlight he saw the face was so *pale*. . .

He shivered, recalling sights best forgotten in battles

years ago. *This man was dead.* He should do something, call for help. Then he saw the stranger's eyes, staring, boring into him. They chilled his soul. His voice froze; his tongue wouldn't work through terror.

Suddenly he wished this pair far away. Alfred dared not even try to search this man for a weapon. When he found his voice again, there was only one thing he could say. "Surely you know you can't go through the gate. Not even the little postern door will be unlocked until sunrise," he said. "Get your cousin to bed in your own house, he needs it." *I'm a coward for saying this, I know. But what else can I do?* Alfred knew the shame he'd feel later. But he'd have to live with it.

"You'd see me here again within the hour, I promise," said the cloaked stranger. "I live in Westcheap."

"I won't let you through. Get back where you came from or I'll have the whole of the watch out," said Alfred, with sudden new spirit. "We'll see how you fare against them."

"This is poor service to a tired man," said the stranger. But he did not argue and Alfred felt a little better.

Soon the anonymous pair were going back along Bowyer's Row. The watchman kept them in sight for as long as he could as they approached the dark shadow of the spire of St Paul's reaching high into the sky. To get back to Westcheap they'd turn left into Sporeneere's Lane, then along Paternoster Row. He watched for their little light to disappear as they left Bowyer's Row where it met Sporeneere's Lane.

But the pair made no left turn. Instead, they went right. This was strange. These were no monks, making for the Convent of the Blackfriars. Nor were they nobles, to lodge with the Earl of Salisbury or Lord Ross in Castle Baynard. No, all they could do was go along

Sporeneere's Lane until they reached the river and East Watergate. But why? Alfred felt another shiver of alarm. Something about that encounter was lodged deep in his mind but he didn't want to admit it aloud because he'd never sleep again if he did.

Alfred was right. The stranger had no intention of calling at any religious or noble house on the way. The lantern was doused; they passed unseen, unheard. Soon the cold night breeze off the river brushed the leader's face. They skirted East Watergate to face the wide Thames itself. Now the leader spoke; his companion did not answer.

"Father Thames will give you cheaper lodgings than any Fleet Street tavern, I think. It's a pity I couldn't put you there further upstream where the tide's weaker and you might have rotted unknown on the river bed. But no matter. I should have remembered how stubborn night watchmen can be. Still, you'll probably drift out to sea now and that will be an end of you."

A push, a splash in the black water and the companion was gone.

Well, the pair were at least gone and out of his sight so no more of his business. Alfred sighed with relief.

But he would have been troubled had he seen the figure cross the end of Bowyer's Row again, then keep going along Sporeneere's Lane, along Paternoster Row as he had said – but after that through Westcheap without stopping, left again up Milk Street making for Cripplegate, where he finally disappeared in the narrow crowded lanes in the shadow of the north wall, to a house where there was a scrabble of rats, a fearful smell and, day and night, smoke climbing from the roof from a fire which never seemed to be extinguished.

Alfred was troubled enough as it was. He'd fought in terrible wars and had to look after himself in this violent city. He'd killed men – yes, and women, too – and faced death himself many times. The more he thought, the more he was sure. The face of the cousin, the pallor, the staring eyes, the lolling tongue, the way it dropped forward – if he could have pulled that cloak down a little he would have been sure. *That was a dead face, a murdered face, the face of one whose throat had been cut from ear to ear. And he should, he should, he should have stopped that man.* Had he, for the first time in his life that he could remember, failed in his duty?

But if he were to worry about every dead body which was taken down to the Thames and thrown in with its throat cut he'd never have a moment's peace. Too much curiosity and he might find his own throat slashed and him floating out to sea as well.

Joslin de Lay, the sturdy piebald horse that had brought Robin to Stovenham ambling slowly beneath him, sniffed the morning air and wished he could be happier. Alys rode by his side, head down, lost in thoughts Joslin knew would not be joyous. This was the second day of their journey from Stovenham to London and Randolf Waygoode, the master painter. For Alys it would be a bitter homecoming, for Joslin merely a stage on a long journey.

Grief and loss had not deserted Alys. "I'm poor company, Joslin," she had said when he tried to talk to her as Stovenham disappeared behind them. No wonder: her beloved Robin fresh buried in the churchyard and visions of his murder repeated over and over again in her mind, a bright sword flashing, his body pierced, his face crumpling and him with it, no more lovely colours, places, faces to grow in paint under his busy, delicate hands. And no husband now for Alys – or ever one she could love like she had Robin. Joslin knew that. He cast a sideways look at her fair head uncovered in the bright morning light, her beautiful sad face. He felt his own stab of grief. Robin was his friend as well; in a few days he had become the staunchest he could have imagined. At any other time, though, Joslin and Alys might have. . .

No. He must put that right out of his mind. He had not been in England a fortnight, yet already another girl pined alone in a castle for him. Would he ever see Gyll again?

Never. He had too far to go. He was Alys's protector on this journey to London. As soon as she was safe with Randolf, master painter of Cripplegate, he would be gone, travelling west to Wales, "the blessed Saint Ursu. . ." and the mystery of his mother. The locket given him by his dying father was a comforting weight at his neck, reminding him of his purpose. The murders in Stovenham had held him up long enough; he had his own mystery to solve.

Yesterday they had followed the road south and west through Suffolk. September was nearly gone. The weather had cleared again: the sun had returned and autumn with it. The air was filled with its delicate scents, leaves were starting to yellow, the way was littered with horse chestnuts shiny and brown where they fell and their shells split open. At any other time Joslin would have taken his harp, sat under a tree and sung songs of praise to this most beautiful season.

Still, it was good to ride through England and not feel hunted. They had stopped for the first night in Colchester. A smart and well-found tavern was happy to

14

take them. They still had money for their lodging, but when the landlord saw Joslin's harp he begged him to give an evening's entertainment. Minstrels were not so common that a chance like this could be passed up. So Joslin did what he had hoped he would do all across England: he sang and played, songs and ballads for the townsfolk, hour after hour, until he had paid for their lodging five times over and put coins for the journey in his money-belt.

Next morning they left early, on the best of terms with the people of Colchester, and carried on through Essex, towards Chelmsford where their next night would be spent.

Now, as their horses ambled along, Alys spoke. Joslin was quite surprised; he jerked quickly out of dreams of Wales, his mother and his murdered father. "Joslin, have you ever been to a place like London?"

"No," Joslin answered. It was true, he could remember nothing except the castle in the Cotentin and the French countryside round about where he had grown up.

"People up from the country sometimes can't take in what they see," said Alys. "I've lived in London all my life, but it still holds terrors. But it's wonderful, too. So many thousand souls squashed into the streets, noise, smells, colours, how *busy* everyone is. You'll love it, Joslin, I know you will. And there are rich pickings for a good minstrel."

"I can't stay a moment longer than I have to," Joslin replied. Did he notice the tiniest flash of regret in her face at that?

"But there are things you have to know," she went on. "You must be careful. It's a dangerous place. Murderers don't need long revenges to use their knives in those dark, narrow lanes. And the plague's never far away where so many are huddled together. It came back this year and took the young this time, not the old."

Joslin shivered. He was not born when the plague first rent Europe in half but he knew it sometimes revisited. Its appalling fingers had never reached into the castle in the Cotentin, but he had seen its efforts in the villages – corpses carried away for quick burial and folk's grief, terror and wild railing against God at losing whole families in one night. Besides, only a few days ago, he had seen in what fear the people of Stovenham held the deserted, deathly plague village of Cry Ashbourne.

"Then I won't come inside the city gates," he said. "I'll just leave you outside and go."

Alys leant across and touched his arm. "Don't worry," she said. "You must spend a night with us at least and eat at Randolf's table before your journey. Randolf will want to meet you and thank you."

*More likely scream with hatred for bringing such terrible sorrow*, thought Joslin. "Randolf doesn't know Robin's dead," he said aloud. "It will be a fearful shock. What about Robin's parents? Who'll tell them?"

"Robin's parents are long dead," Alys replied. "Randolf became his guardian and then took him as an apprentice."

"What about yours?" asked Joslin.

"Dead as well. I'm also Randolf's ward and I live in his household waiting for marriage or a place in the house of a great lady."

"So you both lived in Randolf's household," said Joslin. *How terrible the next months are going to be for you*, he thought but did not say. Alys would have worked that out for herself.

"Randolf's a rich man," she answered almost as if she were apologizing for the fact. "He's got a lot of mouths to feed. He's well known as a painter. He paints for the King. Because of that, people from all over the city and the rest of the land want his work."

"Even in Stovenham," Joslin said grimly and at once wished he hadn't. Why keep *reminding* her? She seemed not to have heard. They were passing through a village with a church of flint standing on a little rise.

"There could be paintings by Randolf in there," she said.

"Would Randolf come so far to such a small place?" said Joslin.

"He'd never trust an apprentice," Alys replied. Then she stopped and tears coursed down her face. Joslin could have bitten his tongue off for the thoughts his words had started in her. When she could speak again, Alys murmured, "Robin was different. To Randolf, Robin was the best apprentice of all, a finer painter already than he was, who'd take over the workshop one day and make it even richer and more famous."

Joslin said something which had been on his mind a lot. "Our news will be a terrible shock. If only we could have sent someone on ahead to break it before we arrive."

"I know," said Alys. "But who?"

There was no talking now. The journey was long: the day wore on. They spurred their horses into a canter to reach Chelmsford by nightfall.

A second night passed in a well-found tavern where Joslin sang for their supper and was cheered to the echo. Joslin was thinking he could take to the life of the travelling minstrel with no trouble. He remembered John Hammond on the quayside at Ipswich. "*Follow the sun*

17

*and sing your way to Wales.*" Yes, he'd do just that.

Next day, before the eighth hour, they were on their way. They left Chelmsford at a brisk canter; there was still far to go to be sure of reaching London the next day with their terrible news. Several miles passed before they let the horses rest and graze. The good weather was holding so they sat under a tree and talked as the horses munched contentedly. Alys started almost where she had left off yesterday.

"Randolf's wife's name is Lettice. They have no children."

*That's why he thinks so much about his wards,* thought Joslin, but this time said nothing.

"They have two servants for the house. Randolf employs three labourers for the workshop and two ostlers for the stables. There are four other apprentices as well. Few craftsmen in any trade have so many. They are Alexander, John, William and Hugh. They're good people. But Hugh. . ." her voice changed. "I stay clear of Hugh."

"Why's that?" asked Joslin.

She did not answer and Joslin at once had a good idea of why. There had been a touch of jealousy there.

"So many apprentices," Alys continued. "It shows how good a painter Randolf is."

"You could be an apprentice," said Joslin. "You're a better painter than any of them." He knew this; he had seen her at work on the Doom.

"*Never* tell anyone that," she cried in alarm. "If we thought we'd ever see you again we wouldn't have told you."

They stopped at High Ongar near midday and bought bread, cheese and ale at a little tavern by the wayside. The weather would soon break; the sun was gone and clouds covered the sky. Joslin shivered as they set off again across the North Weald and wished he had taken his father's cloak out of the roll of clothes slung at his saddle.

The way became rougher. By mid-afternoon they were following the road through the King's forest by Epping. Joslin shivered in fright. For the first time on this journey he felt as he had on those first fearful miles away from *The Merchant of Orwell* which ended in Cry Ashbourne. This forest was a place of shadow and hiding. Twisted branches and gnarled trunks provided cover for robbers and worse. After all, to Joslin from the Cotentin this was still enemy country. A beautiful girl and a frightened man supposed to protect her would be rich prize and easy prey. He hadn't escaped murder to come to that.

"We should have gone another way," he whispered. "This is no place for us."

Until now he had forgotten that strange feeling as they left the church in Stovenham for the last time, after he had seen the Devil's work on the Doom and a third, unseen traveller had seemed to leave with them. Now he felt it like a face looking over his shoulder. He shivered.

But when, as evening came, they arrived safely in the little town of Epping, he was mightily relieved and pleased also when they found another friendly tavern in which to stay the night.

Next morning was dull, grey, cold, with a fine drizzle. Both Alys and Joslin wrapped themselves in cloaks for the final stretch, the long slope down to the Thames. Now they were near their journey's end, Joslin had few words to say. The thought oppressed him that he was soon to be in the foremost city of an enemy land – and a plague city at that, where the dead might show themselves in different guises from those he had seen already. By early afternoon, with the drizzle well set in and damp cloth clammy on their bodies, they were crossing Hackney Marshes, the horses picking their way delicately across narrow tracks.

Yet, even though the clouds were low and the sky dark, Joslin saw a flash of gold high in the air yet miles in front of them.

"What's that?" he asked.

"The golden orb and cross at the very top of St Paul's tower. Every traveller coming back to London sees it from far away and then knows home is near," Alys replied.

Soon they were crossing the fields of Shoreditch, with the Holy Well Priory on their left. Finally, they rode down Old Street, where houses either side showed London was beginning, then left down White Cross Street, past the city's outer boundary, to Cripplegate itself. By the gate was the church of St Giles without Cripplegate.

"The painters' church," said Alys. "Randolf will be buried here one day like everyone in the Painters' Gild." She was about to cry again. "Robin should have been," she sniffed.

Then she fought back the tears and faced the great gate. Already Joslin felt suffocated by the busy street leading up to it. The great bulk was awesome to look at, larger than any castle gatehouse, with windows of houses set in its upper storeys staring down coldly, without welcome. On either side of Cripplegate was the high, wide, patched up wall of brick and stone which had marked London's bounds ever since the Romans built it unimaginably long before. He gulped at the sight and followed Alys underneath.

Now the press and jostle of people nearly brought him off his horse, and the noise assailed his ears. The street seemed a trackway on the floors of hell. Upper floors of timbered houses hung over him like the sides of an abyss while the poles bearing signs of shops and trades reached out like branches of weird trees in a petrified forest. The horses' hooves moved through running filth best not thought about.

He gasped and fought for breath. As he followed Alys he felt as though he were being swallowed up and it would be more than just one night before he would be spat out again.

The body had floated downstream unnoticed in the bustle of ships loading and unloading. It had been carried past Blackfriars Quay, East Watergate, Fishwharf, Queenhithe, Winewharf and Haywharf, until at Oystergate it fetched up against London Bridge and stayed there, held by the current, bumping and swaying gently against a stone pile, waiting for someone to notice it and call the alarm so that the terrible secrets it bore could be seen by everyone.

They pushed through throngs of beggars, hawkers and running children. In Silver Street, Alys stopped outside a very large house. Its upper storeys stood out over Joslin's head, ending only a few feet from the jutting upper floors of the house opposite. The many-paned windows were large, the half-timbered walls imposing. "I house a man of substance," they seemed to say. "So be careful."

Alys dismounted. So did Joslin – and had the feeling that never seemed to leave him in England. He was being watched. He looked round furtively. No eyes in all that crowd seemed to be looking at him. Even the one man standing motionless in all that hurrying, whose face was anonymous, whose clothes were unremarkable, turned his face away. Alys led her horse under the main archway into a courtyard. Joslin followed. Once inside, the noise of the street was muted. Joslin felt quiet and at peace. Two ostlers took the horses. "Welcome, Mistress Alys," said one. The other looked Joslin up and down with hostile eyes. Neither asked after Robin. Plainly, they felt it was not their place to.

He looked round. Behind him, next to the archway, must be the workshop. He heard voices, sounds of activity. In front was the great hall. From it came a woman of, he judged, near fifty, a young maid with her. She saw Alys. Her face lit up – but only for a second.

"Where's Robin?" she said.

"Oh, Mistress Lettice!" Alys replied. "Robin is dead. I must speak to Randolf and the whole household."

Lettice's face turned pale. The maid burst out in a howl of grief. Lettice seemed to notice Joslin for the first time. Like the ostlers, her look was hostile.

"Joslin must speak as well," said Alys. "He was Robin's friend."

"Randolf shall hear this first," Lettice cried. "Fetch him." The maid turned and ran. Once she was gone, Lettice dissolved into tears of her own. Alys reached out and embraced her.

Joslin stood alone, oppressed by the grief he brought to this house.

A tall, strongly-built man with a forked beard, wearing a smock smudged with many colours, emerged from the workshops. The maid fearfully followed him. Behind him were four youths, no older than Joslin. Last of all came three men, rougher-looking than the apprentices. Two were older, the third, fair-haired with a vacant look on his face, was no older than Joslin. The tall bearded man, Joslin knew, must be Randolf. His face was grim. Joslin could not help but notice his long, sensitive fingers – like his own. Painter's fingers as well as minstrel's.

Randolf did not wait to be told the news himself. "Into the hall," he shouted. "The whole household, into the hall. At once."

\* \* \*

*Among the hurrying crowds in Silver Street as Joslin and Alys entered, one person stayed still, unobtrusive. He had waited a long time – and for more days than one, watching patiently.*

*At last he had seen what he wanted – and with it much food for thought. "So the fair-haired boy I was told to expect is not with her," he mused. "Is he dead? Has she rejected him for another? Have I been misled? Here's a new one. His hair is black, his wiry foreign-looking face holds too much inquisitiveness for my liking. Why is there a harp on his back? This may alter everything. I must find out quickly – and think even more quickly."*

*He sidled unobserved out of Silver Street, into a narrow alley which led behind and between houses, all the way to Babe Lane and then the city wall. But he did not go much further. For here he would wait until he could find out all the information he wanted.*

Soon everybody was gathered in the high-ceilinged hall: apprentices, house-servants, ostlers, labourers. Joslin stood behind Alys, trying not to be noticed. But he wilted under the strange looks cast at him. Randolf ignored him; however curious he might be about this stranger here instead of his dear Robin, his care now was for Alys. The apprentices stood together awkwardly. Joslin recalled their names. William, Alexander, John, Hugh. And Alys did not like Hugh.

He tried to work out which Hugh might be. One had a thatch of red hair and was thin, tall and gangling. Another was of medium height, sturdy, strong, with brown hair. A third had long, fair hair. He also was tall, but languidly graceful in the way he moved. The fourth was small, dark, sallow-complexioned with black hair. His eyes darted from one person to another. When they fixed on Joslin, they flashed suspicion.

Joslin remembered Alys's saying she kept out of his way and he knew why at once. *That*, he said to himself, *is Hugh*.

Everybody fell deathly quiet as Alys, quickly and in a low voice, told of the events in Stovenham. When she finished, there was silence except for more quiet tears from Lettice and her maidservants. But Joslin felt anger course through the air.

Randolf spoke. "Thank you, Alys. So we know that Robin died at the hands of an evil man and that by dying he paid a high price for being too good at his craft. But I don't understand *how* he was enmeshed in such evil. Surely only witchcraft could lead him into such straits." His eyes narrowed. "Your companion hasn't spoken yet."

"This is dear Joslin," Alys began. "He has. . ."

"Let him speak for himself," Randolf commanded. There was authority in his voice, such as Joslin knew from the Count, from Roger de Noville, from the Earl's nephew Stephen. Haltingly, for he had no idea how his words would be taken, he started. He knew that the moment they recognized his voice's French lilt, suspicions would rise. London was always full of foreigners, but in these strange times some new voices were more disturbing than others. But he struggled through. He told them about his father's murder, the flight to Cherbourg, the voyage to Suffolk, the start of his quest to Wales, the dreadful night at Cry Ashbourne with the plague dead, sanctuary in St Joseph's church, then the web of murder and revenge which nearly snuffed him out before his quest had started. He said as little as he need of Gyll. But he could feel in the air that some there saw more in that than he had said, that womenfolk were thinking, *Poor man, separated from his love*, while some menfolk said to themselves, *He's a Frenchman. No woman is safe.*

But he was listened to respectfully none the less; one glance from Randolf saw to that. When he came to the end with Robin's death, he felt the silence. It oppressed him; he had to fill it with words. "I know the grief you feel over Robin because you knew him all his life; he was of this household and you loved him. I am a stranger and knew him but a few days. But I tell you this – in those few days Robin came to mean much to me. This was the worst time of my life and he was my firmest friend, save Alys, in a new and strange land. My sorrow may not have the depth of years as yours but it pierces me just as keenly."

He said no more about Alys. But she spoke herself. "If Joslin hadn't been with me these last days, I would have died as well. He's my dear friend and I want him to be yours also."

Once again there was silence in the hall. Then Randolf stepped forward. The thunder on his face had cleared. Joslin knew that he had made up his mind and that the others would take their cue from him.

"Joslin de Lay, welcome to my house. We owe you thanks. Stay here as long as you like. When you leave, go in peace with my blessing." He smiled. "And I hope you'll give us a song after supper."

There was a murmur of agreement. But Joslin was sharp-eared and sharp-eyed. He had been studying the assembly as Randolf spoke and he knew that perhaps not everyone there shared his goodwill. He saw suspicion in the eyes of the apprentice he thought was Hugh. And of the three labourers at the back, only two were still there.

Joslin was shown a bed made up for him with the apprentices above the workshop. He stowed his clothes, made sure his body-belt and locket were safe – and then, on an impulse, placed his father's dagger under the mattress where he could reach it in a trice, just in case. This seemed a friendly house, but he knew better by now than to assume anything. Then he swilled off the dust of the journey in cool water brought in a pitcher by a maidservant and donned – at Randolf's special request – his minstrel's tunic. Before he took his harp and went downstairs, he looked round the room, while it was still empty. He examined the pallets and straw mattresses of the apprentices. He sought clues as to which apprentice was which, whether how they made their beds or left their gear showed what manner of youth each one was. But, no. Randolf ran his apprentices like a castle garrison. The room was as neat, orderly and uniform as the soldiers' quarters in the Count's castle at Treauville. He knew no more about the apprentices – but quite a lot about Randolf.

In the far corner a bed stood bare, with no blanket, no small box of possessions. It must have been Robin's. Was there a meaning, he wondered, in the fact that he had not been given Robin's old mattress but a new one placed as far away at the end of the room as possible?

At supper, with tapers burning in the darkening hall and the wooden beams of the ceiling lost in shadow, Joslin was given a seat at the long table opposite Alys. He felt pleased about this; Randolf accepted him for Alys's sake. But the apprentices all sat at the far end of the table. He wondered if Robin used to sit with them or whether, as future son-in-law, he sat at the top of the table.

He looked at them. The ginger one, the burly one and the fair, languid one were deep in conversation. The dark one took no part but kept his glittering eyes fixed on Joslin. Those eyes worried him; when Dame Lettice tried to ask questions about France his answers were short and distracted. He felt there might be trouble brewing. Perhaps the shorter his stay under Randolf's roof the better. Suddenly his minstrel's tunic looked garish, like a clown's in that sober place.

The supper was everything Joslin expected in the household of a master craftsman of a foremost Gild in the City of London – oysters and salmon from the Thames, geese and a side of beef, fruit and sauces with subtle tastes which showed he was in a great seaport where goods were landed from far away. To drink there was ale, which he expected in England, and wine, which he had not tasted since he left France. He soon forgot his journey. He ate and drank ravenously. He would not have too many feasts like this on the long miles to Wales.

Yet all the while he watched. Yes, this was Randolf's little kingdom. He sat at the top of the table and familiar mastery wrapped round his head like a halo. Every voice, look, movement seemed made in deference to him. There was not a single jarring note – except, for Joslin, the jealous eyes of the apprentice he thought was Hugh.

Supper was over. Randolf called Joslin to his right hand. "Play and sing for us, Joslin," he commanded.

At once, the tunic was no clown's costume but his natural clothing. He tuned his harp and said, "What shall I play?"

"The songs you learnt at home," said Randolf.

Now Joslin felt as much in his element as a salmon in the Thames.

He played and sang, of Roland and how he beat off the Saracens at the siege of Milan, the chivalrous tale of Floris and Blanchefleur and the magical story of Huon of Bordeaux. He felt on his tongue the French words which rolled round his throat like a great comforter, yet reminded him of his old life and his murdered father. After his third ballad he stopped. He could feel the tears welling behind his eyes.

"Take a moment, Joslin," said Randolf. "You've your own sadness to bear as well as sharing ours, and a long journey to make before it's assuaged. We understand that."

Joslin looked at him gratefully.

"You sang a song of Bordeaux," said Randolf. "So take a cup of Bordeaux wine." He handed the drink to Joslin who swallowed a mouthful, turned back to his harp and sang again – this time the mournful *Lay le Freine* – Song of the Ash Tree – in which Queen Beatrice, wife of King Oryens of Brittany, gave birth to twin girls. But the jealous King, sure one of the girls was not his, had them separated at birth and one farmed out to a peasant. When she grew up, Le Freine found her sister and they achieved happy marriages with good men. As he sang of the longed-for reuniting at the end, Joslin thought of his longed-for reuniting with his lost mother – and then he remembered Gyll, vivid snatches of heart-stopping moments, and wondered if there would be any reuniting there as well. Then Fleur, his first love, lost to him now for ever in France. There could never be reuniting there. And – he realized as if a door was closing in his mind – he no longer wanted it.

He looked out over his audience. Randolf and Lettice sat together, their faces relaxed and gently consoled by sweet stories and harmonious music. He saw Alys's expression – a deep, terrible yearning far beyond sorrow. *Her bad times have not even started*, he thought grimly.

Then he looked further, to where the apprentices sat in a little knot in the corner. On their faces were looks he thought he understood – not jealousy or envy but a wish to match him, as if saying, "We can't sing or play but come in our workshop and you'll see what we *can* achieve, which you'd never come near in a hundred years."

*Lay le Freine* was over. The last clappings of appreciative hands and murmurs of delight had died away. Randolf rose. "Joslin, we are in your debt for the best evening in this house that I can remember despite the grief that caused it. You'll stay and share what we have to offer for as long as you like before you set off again on your way."

"Thank you," murmured Joslin as Randolf called for prayers for the whole household before they departed to bed. Joslin stood, head down and eyes closed, as Randolf's deep voice pronounced blessings.

Outside, damp air struck chill as Joslin followed the apprentices across the darkened courtyard, with the red-haired apprentice leading the way holding a dim lantern. He did not know that anyone walked beside him until a hoarse voice whispered almost in his ear.

"You may be Randolf's new little pet and you may have blinded everybody with your foreign French ways but you don't fool *me*."

He could not see the mouth from which the words came but he had a feeling he knew whose it might be.

"I know you and what you're doing. Fishing in Robin's pond while better men stand on the bank deprived of their rights. Well, I won't have it. You get on your way out of here or take the consequences."

"Consequences?" said Joslin quietly.

"Yes, *consequences*. I've a knife as sharp as anyone's. I know how to drop a body so no one will find it – or know it again if they do."

"But I. . ." began Joslin – and then, as light from the ginger youth's lantern reflecting off the walls enabled him to see, he realized nobody was next to him now. He was the last in the little troop of five who clattered up the steps.

The red-haired apprentice placed the lantern in the middle of the floor and lit two others from it. Now a shifting, smoky light played round the room and Joslin could see faces. The red-haired apprentice came to him and spoke.

"Welcome, Joslin, to our humble place in Randolf's world. I'm William."

"I-I'm John," slightly stuttered the stocky, burly apprentice.

"I am Alexander," drawled the fair, languid one.

Joslin, in the English way, shook hands gravely with all three.

"And I am Hugh," the fourth said, but made no move to shake hands. Joslin peered at him in the half-light. *Was I right?* he thought.

"And don't you forget it," Hugh continued. Was that a threat even now, in front of the others who seemed friendly enough? Or a poor attempt at a joke? The others seemed to think so. "L-little chance he has of doing that," John said, laughing. "No one could f-forget a stunted ch-changeling runt like you, Hugh."

Was *that* a joke? It sounded more like an insult – yet it was said with a smile in the voice.

He sat on his bed and looked at the four of them.

31

Things were going on here that he could not under-stand. After all, he'd guessed correctly who Hugh was. But was he right about who spoke to him in the dark? It *could* have been Hugh. He thought he recognized the hoarse voice again up here just now. But perhaps it wasn't. That voice sounded almost murderous. It wasn't the voice of someone laughed at by his mates as a changeling runt. Well, it wasn't William, who'd led the way with the lantern. The tall, graceful figure of Alexander was unmistakeable even as a shadow in weak lanternlight. The voice had no stutter, so it wasn't John's. Or perhaps that little hesitation when he greeted Joslin was just a tiny slip. No, he had stuttered when he insulted Hugh as well.

But then Joslin found Hugh must have a friend after all. Belatedly, William said, "Leave him alone, John. Robin's not the only one lost round here. Remember that."

They were making up their beds, spreading rough blankets over prickly straw. William slept at the far end, next to the empty bed. John was next, then Alexander. Hugh was next to Joslin. He worked grimly at making his bed, then said, "I'll hear no more about this. It's no one's business but my own."

"Oh, but it is our business, Hugh Hockley," said Alexander. "We're a band of painters together and Robin's a grievous loss to us. But if one of us loses a brother as well, that's another loss we all share."

"He's *my* brother," muttered Hugh. "I'll keep my wor-ries to myself. If worry I need. He may turn up tomorrow, as well as ever."

Joslin had made his bed. He lay on it, waiting to hear more, wondering if he dared say, "Tell me about it."

No, he daren't. It *was* none of his business.

32

But they were going to tell him none the less.

"Hugh has an older brother, Thomas Hockley," said William. "Thomas is apprenticed to a master goldsmith in Cheapside."

"Their guardian put them to apprenticeships after their parents died," said Alexander. "Hugh to Randolf, Thomas to Walter Craven."

"W-we're all orphans here," said John. "P-put to apprenticeship by our g-guardians while they look after the l-legacies our parents left us."

"But Hugh's legacy is more than most, eh, Hugh?" said Alexander. "Your parents left you well provided for when you're twenty-one."

Mockery again. *Perhaps*, thought Joslin, *they are the jealous ones*. But what a theme he kept hearing repeated. Childless couples, orphan children – if not the way of the world, it certainly seemed the way of London. The plague had much to answer for.

"Randolf's a good master," said William. "He looks after us well, and he's good to his servants."

"He takes in runaway serfs from the country and asks them no questions," said Alexander. "Like that surly Wulfrum."

"And he gives us every Saturday afternoon to ourselves," said William. "And you've always used the time to meet your brother, haven't you, Hugh?"

"That's no one's concern but mine," said Hugh.

"Only last time he wasn't there, was he, Hugh?" said Alexander.

"What does it matter to you?"

"We're worried for you. You were in such a pother when you came back. But you wouldn't let us help you. You'd been to Master Walter Craven the goldsmith yourself and no one had seen Thomas for two days, had they? They thought he'd come to stay with you and Master Walter was very angry, wasn't he? He would have kicked Thomas out there and then if he'd come back, wouldn't he? And what would have happened to the Hockleys then, Hugh, eh?" All this from Alexander.

"Y-yes, it matters a lot to you, Hugh," said John. "So it does m-matter to us. But you'd have it so it matters to no one but you."

"My brother's safe. Nothing's happened to him."

"How do you know? Has someone told you?" Joslin could tell this question of William's didn't expect an answer. Instead, Hugh threw himself face down on his bed. He stayed there hardly moving, but his shoulders twitched and he sniffed faintly.

"Never mind, Hugh," said Alexander. "Perhaps Mistress Alys will comfort you."

Suddenly the atmosphere was dangerous. Hugh sat up, his tear-blotched face contorted with rage. "No, she won't!" he cried. "She'll only comfort *him*. The French fancy-boy is all she can think about."

Now Joslin was angry. "That's not true," he shouted. "Alys mourns Robin and that's all she can think of."

Hugh looked straight at him. His face was twisted, ugly. "Isn't that a pity? You can't wait till she's not mourning any more, can you?"

Joslin clenched his fists. He sprang out of bed and stood over Hugh, daring him to stand up.

"I came here to protect her on her journey," he said, as calmly as he could. "Remember that."

Slowly, daring him to strike out, Hugh stood. He spoke, his voice dangerously quiet. "Put your fists down. You don't know what you might get back."

Joslin never moved. But Hugh did. As if by magic, a

sleight of hand Joslin never noticed, something gleamed in Hugh's hand.

"My knife's as sharp as any razor," he hissed. "And I'd use it, too."

Joslin was hardly conscious of what he did next. As fast as Hugh's hand had moved, his own had scooped under his mattress and snatched up his father's dagger. The wicked, channelled blade, the jewelled handle – they made Hugh's knife look puny, a small boy's toy.

Joslin held the dagger at Hugh's chest. He saw fear in Hugh's eyes. *What am I doing? I'm a guest in this place*, he thought. Why shouldn't Hugh secretly love Alys? Time was when he'd wondered if he did. And now he'd got into a situation that his sense of honour wouldn't let him back down from.

There was no sound except for the two of them breathing hard, fixing each other with their eyes and waiting for the first to blink. He knew the others were fascinated by the dagger, a weapon a knight should have, not a youth of seventeen years. But then William, swallowing deeply because this was a brave thing he did, walked from his end of the room. "Put the knives away," he said. "We want no trouble here."

"Gladly," Joslin replied. Honour was satisfied. He replaced his dagger under the pillow.

"Hugh?" said William gently.

"You saw what he did," said Hugh. "He's not welcome here."

"You started it, Hugh," said William. "Give me the knife."

"Take his first."

"I can't take away the weapon of a guest. It's his right to keep it."

"Then you'll not take mine."

35

"Then keep it close and out of sight. Let's have no more upset this night. If we laughed at you, then I'm sorry. We know this is a bad time for you. Go to sleep, Hugh, and forget it if you can."

He walked back to his bed, dousing the lanterns as he went. Before the last one was out, he said, "That goes for you all. Let's sleep and get a good night's quiet rest before a busy day tomorrow."

*Amen to that*, thought Joslin and closed his eyes. Soon deep breathing was the only sound in the apprentices' room.

A weak sun rose behind low clouds as a lighterman hooked the body out of the Thames on to his boat. He and his mate manhandled the sodden bundle on board. Used to death as they were, they could not help but retch as they saw the sight. The body had been in the water for some days and it was in a poor state. When they tore the hood away, they caught their breath partly with horror, partly because they had somehow known what they were going to see. The white, bloodless line across the throat from ear to ear showed this was no poor wretch who had strayed drunk into the Thames or an even poorer wretch for whom things had been too much and who had deliberately let the cold waters close over his head. A wicked blade had slashed the life out of this one. The two men looked at each other in alarm at who therefore must be walking the streets of London at this moment. Then they thought of something more practical.

"Whoever did this will have taken all he had," said the lighterman.

"You never know," said his mate. "There may be some little picking left in a pocket that nobody will miss."

They undid the cloak and felt in deep pockets for coin or trinket. But they found nothing. So they stripped tunic and hose away to seek further – but when they saw the bloodless body lying bare in front of them, they gulped with even greater horror than before. On chest and shoulders were the tell-tale swellings, great black boils, which meant one thing. This victim was in the grip of the plague when he was murdered and the lighterman's mate had no idea if pestilence still hovered, waiting to cross to new victims now he was dead.

"Shall we put him back in the water?" he asked.

"Best not," said the lighterman. "He'll only fetch up again somewhere else. He's been in the water too long for the plague to spread to us. We'll land him and call the watch."

He poled the boat into the shore, and as he did so a strange question came into his mind. *If this man were dying of the plague, why should a murderer need to cut his throat?*

And then another: *a double death-dealer stalked London with both knife and plague on him. Truly the Devil was abroad in the city.*

oslin suddenly woke, every nerve tingling, cold
with fear, almost more terrified than at any time
since he'd set foot in England. He was choking, para-
lyzed, hardly able to breathe or move. His senses took a
moment to tell him what had happened. A heavy weight
was on his chest and legs, his wrists were pinioned in a
strong grip. A foul-tasting rag, soaked in a noxious substance he didn't recognize, was rammed in his mouth
and reached almost into his gullet.

Worst of all, something cold, hard and sharp was at
his throat. He gulped, choked and squirmed uselessly.
The weight was human; this vicious shadow with the
strength of three, darker than the night shadows, knew
he was awake.

The shadow spoke – the same hoarse whisper as in
the courtyard. "Another warning, Joslin de Lay. Keep
those long, wicked French fingers away from dear Alys.
Pour no subtle songs of false love in her ears. Don't try
to take her away from here on your secret travels. Her
place is with her own kind. Do as I say or. . ."

The cold sharpness at his throat was gone. Even in

the dark, Joslin saw a tiny bright flash, a blade polished to dazzling lifted just above his eyes. Then the sharpness again, pressed hard enough to show what a devilish blade it was, light enough so only a little blood flowed. Then the rag was snatched away, nearly taking his teeth with it. Light footsteps sounded. There was a rustle as if someone hurled himself into a straw bed and covered himself up so as to seem innocently sleeping.

Joslin's cry woke everyone. They shouted, confused. "What?" "What's happened?" "Call the watch!" "Murder!"

William calmed them down. "Wait till I light a lantern."

There was a scratch of tinder. Soon dim light filled the room again. Joslin sat trembling on the side of his bed; William held the lantern high.

Joslin turned on Hugh. "You don't fool me," he shouted. "That's three times you've threatened me. Don't try a fourth or you'll find I'm more dangerous than you think. I've no designs on Alys so forget it, but if anyone tries to harm her, they'll have me to reckon with."

"What are you talking about?" Hugh spluttered indignantly. "You've got me out of the best dream I've had for years."

"You held me down, put your knife to my throat and whispered the same poison about Alys."

"I tell you I slept," Hugh repeated.

"You're a liar," Joslin said.

They sprang out of bed. Though this time neither held a blade, Joslin was ready to fight. His blazing eyes showed Hugh was as well. But once again William came between them.

"That's enough, Joslin," he said. "I know Hugh went too far before but that's no reason to take against him even if he has upset you. That was over the moment you put your knives away. Let's have no more or I'll be falling out with someone I hoped might be a friend."

"You dreamed it, man," said Hugh. "You've had a long day. While I had a good dream, you had a nightmare. I'm sorry for that. As long as we know where we stand, we can get on together, you and me."

Suddenly, Joslin was sorry for Hugh. Ignored by Alys, brother missing – what did Hugh have to give him good dreams? And no, he didn't want to upset William and the others.

"Forgive me, Hugh. And forgive me, William. You're right. I'm overwrought. Too much has happened. I had a nightmare."

"Then let's sleep. We'll have no more disturbance tonight," said William. They dropped on to their beds again, with the same rustle Joslin heard before, and William put the lantern out.

That same rustle. And the taste of the rag still lingered. It was no dream. Who could it be but Hugh? Hugh was someone to be wary of. It seemed that coming to new places meant making new enemies.

No, he had to get on his way. This place boded no good for him. With that thought, he drifted into a deep sleep.


Morning was here. One of William's duties was to wake earlier than the others. Joslin wondered how he managed that. Perhaps being the oldest apprentice now that Robin was not here had wrought a subtle change in his mind ensuring that he did. At any rate, Joslin was woken by bright daylight as William opened the shutters.

"It's the sixth hour," William cried. "Out of bed, everybody."

Four people tumbled out of bed and began pulling hose, tunics and jerkins on. Only Joslin realized that something was wrong.

"Where's Hugh?" he said.

The noise in the room died. Everybody looked at Hugh's bed.

It was empty. The blanket had been dropped on the floor.

The three apprentices looked at Joslin accusingly.

"What have you done, Joslin?" said John.

"Where have you taken him?" said Alexander.

"You'll not be leaving on any quest today, Joslin," said William.

"There's no need for that," said Joslin as they hustled him through the courtyard.

"Oh, but there is," Alexander answered. His elegant grace hid great strength, as Joslin was finding from the grip on his shoulder.

"Master Randolf, Master Randolf," William called as they burst in the hall. Randolf sat alone eating herring and bread and drinking ale.

"Who dares interrupt my breakfast?" Randolf barked. He did not, Joslin thought, seem the easy, gentle lord and master of last night.

"Master Randolf, Hugh has disappeared in the night," John cried.

"Last night Hugh and Joslin argued. They faced each other with knife and dagger. William pulled them apart," Alexander added excitedly.

"Then J-Joslin woke us in the n-night and said Hugh had threatened him again. But Hugh said he was d-dreaming and then J-Joslin said he m-must have been after all." John again.

William spoke in more measured tones. "I believe Joslin's hatred of Hugh had grown too quick. It's the French way, I've been told. I think Joslin feared Hugh as well and knew he had to strike first. So he made away with him in the night while we all slept. And then he was the first to cry out that he was gone so that we wouldn't think he had aught to do with it. But we saw through this and knew that he had."

Randolf rose and looked gravely at Joslin. "Can it be," he said, "that I have given hospitality to a viper?"

"I'm no viper," Joslin began.

"Don't listen, Master Randolf. We'll find Hugh in a ditch, killed by Joslin's dagger." Alexander again.

"You have a dagger?" Randolf enquired.

"It was my father's. He gave it to me as he lay dying."

"Fetch it to me," said Randolf. "William, go with him."

So Joslin and William crossed the courtyard without speaking. As they climbed the steps into the apprentices' room, Joslin was filled with cold apprehension. His dagger would be gone – disappeared as it had at Cry Ashbourne, not to be seen again until he found it plunged into someone's murdered body. Trembling, he reached under his pillow.

His heart leapt. He thanked God. The dagger was where he had put it last night.

"Don't touch the blade," William said quickly. "Randolf must see if there is blood on it still."

Back in the hall, Randolf gravely took the dagger. He peered long and hard at the blade where the cross-piece joined it and examined the channels down which blood should flow. Then he looked up.

"I do not believe this dagger was used in anger

last night," he said.

Joslin sighed inwardly with relief.

Randolf continued to hold the dagger, cradling it, studying it with knowledgeable eyes. "This is beautiful," he said. He felt the jewelled, finely-wrought handle with the gem set in the end. "Craftsmanship at its best. Your father must have performed a nobleman some great service to be given this. That's how most men who are masters of their crafts but not of noble stock receive such things."

"I don't know," Joslin replied. "He never said."

Randolf turned the dagger over in his hand. "Perhaps the craftsmanship is more Celtic than French. It may be from Brittany." He looked again. "Or from these islands. Irish, maybe. Or Welsh."

"My quest is to Wales," said Joslin.

"Then you may find where your dagger came from." Randolf's eyes narrowed. "But you won't see it again until you leave. Nobody may bear arms on London streets who's not travelling in or out of the city. You must give it to me for safe keeping. I'll return it when you leave." The last he saw of the precious object was Randolf slipping it into a pocket in his gown. "But we aren't here to talk about your dagger. My apprentices say you and Hugh argued. Why should that be after a few hours under our roof?"

Joslin thought a moment before he spoke. "When I first saw Hugh, I felt he was jealous of me," he said. "As we crossed the courtyard in the dark someone whispered in my ear. I thought it was Hugh. He said I was fishing in Robin's pond while better men were deprived of their rights. He said that his knife was sharp as anyone's and he could drop a body so no one would ever find it or know it again if they did."

43

"And what did he mean about other men's rights?"

"Master Randolf, I think he was talking about Alys. I like Alys and we have been through much together. But I'd never think of taking Robin's place."

"Hugh would n-never say that about d-dropping dead b-bodies," John interrupted. "He'd k-kill a rabbit but he'd be too f-feared to kill a m-man."

"Quiet, John," said Randolf. "Is that all, Joslin?"

"No, Master Randolf. Before we went to bed he threatened me with his knife and said the French fancy-boy was all she thought about."

Randolf looked at the apprentices. "Is that true?" he asked.

They nodded.

"How dare he speak so of my ward in her sadness?"

"And then he woke me up in the night and threatened me with his knife again and said the same things about Alys."

"That was a dream," said Alexander. "You said so yourself."

"Yes, I said so, but only for peace in the room. But I know it wasn't. I heard Hugh jump into his bed before William lit the lantern."

"Can anyone prove Joslin wrong?" said Randolf.

The apprentices looked at each other, then shook their heads.

"Then I declare Joslin innocent of fault in this. I believe Hugh slipped out in the night to look for his brother. We know how upset he is about Thomas. And if I'm right he'll soon return. You'll treat Joslin as your friend while he's here."

The apprentices looked unhappy. "Master Randolf—" William began.

"Yes, I know," said Randolf. "You're hurt because I've

44

taken a stranger's part against you. Very well, I'll make a pact with Joslin. He'll stay until Hugh returns and he can prove me right. Is that fair?"

William brightened. "Yes, Master Randolf," he said.

"Joslin?" said Randolf.

"I agree," said Joslin reluctantly.

"Now, because I know well the state you'll have left your room in, I want it set to rights in the way that I demand."

"Yes, Master Randolf," all three apprentices said.

"Then be off."

Nothing was said as they returned. Joslin was uneasy. He had a nasty feeling that Hugh would not walk into the courtyard at any moment. Something more deadly was happening. He felt it with sharp instinct honed by bitter experience in the last weeks.

Randolf was right about the beds. They needed making. Joslin did his in the neat, squared-off manner of the others, then turned to Hugh's.

"I'll do that," said Alexander firmly and pushed him away. Instead, Joslin surveyed this newly-orderly chamber. Nice and neat now. Except. . . He started with surprise and looked again.

There was no doubt about it. Five beds, including his own and Hugh's, looked paragons of order. But one did not. Robin's at the far end, not slept in since Joslin was still on *The Merchant of Orwell* sailing up the Channel, was indented with the shape of a body which must have lain there very recently. How could this be?

Something told him this was important. Would the others know? It was on the tip of his tongue to point it out.

Then he stopped. He was, once again, not in a good

position here in England. It was best to keep quiet and work things out for himself.

But it meant *something*, and it was up to him to find out what.

Once again the whole household met in the great hall: servants, cooks from the kitchens, labourers from the workshops. The apprentices stood together by the door. Joslin placed himself far away on the other side. He tried to avoid Alys; there was no point in making more tongues wag.

Randolf did not have to call for order – everyone knew fresh disaster must have occurred. When they saw Randolf's face, scored with too many shocks in too short a time, they were quiet. "Sad I am," he said, "to call you here because of more woe for this household, but Hugh has gone missing during the night, leaving no trace, no note, no word. I hope we can clear this matter up quickly so we only have Robin's death to mourn. Does anyone know where he could be?"

Nobody did. But Alys spoke. "Walter Craven might," she said.

"That's true, Alys," said Randolf. "And I'm minded to send out to him to ask. But I'm not minded to take anyone off their duties today. There are a household and a craft to be kept up and I won't let them slip. Now we have no Hugh, Alexander and John will come with me to our present commission in St Benet's in Gracechurch Street. My wife is responsible for the house and I won't have her leave it. There's only one person I'd spare to go to Walter Craven and that's Alys."

There was an immediate stir. Joslin heard a servant whisper, "He'd never let her go through the streets alone, would he?"

"And to make sure she comes to no harm, I'll send Joslin as well. He guided her safely from Suffolk, so I trust him with her to Cheapside."

Nobody protested. Now Randolf had spoken, they knew better than to try. Joslin surveyed the people ranged in the hall. Five men stood together at the back who did not eat there last night. Two were the ostlers who had taken their horses the day before. The other three wore ragged tunics and aprons smudged with colours, gilding and patches of silver: the labourers in the workshop. When one of them moved, Joslin caught a whiff of a fishy scent. What was it? Of course, *glue*, made from boiled fish heads. Much used, he imagined, in a painter's workshop. Now, which labourer was Wulfrum, who John wished Randolf had not taken in?

Randolf dismissed everybody with orders to keep eyes and ears open and report anything untoward to him. Then he called Alys and Joslin. "You're to find out from Walter Craven not only whether Hugh's there but whether his brother Thomas has returned," he said. "For one brother to disappear is strange, for two to go makes me wonder if there's mischief afoot."

He looked at Joslin. "You'll take good care of Alys?" he said. "The London streets are crowded and dangerous even by day."

Joslin risked something near a joke. "From the little I

saw yesterday, it will be more like Alys taking care of me."

Randolf looked at him severely. "That may be so. But the footpad or thief won't know that. You'll do as I said. Alys, get ready for the street. Joslin, wait in the workshop until she joins you."

So Joslin made his way to Randolf's workshop, which was airy, with big windows to make the most of the light. Inside, the smell of fish glue was strong. Tables for grinding colours, racks of brushes and easels filled the room. The three labourers were there; the two eldest, including the glue-maker, cast more unfriendly glances. William sat at an easel, a palette with dishes full of pigments at his right hand. On the easel was a half-finished painting. Joslin looked over William's shoulder and saw it was of a young girl's face with eyes slightly downcast.

"The Virgin Mary," said William. He was not unfriendly. "For the altar at St Benet's church where the rest have gone. Randolf trusts me to do this alone."

"As he trusted Robin?" asked Joslin.

"He'll never trust anyone like he trusted Robin," William answered. "But at least he thinks I'm a serviceable painter. Enough to be in the Gild one day and a freeman of the city. Anything in this place is worth it to be a Master in the end."

"Is Hugh a serviceable painter?" asked Joslin.

"We're all pretty good," William replied. "Randolf's a good teacher and a hard taskmaster. But Hugh finds it difficult. If Randolf's short-tempered, you can be sure it's with Hugh. Not that Hugh need worry."

"Why not?"

"Hugh came to London from the country, from Stoke Poges in Buckinghamshire. He likes to tell us what rich gentlefolk his parents were and how the priest of the village taught him to read and write and a bit of Latin as well, so Hugh might go to Oxford and be a lawyer or a priest himself. But his father died and his mother married again, a man with property next door so in one day he became twice as rich. Hugh's new stepfather became his guardian, but didn't like either him or Thomas so sent them to London to their godfather, Walter Craven. Walter took Thomas as apprentice goldsmith and Randolf, out of charity and friendship, took on Hugh. And here he's struggled ever since. Well, we can all read, else how would we know what was in our articles or make sense of the commissions which come? Hugh may be able to write and know some Latin as well, but he finds it hard with the brush."

William dipped his own brush in a tray of brown pigment and worked delicately at Mary's eyebrows, his tongue sticking slightly through his teeth. "Still, Hugh's right. Why should he worry? His father left him with a rich legacy, which will be his when he's twenty-one. Ninety pounds, two gold chalices, a silver salt-cellar, a helmet and sword fit for a knight. And domains in Buckinghamshire to share with his brother when the old ones die. That's a lot to keep the cold out when you step into the world."

"Is his stepfather still his guardian, then?

"Oh, no. Hugh's very sure about that. Out of sight, out of mind, that's what the stepfather thought. Walter Craven has that duty now."

"The stepfather doesn't sound a very pleasant man," said Joslin.

"You may be right," said William. "Even so, someone has to tell him. Not that Jacob Gaylor back in Stoke Poges will worry overmuch."

Joslin suddenly risked a dangerous question. "Robin

was a good teacher, wasn't he?"

"Why do you say that?"

"In Stovenham, I saw how he'd taught Alys to paint."

William put his brush down. Joslin feared his response. But there was no need. William smiled sadly and wistfully.

"So you saw that? I might have known. Yes, Alys was as good as any of us. Better if the truth were known. Not that Randolf knew. Just as well. We might have feared for our apprenticeships." He took up his brush again. "I doubt if Alys will come into this workshop now," he said.

The day was grey, sullen and overcast with a cold east wind. Alys appeared wearing a warm outdoor cloak. When he saw her Joslin realized two things. First – it was cold enough for him to wear his cloak as well. Second – William was right: Alys would not walk through the door. Joslin came outside to meet her.

"Wait for me," he said and ran up the steps to his bed. He fished the cloak out of his clothes roll, and made sure everything else was tidied away. Remembering what he'd seen before, he looked at Robin's bed. He hadn't been wrong. Yesterday the top of the mattress was level. Now it was rumpled with a furrow as if a body had lain on it.

Perhaps it was nothing – an apprentice made uncomfortable by a lump, a scratching straw, had briefly changed beds. Perhaps someone used the privy and blundered back to the wrong bed in the dark. As soon as he thought of those answers, he knew they were not true.

Could Robin's ghost have returned, to make sure all was well here without him? Never. A minstrel who had seen death and cheated it should not believe in such things.

Was it to do with his mysterious night attacker? He remembered the blade suddenly taken from his throat, the weight removed from his body, the soft steps, the thump and rustle as if somebody scrambled into bed. Well, it had to be Hugh, taking a few quick paces to his own bed before the lanterns were lit.

Or was it? How many footsteps? Joslin couldn't recall. *But was it more than the two or three which would take Hugh to his bed?* Or was he imagining this to explain something which didn't seem right?

Didn't seem right? This explanation made it a whole lot worse. There was a sixth person in the room, jealous, murderous, invisible, who waited on Robin's bed for them to sleep, then sidled silently out. Was it likely that Hugh, worried sick over his missing brother, could be this dark terror stalking through the night?

Joslin had a lot to think about as he walked downstairs to Alys.

She was talking to William. Joslin looked in at the labourers preparing pigments and making glue. The youngest was vacant-eyed as if there was never a thought in his head. The other two were much older. They looked at him through lowered eyelids and he tried to fathom their expressions.

Alys had said goodbye to William. Joslin walked with her through the gate into the street. At once he felt nearly drowned in its bustle.

"Keep close to me and away from the drains," said Alys. Soon he grew used to the street sellers, rakers clearing filth, beggars, men and women pushing through on urgent business and running, shouting children as much in their element as shoals of tiny fish in a river. As they walked along Wood Street he told Alys what happened the night before. As they turned

52

left by the church of St Alban, she spoke.

"I could never go in fear of Hugh. Whoever came to you last night sounds as if he's one to fear. If it were Hugh, there's more in him than I thought."

"So who tried to frighten me?"

"Joslin, I've no idea."

They were passing St Mary de Aldermanbury church and into Aldermanbury itself.

"That glue-maker looks a strong customer," said Joslin. "He and his labouring mate gave me some strange looks."

"Wulfrum? Yes, he's not one to cross. Though there's no reason for him to take against you. You're a stranger. Wulfrum does harm to those who've done him ill, not those he just doesn't like the look of."

"Could Wulfrum have been the night intruder?" Joslin asked.

"Why should he be?"

"I don't know. He just looks the surliest of an ill-favoured bunch."

"Did he smell of fish glue?"

"No."

"Then there's no chance."

Joslin said no more. They walked along Catte Street, past the Guildhall, then turned down Lawrence Lane into Cheapside, dominated by the great cross of Queen Eleanor. In Goldsmiths' Row was Walter Craven's place.

Alys was known – they had no trouble entering. Soon they stood in front of Walter Craven. He was sweating and red-faced, more from rich food than hard work for his hands were smooth and his fingers were long, well fit for his delicate craft.

No, he'd not seen Hugh and Thomas had not

returned. Walter was angry. "Thomas has broken the rules of his apprenticeship," he fumed. "He's no right to leave without permission. Randolf should be angry with Hugh as well."

"Randolf's first thought isn't anger," Alys said. She told him of the new afflictions in Silver Street. "Besides," she added, "Hugh didn't slide away in the day. He disappeared at night while everyone slept."

Joslin ventured a word. "And there was someone else who shouldn't be there. Nobody saw him but me. He had a knife."

If Walter noticed Joslin's French accent he said nothing. "Probably Thomas come to get him," he said. "You mark my words. They're good at sliding away in the night. Thursday night Thomas goes, Hugh goes last night – it all follows. They've gone home. Apprenticeship has palled. Too much hard work. They'll be on the way to Stoke Poges by now. London doesn't suit them. They'd rather be idle in the country."

Alys considered this. "I didn't know Thomas went on Thursday."

"Well, he did and I washed my hands of him," Walter continued. "So should Randolf of Hugh."

"But they may have come to harm," Alys protested.

"They should have thought of that before they went. Masters have no use for apprentices who run away without leave. Randolf should get a good new apprentice he can trust, just as I shall. Tell him I'm sorry for the trouble that has come on his house, for Robin was all a good apprentice should be, but grief should not make Randolf soft on those supposed to serve him."

After such a tirade, Joslin waited for Alys to say something. When it came, he was surprised.

"Thank you," she said. "We'll tell Randolf what you say. Goodbye."

As they left, he called after them. "Give Randolf my greetings and sympathies. And tell him if he wants Hugh back, he should send to Stoke Poges."

In the street, Alys said, "Take no notice. Walter's bark's worse than his bite. Masters don't like being bested by their apprentices."

"He's wrong," Joslin replied. "I know it."

"How do you know?"

"If we can find somewhere quiet to talk, I'll tell you."

Close to Walter Craven's goldsmith's shop was the church of St Mary le Bow. They slipped inside, to where cool quiet half-light and the colours of saints and angels painted on the walls by painters like Randolf enveloped them.

Joslin spoke. "When I told him someone else was there last night, he thought it was Thomas come to get Hugh. That can't be true. If Thomas was mad enough to break in and take his brother away in secret he wouldn't brandish knives at strangers. Besides, this person thought he knew my business. If it was Thomas, how could he?"

"All right," said Alys. "That might show the intruder wasn't Thomas. But it doesn't show they aren't going back to Stoke Poges."

"But if Thomas wanted Hugh to go, why not come for him at once? Why skulk hiding round London for four days? Why let Hugh get worried? And if Hugh went home on his own, did he just sit up in the night, say, 'Ah, I know where Thomas is' and set off there and then?"

"I see what you mean," said Alys.

"There's another thing," said Joslin. "Randolf sent

round to Walter when he knew Hugh was missing. Why didn't Walter send to Randolf?"

"He just assumed what had happened because it's what apprentices who are tired of London do," said Alys.

Joslin remembered something William had told him. "Why? Walter's their guardian. A guardian should look after his wards like a parent. He's their godfather as well. A double responsibility."

"So they say," said Alys. "Not all guardians are like Randolf."

Joslin was despondent. "All we found was that Walter thinks they've gone home. We don't know when Thomas went missing, whether by night or day, how they found out, nothing."

"Hugh went round to ask," said Alys.

"Then they didn't tell him very much," Joslin answered.

"But Hugh might still have gone to Stoke Poges."

"How could we find out?"

"He would leave London through one of the city gates. He came to London by the road along the Thames, through Ludgate. I remember him saying what a shock such a great mass of stone gave a boy up from the country. But there's no point in us going there to ask. So many people pass through that one more or less would never be noticed."

Joslin knew she was right. He remembered coming through Cripplegate. But that was by day.

"What about at night, after curfew? Are there so many then?"

"No. And the watchmen must open the gate specially for anyone who tries and ask them their business," Alys answered.

"So if we asked the watchman, could we prove that Hugh and Thomas never left for Stoke Poges in the night?"

"We might prove they never left at night through Ludgate," said Alys. "Is that the same thing?"

"It's a start. We'll go to Ludgate then."

"If you want to," said Alys. "But I warn you – this is looking for the needle in the haystack."

The body the lighterman fished from the Thames at London Bridge lay stripped on a table in a guard room at the Tower. Men of the guard looked down on it, wrinkling their noses.

"Bury him quick," said one. "He's been a few days in the water. The plague should be off him by now. But you never know. Anyway, he stinks."

"He must have proper Christian burial," said the captain.

"But we don't know who he is," said another.

The captain looked at the young, disintegrating face. "He's but a lad. Not come of age yet."

"So young. The plague got him before he'd even started," said the first guard.

"It's the young it takes, this time round. The plague of the innocents, that's what they call it. We need a priest," said the second.

"But it wasn't the plague that took this one," said the captain, looking at the white, shrivelled line across the dead man's throat. "I don't like thinking there's a murderer gone unpunished, but how can we find out who this man is? He might be from the city or a ship from the ends of the world, from north bank or south bank, London or country, England or France or Flanders. No, we need the coroner. This was not a rightful death; the coroner must decide what to do. We'd best wait for the priest and the coroner and then let him rest as he deserves."

The streets were still crowded. In Bowyers Row Joslin saw huge Ludgate barring the way ahead and felt as many Londoners must – that it protected them inside their great, familiar beehive against a wide, lonely, frightening world outside.

They called at the guard room. Yes, last night's watch and that of three and four nights before could be found. Who's asking? Well, that's all right, then. Randolf's name is well known and respected. No, there was nothing out of the ordinary last night or any night during the past week. Except – yes, there was one happening recently which seemed strange. Reported by Alfred of Ware. He hadn't stopped talking about it since. Alfred could be a real old yarnspinner when he chose. Yes, he might be able to find Alfred of Ware. A few coins in his pocket? He'd get him straight away.

Soon Alfred stood before them, old, grizzled, scar-faced. Joslin guessed he'd been in the thick of many battles. No, he said, he knew nothing about brothers passing through last night.

"What about other nights?" asked Joslin, thinking of Thomas.

Alfred was silent, as if making a decision. Then he took a deep breath and started. He'd never got out of his mind what had happened a few nights before. That young man. There were so few of anybody at dead of night, you see. Yes, he could have been an apprentice. In the dark, under his hood, he was most likely a man but he could have been a woman, he was so young and smooth-faced. Friday night, it would be.

Joslin muttered to Alys, "Thomas went on Thursday. Hugh first missed him on Saturday."

Why should Alfred remember him in particular? Oh, that face would haunt him for ever. The boy's companion said he was up from the country. No, not Stoke Poges. Barnet. Where the fair is. Staying in Fleet Street in a tavern. Dead drunk; not a pretty sight for one so young. He had to be taken back to his lodgings by someone who knew London. Yes, that's right – the man lived in Westcheap. So he said. But he wouldn't let him through. He didn't know him, you see, so he couldn't.

No, that's not why he remembered it so well. He was an old soldier. He'd seen as many dead men as living, aye, and despatched a good few himself. And this was what had kept him awake at night. This boy was no more drunk than he was now.

What was he then? Why, he was *dead*, wasn't he, and propped up by the man who'd killed him. Yes, *killed* him. He'd stake his life on it. He knew his mates thought he was an old liar and perhaps he was sometimes. But not this time. Pull that hood away, that cloak aside, and you'd see a slit throat and a bloodsoaked tunic. That young man was for the river, not a comfortable bed for the night.

What had he done? Why, sent them both back, that's what. Like his duty told him. What else could he do? By the time he'd got the rest of the watch out the man would be gone anyway. Besides, his shift was nearly over. He wanted his bed. And another thing. . .

"What was that?" asked Joslin.

"That man. Whether he had killed the boy or not, even if what he said was true, there was something about him that made me. . ."

"Made you what?" said Alys.

"That made me feared, that's what. There, I've said it to you, who's no older than the boy himself, and me an old soldier who's been all through France for the King and come home without a hair on my head harmed. I should have called out the rest of the guard there and then, but I couldn't, for fright. What made me feared? I couldn't tell you. He was ordinary. I can't recall anything about him. But he struck terrors of hell into my soul. I'm shamed about it, but I have to say it, even to strangers who could get me into trouble. I should have pulled that cloak aside and seen the lad properly. It was my real duty, not just sending them back. But I didn't. I daren't."

Joslin and Alys looked at each other.

"Did he take his companion home?" asked Joslin.

"How should I know? Except that I fancy instead of going left when they reached the end of Bowyer's Row as it should have done for Westcheap their light went right."

"Leading to where?"

"In the end, the river. And afterwards, in my dreams, I've seen the young man end up in it."

"Why should he bother coming through the gate?"

asked Alys. "Why not put the body in the river long before, near London Bridge?"

"Ah, I've thought of that," said Alfred. "The further from the city and the weaker the tide, the less likely that we'd see the body inside our city boundaries." He looked guiltily round. "I've said too much. I've never been a blabbermouth until this happened and now I can't stop talking about it. You wanted to know about apprentices coming to the gate at night. Now I've told you. I'm sorry if it's bad news. Don't tell the constable, will you?"

"Never a word," said Alys.

"Thank you," said Joslin. "What you've said could matter a lot."

"You speak like my old enemies," said Alfred, suddenly truculent.

"I come as a friend," said Joslin quickly. "I'm a travelling minstrel welcomed in England."

The watchman's brief anger subsided. "Good enough for me," he said. He left them and they walked through the now open gate and beyond the walls to stand on the Fleet Bridge. Close by was the Fleet prison. Upstream, London Wall curved round to Newgate, even bigger than Ludgate, with its own prison attached like a great brick cancer.

"Randolf said he feared mischief afoot and I think he was right," said Joslin. "Is it possible Alfred's dead man could have been Thomas?"

"That's too big a jump," Alys replied.

As they walked back through the gate, Alys asked, "Joslin, when will you leave us?"

"When Hugh returns," he answered. "I agreed that with Randolf."

"Stay longer," said Alys. "For me. Please. I know

Randolf's right about mischief and I feel lonely here without Robin."

"But you're surrounded by friends," said Joslin.

"It's not the same."

Joslin thought. He needed to be on his way. He'd been delayed enough since coming to England. But would a few days make any difference? And especially for Alys?

"Very well," he said at last. "For you."

"Thank you," Alys answered.

Joslin was thinking on. "Big jump or not, I have a strange idea it's in the river we should look for Thomas and, I'm fearing, Hugh as well. . ."

"If it is, you'll never find him," said Alys, looking down into the Fleet's dark waters. "You may as well seek one particular fish."

They looked downstream, where the narrow Fleet flowed to join the great Thames itself. Their search seemed hopeless.

"We must go back," said Alys. "We've been too long away already. Dame Lettice will fret."

When they went back through Ludgate, Alfred of Ware had gone. They pushed along Bowyers Row, then through the twists and turns to Silver Street, Alys leading. Joslin felt more at home in London now, though he had not been in the city twenty-four hours. Enough had happened to fill half a lifetime already. Add to what he had gone through since Jean had woken him in the castle in the Cotentin not three weeks before and it seemed like five. Nothing could shock him: there was no challenge he couldn't meet. Or so he thought as London's streets, hard, dry, muddy, filthy and wet by turns, passed under his feet.

It was midday when they arrived back. Dame Lettice was for sending to Randolf at once to let him know. But

Alys disagreed. "What is there to tell him? Randolf won't be interrupted while he's at work on an important commission away from home unless there's something he can do. There's nothing he can do, so he won't leave."

"Randolf alone must decide what to do," said Lettice. "But you're right. He'll be home when the light dies. But I want you with me now, Alys. Joslin wouldn't know where Gracechurch Street is anyway. Randolf wouldn't forgive me if I took William off his work."

So Joslin was alone, as if the women had dismissed him. What could he do? He'd given his word to both Randolf and Alys that he would stay. Anyway, he couldn't deny that he wanted to see where this mystery would lead. "Big jump," Alys had said when he said the dead man might be Thomas and, "You may as well seek one particular fish," when he suggested looking for him in the river. And she was right.

Even so. . .

Deep in thought, he wandered to the workshop. William still worked at the painting of the Virgin. The labourers had gone; the smell of fish glue had almost disappeared.

"The glue's gone to St Benet's and Wulfrum with it. Thank God," said William. "It's needed to fix the altar panels on that we painted here. Perkin and Herry have taken new pigments for Randolf's wall paintings. So I'm on my own. I like it that way." He laid his brush down. "What did you find out?"

Joslin told him about Walter Craven. William wasn't surprised. "The man's a fat rat. I know who I'd rather be apprenticed to."

Then Joslin told him of their suspicions and the walk to Ludgate. William was not impressed.

"No," he said. "Don't worry about that. Walter's right.

They've gone to Stoke Poges. They didn't like London."

"What about last night, when I was threatened?"

"Well, put yourself in Hugh's place. Robin dead, then his one chance to impress Alys taken away by an upstart Frenchman – he pondered on it and decided he'd had enough. Thomas must have gone home, he thought. So he got up in the night and went after him."

"But he never went through Ludgate."

"Then he went through Newgate, Aldersgate or Cripplegate. London's ringed with gates to go through."

Joslin wondered if he should just ask at the other city gates.

No, William was wrong. William believed in the simple way because nothing had ever happened to make him think of any other. There was a lot more to it.

So what should he do? Stand and brood while William painted, and Alys was wafted off by Lettice to spin, weave tapestries or whatever ladies of the house did when menfolk weren't around? Never. He'd follow his wild idea. Why *not* seek one particular fish in the river?

"I'm going out into the city again," he called to William.

William did not even turn his head. "On your own?" he said abstractedly. "Don't get lost."

No, he mustn't. London with no guide was a fearsome prospect. But travelling through England had given him a keen sense of direction. North, south, east and west he knew from the sun. When he arrived, they had come south to Silver Street from Cripplegate. This morning they had gone east to Catte Street, south to Cheapside and then west to Ludgate. If he were to do what William suggested, he would go north again to Cripplegate, north-west to Aldersgate and west to Newgate.

Wherever he went, he would not have to walk far; between its walls and the river, London was barely a square mile.

But he would not do what William suggested because he was sure it would get nowhere. No, he would go south, to the River Thames.

In the street, he felt very hungry. He had not eaten that day; last night's feast was a long time ago and he had only vaguely noticed the remains of a shoulder of mutton, bread and ale at William's side. But Silver Street echoed with vendors' cries. A voice almost in his ear was too much to resist: "Hot pies, hot! Good pig and geese." Yes, here was a cook and his knave, there were the pies with an irresistible smell and he had money in his belt. Soon, Joslin was taking ravenous bites from a pie as he looked up into the sky and worked out where the sun was.

Past its zenith, certainly – more than an hour must have passed since midday. Were it to come to earth and start walking, it would go due west along Silver Street. So to find the shortest way to the Thames he must go the opposite way and then turn south. He did, down Wood Street, into Tad Lane, then down Milk Street and Bread Street – until a cold breeze and the rank smell of the river came up and he saw leafy Southwark on the south bank. He had come to Fishwharf: a jetty set on wooden piles. Gleaming fresh fish were tipped out of boats to be gutted on the bank. Above, gulls screamed and dived for the scraps.

The smell of fresh fish was in the air. He stood on the wharf and looked into the water. The tide was on the turn. Suddenly, a feeling of complete futility came over him. What did he expect to find? A body floating right where he looked, obligingly face up and enough like

Hugh to recognize at once? Or Hugh himself, so he could say, "Hugh, you're here. Now I know what happened we can avenge you," and set off back to Randolf's with real purpose? No, the Thames was huge and the wharves and gates along its north bank were many. London Bridge, loaded with shops and houses, bestrode it eight hundred paces to his left. Beyond that the river widened, out to the great, cold ocean stretching who knew where.

Besides, what a wild idea it was. Whoever was dropped in the water might be found by now – or drifted far away from anyone's reach. Oh, how useless it all was. If Thomas was gone, then so was Hugh.

He stood still as gulls dived and cried overhead. Joslin de Lay, pitted against Death and the Devil. Not for the first time in England. Well, he'd been dragged out of the depths of despair before by sudden turns of Providence. Why not now?

He made up his mind. He'd follow the river eastwards, at least to London Bridge, peering in the water as he went. If Thomas and Hugh *were* dead but weren't by Fishwharf, then why not further down?

There were steps down from the wharf to the foreshore. The retreating tide had left a narrow, muddy strip along which he could walk. So he set off slowly, trying hard not to slip, his shoes sodden and smothered in filth and his stockings wringing wet and cold to his skin. After what seemed hours he reached Timberhithe. Here was an inlet he'd never cross without being knocked over by currents and taken out to sea himself. He panicked. Could he manage half a mile of this? Was it worth it? Was it likely he'd find a body conveniently waiting? No, he had to get back on dry land. There was a little wooden jetty nearby that he could reach without going deep into the water. He scrambled for it, clambered up to its rough planking, and looked east again. If a floating body caught in the current was checked it would surely be at London Bridge, whose vast stone piles made huge obstructions in the river. He could reach London Bridge along a dry street, surely. If he had no luck there, he'd retrace his steps and look at each wharf and jetty in turn. So he turned inland again along Broken Wharf and Old Fish Street until he reached Thames Street. Then he set off east to Oyster Hill, St Botolph's wharf where the passenger ships tied up, and London Bridge itself, loaded with shops, houses and chapels. The great stone piles on which its nineteen pointed arches rested rose out of the water like small islands. At the entrance was a guard house, topped with the poles where rotting heads of traitors were on display as a warning to the people.

He stood outside these threatening portals and looked down. Below was the nearest of those huge stone piles. A body drifting downriver could so easily fetch up against it. There was none there now but he felt a lift of the spirits. Here at least was a possibility.

He must ask someone. Who? In front of him, close inshore, a man poled a small, tarred boat downstream, just about to pass under the bridge. Might he know something?

He called, "Friend! I have a question."

The man lifted his pole out of the water. The boat drifted for a second, then, as he expertly used the pole as a rudder, turned in towards Joslin and fetched up on the shore in front of him.

The man's ragged clothes were wet from water seeping on to the floor of his boat. "Who wants me?" he said suspiciously.

Joslin told something very near the truth. "I'm a stranger in London," he said. "I'm looking for my friend, who's nowhere to be found and who, they tell me, hasn't been seen since the Thursday before I arrived. I fear he may be dead in the water. I'm at my wits' end and so I'm asking you for help."

The man rubbed his bristly chin. "A young man was he, your friend?"

"Yes," Joslin replied. He damped down a sudden leap of hope.

"I've not found anyone in the water these last days, though if I had it wouldn't be the first. But I know who has."

"Who?" cried Joslin. "Can I see him?"

"There's two. You can if I could find them," was the reply. "Though I doubt you'll want to hear what they'll tell you."

"Why not?"

"His throat was slit. And there's worse."

"What could be worse?"

"He had the plague on him. The black boils still showed though he'd been in the water more days than one. There, I've said it myself, just as they told me. They wouldn't lie. Not about that."

Could this be Thomas? It couldn't be Hugh. But how could Thomas have picked up the plague? There was no plague in Walter Craven's place, surely?

"What happened to the body?"

"They took it to the Tower and gave it over to the Guard. He'll be deep in the ground now, I shouldn't wonder. Out of sight, out of mind. That's the best to be done for the poor soul and for the rest of us."

"Can you take me to the men who found it?"

But the boatman seemed already to be thinking better

of his first offer. "No. I've no time, I don't know you and I don't like your voice. Besides, the tide's well turned. It'll pour under this bridge like a weir and sink me if I don't get through now. You go to the Tower yourself and ask for the Guard. They'll know what's happened since."

Without another word, the boat was turned. The last Joslin saw was his short-lived helper energetically poling it through London Bridge.

Through the arches he saw the squat Tower upstream. Forbidding though it was, reputed all over Europe as a terrible place, that was where he must ask next. He felt as if he were being led and uneasily remembered that strange feeling as he and Alys left Stovenham and Robin's Doom, that there was a third with them, darkly invisible.

He had turned then and seen nothing. He turned now – and saw a presence all too solid. *Someone stood not twenty paces away, surveying him.* A man in a brown tunic and hose with a half-length coat of grey, able to merge into any crowd. How long had he been there? Was he a mere passer-by, there by chance? Or had he been following Joslin?

If so, since when? From the moment Joslin left Randolf's? From Fishwharf? Or more recently, as if this man, too, was wondering if a body might have fetched up against the stone piles of London Bridge?

If he was here by chance, he would surely answer a greeting. "Good day, friend," Joslin called.

There was no reply. Joslin tried to memorize the face, so he might recognize it again. What was memorable about it? Nothing. Forgettable, anonymous, almost blank in the way nose, eyes and mouth combined into sheer ordinariness.

So why was there a sudden chill in Joslin's heart?

The man returned Joslin's gaze. Then he turned away. Joslin could not know the thoughts which passed through his mind.

*So you are a danger. You're finding out too much. Everything I hear about you points one way. My spy is right. Behind those keen eyes there's too much inquisitiveness for my liking. It could be my undoing and that I can't risk. But it may be yours, too. So, unwanted guest, I may have to send you further away still.*

*And your boatman informer is sending you to the Tower, is he? Then I must go, too. But not trailing behind as I have since I saw you come into London. I'll take the paths I know so well. I'll leave the river by Churcham Lane, then east along Oyster Hill, Billingsgate Street and Thames Street and cut you off there as you reach the Tower. I know the streets of London like I know the lines on the palm of my hand. I don't want to kill a stranger. I'll make one attempt to frighten you away from here. If that fails, then you face a nasty and inevitable death.*

**R**andolf's frustrating day in St Benet's in Gracechurch Street was nearly over. He had left William behind to finish the last panel for the altarpiece but he wished he was here instead. Now Robin was gone – he fought tears away at the thought – William was the oldest and most trustworthy apprentice. Alexander and John were younger, not so skilled, less dependable. His throat was hoarse with shouting at them – and in God's house, too.

And the finished altar panels they had brought from the workshop didn't *quite* fit; there had been hours of shaving down – not painter's work – and touching in. He got rid of some of his anger when Perkin and Herry were clumsy with the dowelling. More was expended on Wulfrum when he arrived an hour late with the fresh-boiled glue to fix them with. Then the herrings for their meal, whose dissolved heads were securing the panels, were still full of sharp bones, the bread was a mass of puddingy dough and the ale was flat. But this *was* God's house. If he wanted to swear he'd have to go outside.

Well, he did, so in mid-afternoon he left the nave

without checking the mess on the wall that Alexander was making of Herod and the Innocents, stood in Lombard Street and cursed at the top of his voice so the passing population stopped to listen. Then, much relieved, he stepped back inside.

But his happiness did not last long. Herod's head was far too big for his body. Randolf roared at Alexander for being a worse painter than the most untutored clodhopping country serf. He ignored Alexander muttering that if Herod was such a great monster then he ought to look like one. Instead, he roared at John for not mixing the pigments perfectly. Then he roared at William for not being there but working quietly back in the workshop where he couldn't hear him. Then he roared at Wulfrum for being a surly, uncouth wretch only fit for mixing glue and that too slowly, too late and – as he sniffed with shame – too stinking by half for God's house.

But Wulfrum, who was just a labourer, said nothing but stared back with a balefulness that quietened Randolf's anger at once. No servant would cow Randolf – but he'd heard about unrest in the countryside, Kent, Sussex, Suffolk, where working men were still in short supply after the plague twenty years ago and serfs demanded higher wages and more rights. Wulfrum was a serf once. Randolf well remembered the day he took the shivering wretch in off the streets and listened to his incoherent story of starving in the country and running away from a cruel master to London hoping for a different life. Well, Randolf was a compassionate man and had taken him in. But was it a case of "Once a serf, always a serf"? Serfs in the country had much to complain about. One day, he feared, it might end in rebellion and bloodshed. Ah, but never in London, which drew people in like flies to a spider's web, where men were content working for masters who were busy merchants and craftsmen, not idle barons.

But then he saw Wulfrum's face and he wondered. Not much contentment there.

Ah well, this cursed day of incompetence was his own fault. He should not have been so keen to get to work without losing time. Robin should have been given a time of quiet mourning. More haste, less speed. They were none of them working as they should and no wonder.

At last Wulfrum turned away and busied himself with Perkin and Herry. There were tasks for them all now. The panels had to go perfectly in place with dowels, glue and clamps to hold them firm till next morning. Alexander and John ceased painting to join in this last effort before sundown while the glue was still useable.

It was hard but delicate work. The centrepiece of the great threefold wooden panel behind the altar depicted the Crucifixion. Flanking panels showed on one side the body taken down from the cross, on the other the empty tomb. Overlooking the whole, on a panel which needed the most delicate fixing of all, was Randolf's own masterpiece, the risen Christ. He had painted this to fulfil the commission and for God's greater glory but deep down he felt a secret pride that he could express to no one. For after all, his talents were gifts from God which he should not hide under a bushel. They were *not* his own possessions. The scriptures told him so.

Now the whole altar wanted just one more item – the final panel showing Mary, mother of Jesus, to be fixed above the empty tomb where there was now a gap like a tooth knocked out in a fight.

So they weren't finished after all. Wulfrum would have to mix more glue. Perkin and Herry would have to hope the panel fitted first time. But if William had Hugh to help him, the panel would have been finished early enough to bring round and fix before the light went.

"You'll have to offend our noses again by morning, Wulfrum," said Randolf. "But only enough glue for one panel. No more, no less."

"We could have finished if Master Hugh were here," said Herry.

Randolf did not answer. He'd hardly thought about Hugh since they set off that morning for St Benet's. He was ashamed. But Alys would soon give him the news he wanted. Hugh was probably with his brother at Walter Craven's. Of course, Walter should have sent him back at once – but then, Walter had cares of his own. Oh, why didn't he think to give Alys authority to order Hugh to St Benet's straight away?

And did young Joslin look after her well through the streets? A likely lad that, very sad about Robin – as well he should be – and with strange tales to tell.

Now Randolf fell to different musings. He had the proper ambitions of any Gild man. Besides being known as a painter to the king, he wanted to be warden of his Gild, sheriff of the city, perhaps in the end even Mayor of London. Craftsmen didn't often reach such heights: most sheriffs and mayors were merchants. He remembered the night before: that sweet harp and tuneful voice taking them to times and lands unknown and heroes hardly imaginable. But soon Joslin would go – might even have left. He hoped not. He must try to persuade the young lad to stay. If he had his own living-in, full-time minstrel, good enough to play for a duke or king and so young he could only get better, would that improve his chances of being mayor?

Ah, but was he right to want it? Was ambition a sin?

75

He had thought much about this. No, he would use his position for good works, charity and the glory of God. His conscience was clear.

As dusk approached and they loaded their tackle on the handcart outside ready to leave, Randolf was in a surprisingly cheerful humour. Not even Wulfrum's sour face could depress him.

A man sat in the Guildhall, seriously worried. His name was Simon of Chichester and he was the city coroner, appointed by the King and answerable to him alone, but serving James Andrew, master draper, whose year of being mayor was nearly at an end. And he had done something which worried him.

The previous day he had been called to the Tower. This was strange in itself; the Tower was outside the boundaries of the city and the mayor's writ did not run there. But fetched he had been nevertheless, to find a woeful sight indeed. A young man, dead, the plague about him and a slit throat as well. Unknown and with no way of telling who he was. He could have been thrown overboard off a boat at night and his killers still on board a ship full of plague well out to sea and on the way to Flanders by now. If so, good riddance.

Yes, he knew why he'd been called. The body was fished out of the river by London Bridge. Nobody in the Tower would take the responsibility. So what could he do?

"This was not a rightful death," he said at once when he saw the knife stroke which had taken the life out of the lad. Then: "But this was the will of God," he said when he saw the plague swellings.

Guards and priest looked unhappy. They wanted a decision. So he made it.

"He's beyond our help and our knowing. I believe the poor soul is a Fleming or a German. Those who made away with him won't be seen again here in life or in death. So I say we commit him to the ground, say our Christian prayers over him and then forget what we saw. Least said, soonest mended."

He knew this was not the first time coroners had acted thus. He had done it himself and never heard another word. His job would be impossible if he did not.

"We can't bury him in Tower grounds," said the guard captain.

"Then we must take him secretly to the nearest church in the city," Simon of Chichester had replied, and had felt worried ever since.

Joslin had picked his way along Tower Street from London Bridge to the Tower. No, he wasn't followed. Perhaps that man had been a chance passer-by after all.

Now the White Tower stood close to. There was no castle Joslin had ever seen, no, nor no city gate, which had not at least said, "Come in and be welcome if you're a friend," even when it cast threats at enemies. But the conquering Normans had built this pile two centuries before simply to say, "We're masters here now. Defy us if you dare, worms."

Well, Joslin didn't know how the common folk of England saw it, but he – a foreign and, the King would say, an *enemy* foreign – was struck fearful. Go in and ask the Guard? He'd rather try to fly back to France using his arms as wings. So what could he do? He sat on a stone to think. The boatman said that the body had a slit throat and plague boils as well. So a chaplain in the Tower might well have shriven him even though he was dead. And then what? Buried? Would the Guard have started a hue and cry for the murderer? Should he go in and say, "If you've seen a body I know whose it may be?"

But then there was that dreadful thing the boatman said. The body had a slit throat and the plague as well. How could it be Thomas?

What should he do? Go in that forbidden place, not know what he wanted to ask and end up in a dungeon? Or go back to Randolf's after a wasted journey? But why should it be wasted? He would walk around for a while and make up his mind what to do.


All Hallows Church stood at the end of Tower Street, not a hundred paces from the Tower Ditch. Nobody was watching. Joslin slipped cautiously into the graveyard. If he had to think about the dead, then this was the best place to be. He soon made up his mind. He'd wasted his time. He'd followed a daft idea and got nowhere. He'd rest a while and then set off back.

Before he went, he looked round. Headstones, larger tombs of local magnates, a few fresh-dug mounds. In a far corner earth flew into the air. A gravedigger, hidden by the depth of his new pit, dug furiously.

Well, if anyone knew about dead bodies he would. It might be worth a last try. Joslin approached and looked down on him, standing on the floor of his new grave, sweating, near exhausted. He leant on his spade, glad of a rest.

"Friend," said Joslin, "I seek news of one who may be dead."

"Can't you tell the difference between the dead and the living? I fear you'll never make a gravedigger, then."

"I mean a friend of mine whose fate I don't know."

"And why should I be able to tell you?"

"You must know about dead bodies."

The gravedigger shoved his spade deep in the earth. "We all know about dead bodies seeing as everybody will be one in the end."

Joslin had a sudden wild idea. "I mean one who's been buried lately. In the Tower."

The gravedigger leapt out of the grave to stand beside Joslin. His doubts seemed to have gone. Had Joslin hit an impossible target?

"Ah," he said, "I begin to understand."

"I'm looking for a friend," said Joslin. "I'll gladly pay."

"Don't worry, lad. I believe you. You may settle a doubt which I don't like. I'll tell, but you needn't pay."

"You mean you can help me?" Joslin could not believe he'd found such light.

"They can drag me out of my sleep to dig a cover for bodies at any time. But here, not in the Tower."

"I don't. . ." Joslin began.

"Listen before you speak," said the gravedigger. "Last night, four hours after curfew, there was a thumping on the door of my hovel. When I opened it, there stood three of the Tower guard and a priest I didn't know. 'Up,' they said, 'and dig a grave before sunrise.' They had a wooden coffin with them and wouldn't let me delay. Well, if they pay me – and they did, handsomely for the inconvenience, I'll give them that – I'll do my job for anyone any time. So I selected a place out of sight by the wall and set about digging. They wouldn't let me dig as deep as I'd like; they said there wasn't time before daybreak. I'd got down hardly ten hand spans before the priest said, 'That's enough.' So they pushed the coffin into the ground and the priest muttered his prayers over him, though much good they'd likely do the poor soul, the state he was in, and left me to fill the grave."

He beckoned to Joslin to follow him. "It's over here," he said.

They walked to a dark corner in the shadow of the wall. Fresh earth in a mound, unmarked, soon to be forgotten.

"So you did what they told you and that's all," said Joslin.

"No, it is not," said the gravedigger. "Some grave-diggers might not dare such desecration, but why shouldn't I see what it is they were so secretive about? Strange things best not thought about can happen in that Tower. Why, I wondered, should the Guard and a priest be so keen to have this poor wretch shoved hugger-mugger out of the way? I pushed my spade into the coffin lid and prised it open. I pulled the body's shroud aside and looked. And by the light of my candle I saw them. A slit throat and the plague's shilling in the armpit. A mere youth, dead in two ways. Why? I wondered. Why murder a man the plague has already condemned? I covered the body up, put the lid back and replaced the earth. Then I came back to my bed and stayed awake for many hours. I was very afraid."

"Why?" said Joslin. "What had this to do with you?"

"Because I'd a fear that I'd seen what I shouldn't have seen. I feared that should it be found out it might go badly for me. Information is good and sometimes use-ful, but now and again it can be your death."

"Then why tell me?"

"God help me, I can't help myself. You're his age. If there's a man stalking the city with a knife sharpened for the throats of the youths of London you above all should know, to be on your guard."

Joslin clasped the gravedigger's hands in his own.

"What you've said stays secret. Nobody will know how I found out. I swear it."

The gravedigger looked at him. "I trust you," he said. "Will of Essex is my name and if I can help you any more I'll gladly do it. If you've found what happened to your friend then you'll know you've got a dangerous enemy. No, two – a murderer and a pestilence."

Joslin felt in his belt for coins. "No," said Will of Essex. "I reckon I've given you the worst news that I could. I won't be paid for that."

"Then you have my thanks," said Joslin.

"That's enough," said Will. "So I'll bid you farewell."

Joslin walked slowly away. The boatman's story was proved. Something devilish had happened to *someone* – and it *could* have been Thomas. Which meant Hugh, if he wasn't already dead, might be condemned to a hateful death as well. This was a Devil's web spun even closer than the one he had unravelled in Stovenham.

Will of Essex watched Joslin disappear out of the churchyard into Tower Street. Poor lad. He had something to think about now. Still, it wasn't his business. He jumped back into the grave he had nearly finished and started to dig. Then he was aware of movement above that shouldn't be there. He sprang out again – to see someone sidle through the gate into the street. Brown hose, grey half-coat. When had he entered? How long was he there? What had he heard?

Will of Essex returned to his task, troubled in his mind.

Joslin looked up at the sun, now far spent to the west. He panicked: how was he to cross this close net of streets eastwards and hope to light on Silver Street without getting lost? Steering by the sun might take him to a wide river, but wouldn't lead him to a small house. He must go back along Tower Street, down to London Bridge and along Thames Street until he found Fishwharf again, then turn inland and retrace this morning's steps. Besides, the image of the stranger by London Bridge would not leave him. How would he know if he were followed in the packed, jostling streets? But near the river – well, he might have a chance of seeing a stalker.

So back past Tower Ditch he walked, then east, by London Bridge, until he came down to Fishwharf, nearly deserted by people and screeching gulls alike now the morning's catches had been unloaded. Away from the river now, Bread Street, Milk Street, Tad Lane, Wood Street – and at last he was on paths remembered from the morning which would take him unerringly back to Randolf's.

The stranger paused a moment by the churchyard gate. Then he slipped into the porch of All Hallows. Here, he observed Joslin unseen – and it was almost as if he could see how his quarry was thinking.

He laughed quietly and mirthlessly as Joslin turned south towards the Thames.

"That's right," he said aloud. "Feel safe, my fine fellow. Even though I'm watching you."

The three labourers and two apprentices took it in turns to push the handcart. Randolf walked behind. Dusk was falling as they turned in through the gates. In the courtyard, Randolf, thinking he'd trust them for once to do something without supervision, ordered Perkin, Herry and Wulfrum to unload the handcart and Alexander and John to prepare materials for next morning's work. Then he strode to the hall and roared for Lettice, who appeared at once, Alys with her. Randolf, with cares of his own, never noticed her worried face.

"All right. Where's Hugh? Let me give him a piece of my mind."

Lettice hated Randolf in this mood. "Husband," she said. "You won't find him. Alys and Joslin will tell you."

Alys told him about their visit to Walter Craven. Randolf listened, his face darkening. When she finished he burst out, "And Walter's right. Hugh's gone home with his miserable brother. But I'll bring him back, roped to a hurdle. I'll have him put in the stocks as a common thief, because thief is what he is, or as good as." All the outrage of the master whose bond had been broken rose in him.

"I haven't finished," Alys murmured.

"What more can there be?"

"Joslin and I tried to find out more." She told him about Alfred of Ware and his strange story. "Joslin had this idea the dead man might be Thomas. If it is, we fear Hugh will go the same way."

For a moment Alys thought Randolf would burst with anger. But he controlled himself, enough to say without shouting, "Nonsense! Hugh's gone to Stoke Poges. I'll send to his stepfather Jacob Gaylor to bring him back."

Lettice laid her hand gently on his arm. "Randolf," she said. "I know it's hard to believe there's another death among the apprentices so soon. But we must think about it, in case it's true."

"Joslin would tell me a different story," Randolf replied. He looked round suspiciously. "Where is he?"

"We don't know," said Alys. "We've not seen him since he and I came back."

Now Randolf roared again. "He's left us as well. He's gone to Wales without a word of farewell. He saw what a desperate place this household is and went while he could."

"Never," said Alys. "He wouldn't go like that. He'll be in the workshop."

She came back a few minutes later. "He's not. But William says he went back into the city. His clothes are still by his bed. So's his harp. He'd never leave without that."

"Yet now darkness falls and still he's not here. What foolery let him loose in this town which even I hesitate to cross without company?"

"Joslin can look after himself," Alys replied. "He's

gone through worse already, more than we can imagine. He'll have to suffer even more before he reaches the end of his journey."

"But he's not here *now*," said Randolf. "And I want to know why."

The stranger passed quickly, as one who knew the place well, along Tower Street, Eastcheap, Candlewick Street, Bridge Row and Watling Street until he turned north along Cordwainer Street and Hosier Lane, over Westcheap where he kept himself close and unobserved, along Lawrence Lane into Catte Street and finally, by way of Aldermanbury and Wood Street, into Silver Street. Here he hid in a doorway opposite Randolf's house where he could watch and wait.

He knew how easy it would be to overtake this inexperienced youngster and be here to watch him end his journey. Half an hour had passed and dusk had well thickened before Joslin appeared. The stranger watched as he reached the gateway and disappeared inside.

"Safe for now," the stranger murmured aloud. "But don't rest easy. I'm still watching you."

Joslin reached Randolf's gateway with a calmer mind. He wasn't followed home. The stranger was just a chance passer-by after all. Those odd premonitions at London Bridge meant nothing.

Except that. . .

As he stood in the entrance to the courtyard, the same chill of strangeness that he had felt at London Bridge came. *A man with a face so unmemorable that he could never forget it was near, watching him. Such an unmemorable man – so Joslin didn't need to see him to know he was there.* Those thoughts were paradoxes.

They made no sense. But they had to. Joslin knew those same eyes were on him and a silent war had been declared.

He entered the courtyard with one thought: *This day has stirred up demons.*

The courtyard was empty. Joslin wondered what to do. Much as he would like just to flop down on his bed, sort out the day's events and then sleep, he had to see Randolf and Lettice first. And, most of all, Alys. He did not have far to look. Randolf stood waiting in the entrance to the hall. "Joslin!" he shouted. "Where have you been?"

In the hall, he faced Lettice and Alys as well. He blurted out his story, including the gravedigger and even the stranger. Finally, Randolf spoke wearily, "So what am I to believe? Hugh's gone to Stoke Poges, I tell you. If Walter says so, that's good enough for me. Besides, one mortal blow with Robin gone is enough for any house."

"Randolf," said Lettice. "You should listen to them. There should be a search. We should call the constables out."

"I'll not be made a fool of so rivals can say I wasn't able to look after my own affairs. Why raise a search when its quarry is safe at home with his mother and stepfather?"

"So you think these young people are mocking you and making trouble?" said Lettice.

Randolf growled grudgingly, "No, I don't say that. I think they're trying to spare my feelings, to make it seem that I'm a good master who can control his apprentices."

"But Randolf. . ." Lettice began.

"Silence, wife," said Randolf, quietly but with greater strength than if he had roared. "I've said what I've said.

There's an hour to dinner. I'll go to my chamber and be alone."

He marched out. Lettice followed. On their own, Joslin said, "Everything today happened as I said. You do believe that, don't you?"

"Of course," Alys replied. "But what does it mean? Why murder someone who'll surely soon die of the plague?"

"Maybe the murderer didn't know his victim had it?"

"Perhaps. So the murderer's probably dead of it by now."

"Perhaps thinking Thomas is the murdered man is just moonshine. There was no plague in Walter's house. So how could the man thrown in the river be Thomas?"

"The plague was at its worst in high summer," said Alys. "Autumn's here now. The weather's getting colder and the plague doesn't seem to like that. It will be gone completely by winter. It never spread like wildfire this time, not like they say it did before. It never reached us or Walter Craven, so it wouldn't start now. If the murderer *has* died of the plague, it means that we've wasted our time today because he could never have murdered Hugh."

"But it doesn't make sense," said Joslin. "If Thomas has taken Hugh home with him, where was he in the days between when he disappeared and Hugh went missing?"

"Getting drunk? Whoring? Gambling?"

"Someone would surely have seen him and told Walter."

"He might have gone outside the walls and come back for Hugh."

"Why? Why not go home with him straight away?"

"Joslin," said Alys firmly. "There have to be reasons

87

that we don't know but would understand if we did. Thomas *couldn't* have had the plague and whoever murdered that man *must* be dead by now."

"So I've been on a wild-goose chase today," said Joslin. "Ah, well, at least I've seen a lot of London."

He wondered whether to tell her about the stranger at London Bridge. But already she was talking about something as important.

"There's still a mystery to solve," she said. "Who attacked you last night? You say it wasn't Hugh. It might have been one of the labourers. But not Wulfrum because there was no glue smell."

"We'll never find that out either," said Joslin.

"He might try again tonight," said Alys. "You must watch out."

"How *can* I know who it is?"

"There are few to choose from if he comes from within this house."

"He has no stammer so he's not John. Nor is he another apprentice."

"Why so sure?"

"Because he ran into Robin's empty bed. I saw next morning where he lay."

Alys was silent. Joslin wondered if hearing that had upset her. Then she said, "So it's a labourer, an ostler or a servant."

"There was no stable smell on him, or kitchen smell either."

"So he was a labourer."

"Was it Perkin?"

"Perkin and Wulfrum are friends and of an age. But while Wulfrum's surly, Perkin's good-natured. If I feared either, I'd fear Perkin least."

"Well, it's not Herry."

"Why not?"

"Herry's harmless, gormless. He lacks some of God's gifts."

Alys shook her head. "Herry has a strange look in his eye. Vacant; nothing's behind it. Some say such people should be put away. For myself, I have doubts. If God's spirit isn't living behind those eyes as he does in most people, then who might fill his place? What if there's a demon growing there? How might it show itself?"

"That's not fair, Alys," Joslin replied. "I've known people before like Herry. They're harmless and their souls are innocent. I've seen men mock them and make cruel sport. I don't think that's right; they're God's creatures as much as anybody."

"No one here would either," said Alys. "Randolf has a special regard for Herry. That's why he works here. He's happy, fetches and carries and wants no more. But sometimes I see those eyes and I wonder."

"Then don't," Joslin answered.

Alys said nothing.

"So do we look beyond the labourers?" Joslin asked.

Alys looked down, biting her lips. "Joslin, everybody here is well-intentioned and works for the good of the household. If it weren't so, Randolf would send them away. But there are other matters in their hearts which nothing will wipe out. I know there are eyes in this house which follow me. I knew before we went to Stovenham and I feel it tenfold without Robin here. That's why you're feared and warned away. Some don't think you only came here to protect me."

She was quiet again and looking down at the floor. Suddenly, Joslin realized her face had crumpled into tears. "Alys. . ." he began.

She clung to him, crying her heart out. "I'm sure of

nothing any more," she sobbed. "What is there to be sure of now I've lost Robin?"

"Things will get better," Joslin said weakly. "I'll stay for a while."

"No," she cried. "Forget what I asked you. Go when Hugh returns, as Randolf said. This is my life now. The good things are gone for ever."

He tried to calm her, but knew he gave no comfort. Alys was a widow before she was married with nothing but household chores or the nunnery to look forward to.

As he stood there, he was aware of someone in the doorway to the hall, watching. A pale face on a body wearing a clean tunic. The face turned in a split second, giving him an impression of newly wet hair as if from a ducking in the Thames or a cold bucket of water.

He looked up, ready to shout. But the figure was gone, so quickly that he had no idea who it could have been.

A second supper in the hall, nearly as rich as last night's. Afterwards he played and sang as before. But there was no pleasure now. Randolf was restive, not paying attention. Hardly half an hour had gone before he stood up. "That's enough," he said.

Joslin put his harp down.

"You played well," said Randolf. "Don't think I'm displeased. But tonight's not the night for such things. We've too much to think about."

He stalked out of the hall to his chamber. Lettice followed. Immediately, servants appeared to clear the table. Joslin looked round for Alys. She had gone, to brood alone.

* * *

This night, nobody unknown crossed the courtyard with Joslin. The atmosphere in the apprentices' room was quiet, apprehensive – much different from last night. Hugh's empty bed made Joslin feel an outcast. There was little talk. When William announced he was putting the lanterns out, nobody objected. Easy, level breathing throughout the room soon showed sleep was the best way of smoothing out the trials of these strange days.

Randolf often talked with Lettice far into the night about his plans for great things. Lettice, however, had not expected anything like that tonight. So she was surprised with what he had to say.

"Wife," he said, "what do you think of young Joslin?"

Lettice did not think for long. "He seems a good young man. He has his own troubles which sound enough for any one, especially a boy with so few years to bear them, yet he's time for other's woes and treats them with as much care as his own. And what a wonderful singer he is, and what a harpist. I've never heard the like."

"I agree," said Randolf. "Are you thinking what I'm thinking?"

"What, that if he were to stay here he might even be a husband for Alys in due time? I'm sure she has a lot of time for him. And he for her, if truth be known. But he's got his own quest. Besides, he's French. One day he'll go home."

"I doubt that," said Randolf. "His destiny lies in these islands."

"But Alys has many months to mourn for Robin before she even thinks of marriage," said Lettice. "Joslin will have long gone from here."

"Wait a minute," cried Randolf. "I was carried away there by what you said. Alys marrying Joslin hadn't crossed my mind. Though now you've mentioned it . . . ah, but don't forget, I had an offer from a man once – a man who said he'd be rich in years to come. I'm not sure I liked him, but I can't deny he could make Alys a good husband. Now Robin's gone he may come back. Alys should have the choice, at least."

"I remember who you mean," Lettice murmured. "And you'll remember what I thought. I didn't like the man, either. Someone like Joslin would be better for her. It's more seemly that two young people marry than an old man and a maid, however rich the man may be."

"You're right, no doubt, as always," said Randolf. "But I didn't mean marriage. I'm thinking of something much more likely."

"What could that be?"

"That Joslin forgets his pie in the sky in Wales and stays in this household as our own minstrel. Think of it, wife. A minstrel living on the premises, performing to us alone; a minstrel as good as any in mayor's hall, duke's castle or even king's court. Why, we'd be the envy of every master craftsman in the city. With Joslin here I might be mayor myself within five years."

"With all the cares it would bring," said Lettice.

"It's every Gild man's rightful ambition," Randolf replied. "It's not wrong of me, is it? It doesn't mean I'm selfish and grasping? I have proper pride and I work for God's glory."

Lettice did not answer.

"Well, say something, wife," said Randolf. "Aren't I right?"

"Perhaps you are," said Lettice slowly. "But Joslin never came to London to suit *your* convenience and you can't ask him to stay out of selfishness."

"I'd pay him well," said Randolf. "And if he says yes, a wedding between him and Alys might happen one day. That would please you, wouldn't it?"

"It depends on them, not us," said Lettice and would say no more, so Randolf had to spend the night wondering how he could make such things happen without seeming a scheming, selfish hypocrite.

It was the same as the night before. Weight on his chest, smell of sweat, cloth in his mouth, a sharp blade at his throat. And a hoarse voice: "A second visit, Joslin de Lay, seeing as you're still here. If you know what's good for you, get on your way and don't come back. You've spent too long with Mistress Alys today while other men toil and that's an advantage we won't put up with. So *go*. Or there'll be a third young man who'll seem to have disappeared and nobody knowing where to look. This is a warning. There'll be no more."

Joslin stayed dead still, holding his breath. He stared up in the dark, trying to make out any feature of that face. He racked his brains to make the voice resemble one that he had heard in the last two days. He wanted to ask, "Who are you? Why should you say this when I only want to see Alys happy before I go?" But the slightest movement in his throat would make that keen blade draw blood. Besides, how could he know this man would not press further and slice his neck like the throat of the youth who might be Thomas Hockley? He waited, holding his breath, his heart beating wildly.

Suddenly the weight was gone, the rag out, the blade removed. He heard sure-footed steps, heading, he was certain, downstairs. He cried out in relief.

The apprentices woke, at first scared, then grumbling. William lit a lantern. "What happened this time, Joslin?" he said.

"The same as last night," Joslin replied, still shaken.

"Th-then where is h-he?" said John.

William lifted the lantern high. "Every spare bed's empty," he said. "Nobody's hiding. It was a dream, Joslin."

"It was no dream," Joslin replied. "Whoever it was ran downstairs."

"Then run after him," Alexander muttered. "And don't come back unless you can keep quiet for the rest of the night."

"At least I know it was none of you," said Joslin.

All night there was silence throughout Randolf's household. Nobody stirred to disturb the peace. But outside, just before dawn, things were different. Something was happening in the street which would shatter every nerve in every person who lived in that household.

Joslin woke early. Light was filtering through the window. Something had woken him up. What was it?

Yes, now he knew. From the workshop underneath. Someone had been stirring early. Wulfrum was preparing for the day's work at St Benet's. The rank smell of boiling fishheads rose through the floor. The other apprentices, used to it, slept on. To Joslin it seemed an offence.

The smell brought back that little niggle of the day before. *Something about making glue didn't add up and made a nonsense of what he was thinking.* He strained his mind to work out what it was, but no flash of understanding came. He lay back on his tickling straw pillow.

*Give it time*, he thought. *It will come.*

The apprentices scrambled out of bed and pulled their clothes on, made their beds and squared off everything in the room till it looked the acme of order. Joslin, to keep the peace, did the same.

Then they rushed downstairs for their frugal breakfast of bread, cheese and ale. Afterwards, they loaded up the handcart for the walk to Gracechurch Street. William was to go today now his panel depicting Mary was finished. The stinking, bubbling bucket containing just enough glue to fix it on the altar was loaded, together with pigments and brushes. Last was the panel itself, carefully wrapped in sacking.

Joslin watched. Yes, Perkin was ugly. But was he harmless? Could he have been the night's intruder? Or Herry? Joslin watched him as well. Small, fair-haired, good-natured – and, there was no denying it, vacant round the eyes. No, he could *never* utter threats and wield a knife at dead of night. And Wulfrum, surly, taciturn. Wulfrum looked different today. He had changed his tunic and hose. His face had somehow altered. Joslin could not work out how, but somehow the change rang a bell in his mind.

But did it matter? Joslin, before he slept last night and again when he woke, had thought hard about that latest threat. And what Alys had said to him that evening. "Go when Hugh returns, as Randolf said." So she had changed her mind from the morning. Then he'd take her at her word. It would be best. Yesterday seemed like a bad dream. He'd wasted his time on a wild-goose chase. What the gravedigger told him had nothing to do with Thomas, and Walter was right. Hugh would soon be found, either returning apologetically or happily far away at Stoke Poges. Nobody now thought he had anything to do with it. He'd ask for his dagger and go. He approached Randolf.

"Randolf," he said. "I have to go now. Please release me from my promise. Hugh will soon return. Thank you for such rich hospitality. I'll never forget it."

"Can't I persuade you otherwise?" Randolf asked. Joslin saw the disappointment in his eyes. "Wouldn't you like to stay here and be our own minstrel, well paid, well fed, comfortable and respected?"

Joslin stepped back, dazed. This was a temptation like John Hammond's on the quay at Ipswich. It would not be the last put in his way before he reached his journey's end, of that he was sure. For a moment he was tempted. But he fought it off. "There's too much ahead that I have to do. I owe it to my father. I'm sorry," he said at last.

"And so am I," said Randolf. "More than I can say."

He turned away, his shoulders hunched despondently. Joslin watched the little procession move out of the courtyard into the street.

Now he had a lot to do. He had to prepare for his journey, say proper farewells to Lettice, to Alys and then. . .

The cry of horror from the street carried back into the courtyard. A second later the handcart came bucketing in, with the apprentices, labourers and Randolf himself pushing it for all they were worth.

And jolting on it, sharing the space with the painted panel of Mary and a bucket of fish glue, was a limp, lolling body.

"Stop!" commanded Randolf. Servants, Lettice and Alys appeared as if from nowhere. All eyes looked at who was on the cart.

Unmistakably Hugh. As Randolf removed the cloak, they saw the equally unmistakable signs. A slit throat, a tunic stiff with blood and, on neck and under armpit, the black boils of the plague.

Serving girls screamed. Lettice sank to the ground, covering her eyes. Randolf ran to support her. Alys stood silent, her hand over her mouth. Ostlers, cooks and labourers stood apart, staring disbelievingly.

Joslin went close to the handcart. Yes, that was Hugh right enough, familiar though he'd seen him so little. He remembered the last time – dimly in lantern light, with him holding his father's dagger to Hugh's throat, Hugh's own knife gleaming in the half-light. Not thirty-six hours before. The slit throat, the tunic stiff with dried blood, those dreadful swellings like burst black peas: this was what the young man who'd once drawn a knife in anger had come to. Biting back his revulsion, but sure he'd heard somewhere that you couldn't catch the plague from a dead man, Joslin stretched his hand out, lifted Hugh's hand, then let it drop. He had become used to the sight of death in his time in England, but this was crueller than any yet save Robin's.

He moved close to Alys. He knew what she was thinking. *Alfred of Ware was right. Thomas is murdered, too.*

Besides, the boatman and the gravedigger had given the proof.

One thing was clear. Nobody would let him leave for Wales today.

"He was lying in the drain," said William. "Face down. There wasn't much blood. It had dried on his tunic. People must have seen him before we did. They'd think he was drunk and sleeping it off."

"It w-was his h-hair made us stop and t-turn him over," said John. "When w-we saw who it was, P-Perkin and Wulfrum p-picked him up and p-put him on the handcart. We pushed the paints and g-glue over to one side to m-make room for him."

"I took my painting of Mary and carried it myself," said William. "It would be blasphemy to let her stay next to a murdered man."

"You're all good lads," said Randolf.

Herry, Joslin noticed, did nothing. He stood by the handcart, looking at Hugh, a vacant half-smile on his face. Then, unexpectedly, he said something which Joslin heard but nobody else noticed.

"He was put there for us to find him. Nobody else."

"Randolf," said Lettice. "You must fetch the sergeant."

"One man to keep the law for the whole ward," scoffed Randolf. "What can *he* do?" Nevertheless, he detailed William to fetch him. "Giles Worsdell's all we've got," he said. "Justice will be hard to come by when a boy like Hugh can be left dead in the street."

William soon returned with Giles Worsdell the sergeant, a dark, square-jawed man. He nodded to Randolf, then looked at the body. When he saw the plague swellings, he recoiled. "Is there plague in this house?" he demanded.

"Look round you, man. Does it look like it?" Randolf

retorted. "This is how the poor wretch was found out-side."

"Do you know who he is?"

"Hugh, my own apprentice."

Giles gave Randolf a long, suspicious look. "Show me where you found him," he commanded.

Randolf led him outside. After a moment's hesitation, Joslin and Alys followed.

"Here," said Randolf. They were hardly ten paces from the gates.

They all looked down at the channel running along the middle of the cobbled street. Joslin noticed some-thing.

"Hugh must have been placed there after the rakers had been through cleaning the street," he said. "The drain's still clean, so it couldn't have been long ago. Yet the blood on his tunic is dry. His body isn't stiff in death yet, though it's cold. . . He must have been killed in the night, away from here, and brought to be left outside his home like a parcel half delivered." *And Herry was right,* he thought. *But why, when Thomas disappeared so completely?*

Giles Worsdell looked up. "Who are you?" he said.

"Joslin is my visitor and my guest," said Randolf firmly. "He has nothing to do with this death."

Giles grunted. "He only says what I would have found for myself."

Back in the courtyard, Giles looked down again on the body. "The plague's already well advanced. He must be buried quickly. Yet his slit throat tells me he met no rightful death. I shall have to fetch the city coroner. There's no time to lose if we've to look for a murderer. A jury has to be called." He turned to William, who, he seemed to think, was messenger for the household.

"Fetch a priest," he said. When William was gone, he spoke to everyone else. "This must be a murder because the plague isn't so advanced that it would have taken him yet. Perhaps to slit his throat was a kindness to the poor fellow after all."

"But you must see," said Randolf, "that he was murdered far away from here and that nobody in this house could be responsible."

Giles Worsdell did not answer but made commands before he left.

"Stay here. Nobody leave the courtyard until I return. Above all, nobody touch the body. Not even the priest when he comes."

Then he was gone, leaving everyone stunned.

William returned in a few minutes with the priest from St Olave's in Silver Street. The old man showed no surprise at Hugh's body; plague, rebellion, murder over many years meant there were no surprises left for him. He performed the rites in a low mumble, then, when he had finished, Randolf spoke.

"You'll have a burial soon when the coroner's seen him, Father."

"The coroner must call a jury," the priest replied. "But you're right, I'm sure. This poor fellow mustn't stay above ground longer than can be helped." He stood up. "I'll wait here for Giles Worsdell."

Nearly an hour passed before Giles returned, Simon of Chichester with him. Simon of Chichester was still worried. Should he have had that poor wretch in the Tower buried at once? Had he been too hasty? Was it purely through fear of those boils? Some said the plague did not spread from a dead man but he had no proof of that. For all he knew, it could spread and kill everybody who had been in that room. Some wise men said the

101

plague moved invisibly through the air. Others said it was all due to the unlucky conjunction of the stars. They could say what they liked. *Nobody really knew.* So should he have called a jury, to make at least a token attempt to identify the body?

And now Giles was describing a death to him which sounded exactly the same. This appalled him. It could not be coincidence.

He followed Giles into Randolf's courtyard and saw the new corpse. Yes, if ever there was a death which was not rightful, this was it.

He looked closer. Exactly as before: same slashed throat, though this time not bleached by days in the water, same boils of the plague. Which had killed him first? And why use a knife when the plague would finish him anyway?

This was devilry. Worse – this mysterious son of Satan had struck twice. The two dead faces were so similar they had to be brothers.

"Who is this man?" Simon of Chichester demanded.

Randolf told him.

Simon asked the question which would solve so much but could also mean trouble for him. "Has he a brother?"

"He has. Thomas, apprentice to Walter Craven of Cheapside," Randolf replied. "We thought Thomas had gone home to his mother and stepfather in Stoke Poges and Hugh had followed him."

But when Joslin heard the coroner's question he could not stop himself. "I believe Thomas may be dead as well, in the same way as Hugh, and buried at All Hallows in Tower Street."

Trying not to show the turmoil he felt inside, Simon turned a stern face to Joslin and spoke severely.

"And why should you think that?"

Quickly, Joslin recounted yesterday's events, leaving nothing out except the stranger, and ending with his talk to the gravedigger. Simon of Chichester never took his eyes off him. When he had finished, the coroner said, "I see. And where in France do you come from?"

Oh, that was it. Never trust your enemy. Joslin could have bitten his tongue off for blurting out all he knew in his unmistakable accent.

Randolf came to his rescue. "Joslin is my honoured guest. He's performed great services to this house. I believe he's as honest as day itself and I'd trust him with my own life. Besides, Thomas disappeared before we even knew him."

"That in itself could be a suspicious circumstance," said Simon of Chichester. "Perhaps new arrivals and new deaths go too easily together."

Randolf was having none of this. "Rubbish," he said. "Joslin and Alys were still in Suffolk. And besides" – daringly now, for this was a representative of the King he was talking to, even though he'd known him for years – "is there not therefore a body buried at All Hallows of a man who suffered the same death, which you either never knew about or allowed to be put in the ground without proper enquiry?"

Perhaps Randolf had had a brainstorm and thought his ambitions were fulfilled and he was mayor already; perhaps Simon of Chichester remembered Randolf's respected place in his Gild and his reputation as King's painter and had decided that one day he might be. After all, October was close and the yearly change of mayor with it. James Andrew would soon be succeeded by another Simon, Simon Mordon, fishmonger. But who would be mayor next year? Or the year after that? One day it might be Randolf Waygoode. The coroner thought he'd better be careful. King's man he might be, but he depended on the people's goodwill. Besides, this Frenchman's story had a certain ring of truth. Witnesses would not be hard to find – boatman, gravedigger, watchman on Ludgate. Even if it reflected badly on him, the truth had to be found. To start with, there was something they could do at once – though he hesitated about it because it was in itself a sin and they'd be no better than scavengers looting soldiers' bodies left on battlefields when the fighting was over. But there was no alternative.

"Very well," he said. "All you are saying leads me to a serious decision – the disturbance of a body laid to rest. We must dig up the grave at All Hallows. It's the only way to settle the matter." There was a horrified hiss of indrawn breath from everyone there. This was a terrible thing to do. Simon went on. "I must seek dispensation from the dean of St Paul's as well as tell the priest of All Hallows. Nothing must be left to chance. There must be no way in which we could be called to account for such a violation."

He turned to go. "You'll hear from me," he said. To the priest of St Olave's: "This body should lie in the church overnight before burial tomorrow." To Randolf again: "I suggest you get word to his stepfather in Stoke Poges – and also warn Walter Craven that by tonight he may know exactly where his missing apprentice has gone."

With that, he left them in the courtyard with much to think about.

Simon also had much to ponder on. His fears had good foundation. He had been wrong to order the quick burial of the corpse in the Tower, wrong to think it was just the body of a passing foreign and – which worried him even more – wrong to order such a thing on land outside the boundaries where he had no authority, even if the body had been found on the city side of the wall. The gravedigger was wrong to open the coffin afterwards – but what was there to be done about that if he were in the wrong as well? What if these London people – mayor, sheriffs, even Waygoode – complained to King Edward about him? He comforted himself with a good thought. The Tower people might want to keep quiet about it as well – he hoped. . .

The corpse might not have been a passing foreign after all, but he had *found* a passing foreign none the less. A Frenchman, not a citizen, not even trying to be a citizen – not like so many other foreigns who arrived in London – and staying in Randolf Waygoode's house. Was he a fellow-painter from Paris, exchanging skills, learning new ones? Perhaps. But it was something out of the ordinary. Simon of Chichester, when he investigated a death which was not a rightful one, did not like things which were out of the ordinary. He must learn more about Randolf's foreign guest, who knew a remarkable amount for someone who hadn't been in London for two days yet.

Randolf, meanwhile, was not lost in thought. He was issuing orders.

"Unload the cart and straighten poor Hugh's body on it respectfully," he said to apprentices and labourers alike. "Perkin, you go with the priest to St Olave's and bring the cart back empty. Then scrub it to make sure no trace of Hugh's last journey is left. William and Wulfrum, take horses and make ready for a journey. I'll give you money and food. You'll reach Jacob Gaylor and his wife in Stoke Poges by tonight. If they want to come back and stay here, all well and good – they're welcome. If they don't, that's their business. Remember, I'm sending an apprentice and a labourer together because if you meet trouble on the way I'd rather lose one of each than two of the same."

Whether William and Wulfrum found that comforting, Joslin did not know.

"Meanwhile," Randolf continued, "I must see Walter myself."

Within ten minutes, William and Wulfrum came from the stable leading the same horses that Joslin and Alys had ridden on from Stovenham. Their packs were loaded with bread, cheese and a flagon of ale. Randolf solemnly gave them twopence each with orders to give it back if they never needed it. As an afterthought, he said, "Stay there," and went into the hall. A little later he appeared with two short swords which they each secured at their belts. "The road westward can be dangerous," he said. Joslin shivered, knowing he was soon to follow this road. They awkwardly mounted the horses, sat looking unhappy and then clattered out of the courtyard. Perkin returned with the empty handcart which he commenced to scrub down outside the workshop. Randolf marched out of the gate to Cheapside and Walter. Lettice beckoned Alys to her and they left. All the servants went indoors to get on with their work.

Joslin felt at a loss. He had nothing to do. Everyone else seemed to be busy over matters which did not concern him. But he had to do something. Wandering aimlessly was no use. Alexander and John were busy in the workshop; Joslin guessed that even when the day's work at St Benet's was cancelled, there was still much to do. Well, there was one thing which he always did when at a loss. He went upstairs, took his harp and played and sang.

But today the magic would not work. Fifteen minutes passed; he had sung enough. Besides, in a house as broken as this, it was not right. He came downstairs again. Then he saw someone standing outside the workshop, looking as vacant and aimless as he was feeling.

Of course. Herry. John and Alexander were busy and so was Perkin. So there was nobody free to tell him what to do and he hadn't the wit, it seemed, to see for himself. Therefore he was doing nothing.

Joslin couldn't believe that it was Herry who had stuffed rags into his mouth and held a knife to his throat at dead of night. But now was a chance to find out – and perhaps more as well. So he went over to him. Herry saw him coming. He lowered his eyes, whether from shyness or fright, and turned to move away. But Joslin stopped him.

"Herry," he said, reaching out and taking him gently by the shoulder. "Don't go. I want to be your friend. I'd like to know you better, even if I will be leaving here soon to get on my journey."

"Oh, I don't know about a friend, you being foreign and all that."

"I'm a friend to others here, so why not you?"

That seemed to calm him a little. Out of the corner of his eye, Joslin could see Perkin still scrubbing the cart. He seemed to be neither watching nor listening. Even so, Joslin wanted to be out of his way. So he led Herry over to the staircase to the apprentices' chamber and, once out of sight, started his questions.

"What's it like here, working with Randolf?"

"Why do you want to know?" Herry still sounded suspicious.

"Well, you never know, I might end up working here as well."

Herry was suddenly frightened. "You won't take my job away? You won't have me put out on the streets, will you?"

"Of course I won't," Joslin replied. "I wouldn't be in the workshop. Randolf wants me to be the minstrel here."

Now it was out, he couldn't believe he'd actually said that to somebody, even if it was only Herry. Perhaps deep down he really did want to accept Randolf's offer after all.

But Herry only saw it as far as it affected him. "That's all right," he said. "I wouldn't be no minstrel. I don't know any songs or stories."

Then Herry said something which surprised Joslin and pleased him as well. "Master Joslin, if you do stay and be Randolf's minstrel, can you and I be friends? I don't mind you being foreign."

"Of course, Herry," Joslin answered.

"Only I en't got no friends here. They all think I'm daft. I am, too. But I'd like to have friends."

Joslin thought they'd better get away from that line of thought. So he asked another question. "Herry, where do you live?"

"Here."

"In the house? I've only seen you when you're working. I thought you lived somewhere else."

"I en't got nowhere else to live. I sleep in the straw over the stables. Wulfrum and Perkin sleep there, too, and so do the ostlers."

"And aren't you friends with them?"

"No. They laugh at me because I'm daft and they slip out at night after curfew and go drinking in the tavern and Master Randolf don't know about it." He suddenly put his hand over his mouth. "I shouldn't have said that. You won't tell him, will you?"

"No, Herry, of course I won't." But there was something here worth knowing. "How do they get out with nobody hearing?"

"I mustn't tell you."

"Oh, please." An idea. "If they won't go with you, perhaps you and I could one night. If we're going to be friends."

"All right, then," said Herry. Joslin felt a sudden stab of guilt at the ease with which he was prising information out of Herry simply through a half-promise of friendship. "When it's dark they slip out of the stable but instead of going through the courtyard they go into Randolf's little orchard at the back and then through the fence where they've made it loose but nobody can see it. And they've never been found out."

"I didn't know Randolf had an orchard."

"Oh, yes, lovely apples there, though we're not supposed to pick them. Randolf won't even let us have the windfalls."

If only he'd known this yesterday. Had he and Alys gone to look, would they have seen footprints still there in the morning dew to show where Hugh had gone?

"Do the apprentices ever get out that way?" he asked.

"They don't know about it. And they wouldn't dare go out after curfew. Master Randolf would kill them."

Joslin fully believed what Randolf might do if he found out, but it was hard to accept that William and the others never tried. After all, they *were* apprentices – and apprentices all over Europe were supposed to be an unruly lot, rioting, getting drunk and not giving a toss for anybody in authority.

He asked another question. "Herry, you wouldn't ever threaten me in the dark with a knife, would you?"

"Why should I do that, Master Joslin? You're my friend. Besides, I en't got a knife."

"Not even for work?"

"Well, work's work, en't it, and I wouldn't go sticking people with knives meant for work."

"Not even over Mistress Alys?"

Now Herry's face turned a deep shade of red. "Mistress Alys wouldn't look at me," he said. "It's no use me even dreaming about her or getting angry if folk misuse her."

"What do you mean, misuse her? Has someone misused her?"

"They wouldn't dare with Master Robin around. But. . ." He stopped.

"Go on," said Joslin.

"Oh, Master Joslin, I mustn't. I've said too much."

"One thing more. Why did you say Hugh was left for us to find?"

"Why, wasn't he? Did I say wrong? I thought when I saw him that he must be."

"And I think you were right," said Joslin slowly.

There was noise in the courtyard. People were coming back. Perkin had finished scrubbing the handcart; Randolf and Walter had returned and Randolf pronounced himself satisfied. The two master craftsmen walked to the hall. Perkin wheeled the handcart to the workshop entrance. Would Herry say any more? Yes, just one thing. "Master Joslin, the apprentices would go out through the orchard if they knew they could. It's hard trying to open the main gate without anybody hearing. And if you do get out, someone might find the bolts undone and do them up again so you're locked out all night."

Herry left the staircase and slipped into the workshop himself. Joslin sat on the lowest step, thinking over what Herry had told him. He had a feeling that everything was important, though at the moment he couldn't quite see how. And nothing was more important than what he had said about Hugh's body even before Randolf had sent for the sergeant. *"He was put there for us to find him. Nobody else."*

No, Herry was nowhere near as daft as people made out. He'd *like* to have him as a friend. He seemed as shrewd as many and quite likely truer than most.

hen William and Wulfrum returned next day they had a strange tale to tell. That each had a different view of what had happened made it all the more riddling.

William rode horses regularly when he was a boy in Kent but Wulfrum hardly ever had, even when a serf in the country deep in Oxfordshire so many years before. Their horses walked through Ludgate, crossed the River Fleet over the bridge, along Fleet Street and the Strand, past the Palace of Westminster in the royal city next to their own – and by now Wulfrum was hanging on for dear life.

"Keep up," William shouted. "We must get to Stoke Poges before nightfall. Today's bad enough without trusting my life to Randolf's blunt sword when the robbers ambush us."

Wulfrum was too out of breath and flustered to answer but he seemed to see the point and by Chiswick he had more or less got the hang of the horse. By noon they were well along the Thames. William knew that following it would take them miles out of their way. They must go the straight way across Hounslow Heath, a wild place. If robbers were to set on them, it would surely be there.

"Then we'll put our swords at our belts," said Wulfrum. "We'll show them we're as wild as they are."

There was no other way. William felt a shiver of foreboding as he buckled the weapon on. Any proper robber worth his salt would laugh at it. Still, what would that robber do if they were unarmed?

The heath was a vast, trackless place. Noon had long passed before they reached the tiny settlement at Heath Row and stopped outside cottages, within sight of peasants working. Here they ate their bread and cheese and drank beer while the horses cropped fine grass.

"Ah, we're well on our way," said William. "We'll make it." Randolf had not needed to tell him where Stoke Poges was; Hugh had told him the way often enough – "The heath to the Thames at Windsor and then within sight of Edward's great new castle you turn away through the beeches of Burnham till you reach Stoke Poges. And it's good to be out there on your own without the press of London folk around you."

But Wulfrum was uneasy. "I reckon if we go on this way we'll come to Thame, where I ran away from all those years ago. I passed by here when I fled. If anyone should see me who remembers, I'll be taken, whipped, branded and set in the stocks. I could be hanged."

William laughed. "Who'd remember?" he said. "That was years ago. And we're not going to Oxfordshire." He remembered something he had once heard. "And your old master's dead, isn't he?"

William was shocked at how Wulfrum's face went suddenly pale. "I wish he was," he said.

"But you'll never see him again. What do you mean?"

But Wulfrum would say no more. His mouth was tight shut and from now on he was silent, sullen, no sort of companion at all. William began to long for the end of their journey.

Besides, Wulfrum's words made William uneasy as well – not for his companion's sake but because two murders had sent them on their errand. As they set off again, he had unpleasant thoughts. These murdered men were apprentices like him. Could he be next? Perhaps they had more than casual robbers or the lord long ago cheated of Wulfrum's labour to worry about.

The sun shrivelled in the grey sky along with the thought as they reached the river and then left it, heading north and hardly noticing the new bulk of Windsor Castle on the other side. Now they passed through dark beechwoods. They shivered for what might hide behind every tree. October was now here: the day drew in and light waned. Ominous shadows under the branches gave William yet more frightening fears.

"Do you feel someone's watching us?" he said. "I do. Bad things are going to happen because of our journey. I feel it in my bones."

"That's all right," Wulfrum replied. "As long as nobody's after me." Away from the river and the road to Oxfordshire, he seemed to have cheered up. William shot him a suspicious look. If it came to a choice between robber band and loyalty to him, he had a pretty good idea what Wulfrum's decision would be.

But nobody stirred behind the thin-barked, muscular-looking trunks except for scurrying woodland animals. Nobody swung down on them from high branches like Robin Hood. The treetops were only disturbed by chattering birds. "You're useless," said

Wulfrum. "There's nobody watching for us. You're frit of your own shadow, you are."

William had to agree. He tried to shake off these evil thoughts.

It was nearly evening when they broke out of the trees into the village of Stoke Poges. They found the manor house in which Jacob Gaylor lived with Cecily, his new wife, mother of Thomas and Hugh. She had brought the house, lands and acres of beechwood as dowry to her second husband. The house showed no signs of life. All William's feelings of foreboding returned.

They crossed a moat. The small gatehouse was deserted. They came to the hall. William dismounted and beat on the door. There was no reply. Wulfrum stayed on his horse, saying nothing. William shouted, "Jacob! Jacob Gaylor."

At last two people came – a young priest and a man, thickset, dark-jowled, bearded, in middle age. William stared at him. "You're not Jacob Gaylor," he said. "You're not Hugh's stepfather."

"No, that I'm not," was the reply. "Who are you?"

William didn't answer that question at once. Instead – "But I *do* know you. I've seen you somewhere before. I *know* I have. . ."

"Well, I don't know you. Who are you? What are you doing here?"

"It's Jacob we want," said William. "We must talk to him."

"Then come to him, by all means," said the man. "And Dame Cicely as well."

He led them through the hall and solar to the first bedchamber. Here was a bed fit for a duke, with posts at each corner and red curtains of some richness. He pulled back the nearest curtain.

On the bed lay, side by side like effigies of a lord and lady on a great tomb in a cathedral, a man and a woman. William knew them – Hugh's mother and stepfather.

"Are they asleep?" he said. "I must wake them and tell my news."

"You can try, but it will take you a long time," replied the man.

Then William realized: they lay still because they were dead. So now a whole family had been wiped out.

Joslin went up to the apprentices' chamber and took his harp. Singing might come easier now. He tried out some old ballads, perfecting weaknesses, inventing variations. Then he mused – here he was in one of Europe's foremost cities in a great realm. He could not leave without a stock of its songs and stories, or without making some himself. He tried chords on his harp and played with rhythms and words.

No, nothing would come – not yet. But of London he would sing one day, when all this was over. And Alys would listen to him. So would Gyll. He remembered the last time he had seen Gyll, in the castle at Stovenham, before he and Alys had left, when he had foolishly thought that no more than a long journey lay in store and violent death was put behind him. No chance. Murder never slept: the dark figure of the killer haunted his dreams – in Stovenham and now here. But what about that first smiler with a knife in the castle in France, whose victim was the closest of all to him? Was it the man with the sallow, pock-marked, twisted face who had leered along passageways, down staircases, round corners before his father was knifed to death? Would Joslin meet him again? And what would happen then?

And would he ever see Gyll? What would happen if he did?

*No, these thoughts bring melancholy. Stop them and do something.* There were things here and now to work out. He put down the harp and walked to Robin's bed. Yes, it was still rumpled as though someone had lain there during the night. Nobody had touched it; each apprentice would only look after his own bed. Last night the intruder had gone straight down the stairs. Why had he not stayed this time?

Who cared, in the light of the terrible death of poor Hugh?

Well, Joslin cared, because it was he who the night visitor threatened.

He sighed and went back to his minstrelsy. Soon he was lost in it again – until a voice downstairs broke his concentration. "Joslin? Are you there?" Alys. He put his harp on the bed and ran down the steps.

"I've embroidered until my fingers are sore," she said.

Though cloud was low, Joslin could see the sun dimly showing through, far to the west. How many hours had he spent alone upstairs?

"Simon of Chichester and Giles Worsdell aren't back yet," she said. "Nobody can do anything until they are."

"Then I've things to tell," Joslin replied. "I've spoken to Herry."

He told what Herry said, especially about how Wulfrum, Perkin and the ostlers got out after curfew. "Let's go and look," he concluded.

They passed the stables. They heard sweeping and washing down but only horses watched them go by. In the orchard, branches of apple trees bearing good fruit reached close to the ground. The fence marking Randolf's boundary was high, wooden and tarred.

"The alley beyond leads to Babe Lane and the city wall," said Alys.

"And here's where the fence is loose," said Joslin. He had tried all the boards one by one and had found one which moved to the side leaving a gap just big enough for an adult to get through. He looked at the ground round it. "Is it my imagination, or is the grass worn here as if this way out's used a lot?"

Alys looked as well. "It's not your imagination," she said. "Is this where Hugh was taken, then?"

"Or went by himself, of his own accord," Joslin replied.

"Do you think that's likely?" asked Alys.

"As likely as anything else. What I can't understand is whether me being threatened every night has anything to do with Hugh and probably Thomas being murdered."

"But you said that at first you thought the person who woke you up with his knife at your throat was Hugh."

"Only because he threatened me before. In a puny sort of way."

"But that's a connection on its own. It's as if Hugh disappeared *because* he threatened you."

"That doesn't make any sense. Hugh threatened me about you. Then someone else threatened me about you. And don't forget I was threatened about you even while we were still in the courtyard. That could have been by Hugh or by the second one or by someone else altogether. It was in the dark and I didn't know anybody then. So if anyone had disappeared and been found dead afterwards it ought to have been me."

"So what are you saying?" said Alys.

"I think there are three possibilities. The first is that Hugh knew he was going to leave that night, waited until everyone was asleep, then stole down to the orchard and through the fence on his own. The last thing Herry said to me was that the apprentices would go through the orchard if they knew they could. Well, perhaps they did. The second is that the person who attacked me hid on Robin's bed until everyone was asleep, then took Hugh out with him. Nobody heard, so Hugh must have wanted to go and wasn't surprised, or whoever took him somehow made sure Hugh couldn't make any sound. The third is that my attacker has nothing to do with it. Someone else altogether came in and took Hugh. That person might have been the one who hid on Robin's bed."

"And which is it?"

"I'd say the second – if he hadn't come again last night. I don't understand that. Surely he wouldn't want to risk being found out?"

"Unless you're his real target."

"How can I be? Nobody knows me. If it wasn't for you, they'd never bother about me."

Suddenly something clicked together in his mind. He stared at her. "Alys, *you're* the only connection. Everything that happens, except Thomas's disappearance, seems to be to do with you."

Alys shuddered. "Don't say that." She paused, then continued. "There's something that's been at the back of my mind for a long time," she said. "Since we've been home I've thought about it a lot."

"What is it?" She did not answer at once. "Don't tell me if you don't want to," he said. "It's none of my business."

"Oh, but it is – especially if it's connected." She was silent again, as if collecting her thoughts, then started. "A long time ago, when I was only thirteen, Randolf told me that a man had asked if he could marry me. This man said he had a good estate, or soon would have, and would make as good a husband as any girl in my position could expect. All he wanted from me was a sufficient dowry, and he knew enough to be sure I'd bring it to him. Well, Randolf told him I was too young and there was an end of it. But when the man had gone, Randolf told me."

"And who was this man?" Joslin asked.

"Randolf wouldn't say. I thought he was just trying to make me feel good, to let me know I was in demand and I'd never have to starve or go into a nunnery. He said I wouldn't want to know, he'd sent him away and there was an end of it. Anyway, Randolf was right, I didn't want to know. But I've thought a lot about it over the last two days."

"But *is* it connected? And if it is, why should poor Hugh and Thomas have to die?" He sighed. "This is like a great mire. We'll never reach the firm ground."

"But we have to," said Alys.

There seemed no more to say. They left the orchard and entered the courtyard just as Simon of Chichester was coming through the gates and shouting for Randolf.

William stared at the two prone bodies. So much death at home – and then to come all this way to find more. He tore his eyes away and turned to the bearded man.

"But when?" he gasped. "How?"

"How indeed," was the reply. "As to when, just an hour before you arrived."

*Yes*, William thought, looking at the man. *I know that face. But where have I seen it? And who was he, this interloper in the house where once lived their dead workmate?* His hand straying towards Randolf's sword, he asked. But he need not have worried. The man answered easily and frankly. "I'm Edward Gaylor, brother to Jacob whom you see lying here. So you find me in a brother's grief."

That meant he was a sort of half-uncle to Thomas and Hugh. He ought to hear their news. But how, William wondered, to break it?

Edward saved him the trouble. "But I forget myself. You have terrible news yourselves, you say. Then you must give it, even if the ears it was meant for will never hear it."

"Just as well," growled Wulfrum.

Now William found words pouring out of his mouth: Thomas disappeared, Hugh foully murdered, the likelihood that his brother had suffered the same fate. Edward Gaylor listened gravely, while William reasoned: *if he's their stepfather's brother, he might have come to visit them in London and I saw him in passing.*

Edward Gaylor heard him out. At first he merely nodded – almost, William thought, as if he were not surprised. Then he looked at the two bodies. "I'm almost glad they weren't alive to hear that, for all that Jacob wasn't overfond of his stepsons."

"But how long were they ill?" asked William. "And do you live here with them?"

"No, I don't live here. I count no place as home. I wander, I travel, across England, Scotland, all Europe, making a living as I go. Jacob was my elder brother. We got on well before our father died. Why, together our family once helped in a great service to our King, for which he never showed proper gratitude. Jacob, of course, inherited our family estate and gained the estate next door when he married Cicely. That wasn't for me. I wanted the whole world."

William, bound apprentice to a stern master, with a craft that would never let him starve, whether as journeyman or master, shivered at the thought of such a journey into the unknown. "I arrived here but seven days ago," Edward continued. "And I found them, as far as I could tell, in good spirits. But since then, their decline to death has been swift and sudden, awful to behold – as though God decided He had no use for them after all. They started the day well, then shrivelled before my eyes this very morning. I could do nothing. I'm no physician and didn't know where to find one. They took to their bed by the eleventh hour howling with pain and died an hour before you came. But they didn't die looking as they do now. I laid out their twisted bodies to show respect and for when the priest came, too late, alas, to shrive them while they lived."

The priest spoke. "Edward's been back here seven short days. It's a cruel thing for him to come home at last just in time to see his nearest die before his eyes."

William said nothing. How shattering were the ways of God when He gathered up His thunderbolts to hurl at His target. Thomas and Hugh Hockley, Cicely and Jacob Gaylor, all in different places – but God on high could see all four at once. They must have displeased Him, so He had said, "*Now!*" and in the twinkling of an eye all were gone. Such was the way God disposed of humankind, and there was no arguing with it.

There was only one thing to do. They had to get out of this new house of death. "We must turn round and go back home," he said. "Randolf must know of this at once."

"I'm not going through those beechwoods in the dark," said Wulfrum. "Or across Hounslow Heath."

"I'd not hear of such a thing," said Edward Gaylor.

"You'll stay here until morning. Don't worry, the dead won't rise up and harm you. There's a bed for you, William, and good straw over the stables for the servant. But first you must eat and drink."

He led them into the kitchen. "Dame Cicely made good capon pies," he said. "Here are two they'll never eat now. And strong ale as well."

There was a flagon on the table and William picked it up – just a second before Edward could take it himself. It was a quarter-full of wine. William took a beaker and was about to pour himself a drink.

"I'd rather wine than beer at a time like this," he said.

But Edward moved fast. He dashed both flagon and beaker away, strode to the door and emptied the contents on the ground outside. "That would be impious and wrong in the sight of God," he shouted.

"Why?" asked William, puzzled.

"Because it was from that flagon they were drinking before they left this kitchen for their last rest."

"What do you mean?"

"That good Rhenish wine was their last earthly sustenance, so no others should share it. That would be a sin before God."

"Rubbish!" Wulfrum shouted.

"No," cried Edward. "I'm right. Such a flagon is made sacred because Cicely and Jacob drank from it before they died."

He stood in front of them, breathing heavily, his face flushed, suddenly angry. William was immediately struck fearful, sure of something else that was evil. These poor people were *poisoned*.

Edward was looking intently at him. "Yes, I know what you're thinking. But if what killed them lay in the wine it was not put there by me or anyone in this place.

That flagon was a gift from a stranger from far away, for those two and no other, as a sign of goodwill to *me*. Believe it, please. I'd not knowingly harm my own kin."

*Funny sort of goodwill*, William thought. But he returned Edward's intent, earnest look. Yes, this man meant it. And if he didn't – well, best that William believed him all the while they were here. "All right," he said equably. "I'm sorry." He settled for pie and ale. In spite of everything, they went down very well. And Edward Gaylor regained his friendly manner at once.

By now, darkness was well descended. Edward Gaylor showed them where to sleep. He took Wulfrum to the stables, then came back to William. "Have a good, quiet night and forget this day's trials," he said. "Be gone when you like in the morning, don't worry if you don't see me, take what provisions you want for your journey and make good speed to London. I may stay here a few days to see everything decently carried out, then be on my way. I doubt that we'll meet again."

He left, the priest with him, and William prepared for bed. He slept well, was up – through habit – at daybreak and found Wulfrum already in the kitchen. There was no sign of Edward Gaylor. Had he changed his mind about staying? William took a game pie and a mutton pie for the journey, then refilled Randolf's flagon with ale. Together they breakfasted on bread, cheese, apples and a freshwater trout. Wulfrum had seen to the horses; a weak sun rose over the treetops as they mounted and were on their way.

Neither spoke for a long time. Wulfrum broke the silence.

"You caught him on the hop last night. He'd meant to get rid of that wine before anybody saw it."

And as his horse trotted along the track through the

beechwoods, William wondered if Wulfrum was right and Edward might not be as innocent as he seemed. Then he remembered that earnest, intent look as he insisted on his innocence. No, this Edward Gaylor had *not* poisoned his own brother and sister-in-law. He was sure of it. But he reckoned Edward knew who had.

The darkness of All Hallows churchyard was dimly
lit only by a few lanterns. Round the grave stood
Simon of Chichester, Randolf, Walter Craven, Will of
Essex, Joslin and two constables. Randolf and Walter
were there to identify what might be a disintegrated body;
Joslin was there to prove his story with the gravedigger.
Also, there was the parish priest, to ensure there was no
desecration and that everything was done in a seemly
manner.

The night was chilly. There was a low moon. Frost
would come tonight; the coming winter would be hard.
Joslin shivered. It was easy to believe the souls of the
dead would rise up from their coffins in fury at the peace
of one of their number being disturbed. The mood
round the grave was tense; others must feel as he did,
even those as used to death and its causes as Simon of
Chichester.

Will of Essex knew Joslin at once and corroborated
his story. Then he dug quickly through the loose soil
and piled it up high on one side. He and a constable
jumped into the grave and lifted the coffin out. Carefully,

because soon he would have to replace it so it would last until the Day of Judgement itself, Will prised the lid open. He leant down and shone his lantern on the dead face.

Everyone recoiled. Joslin had a sudden flash of confusion. *What if it's not Thomas? What if it's someone we don't know who's met the same death as Hugh? What if Thomas is still alive, watching us, laughing at us, for strange, unknowable reasons of his own?*

Randolf and Walter bent down to the body. After five days, three of those in water, it was a ravaged sight. Even so, they were in no doubt – and, yes, Joslin had known really what they were going to say. "That's young Thomas all right," said Walter. "The poor lad. I had my ups and downs with him, but what had he done to deserve that?"

Simon of Chichester motioned to Will to close the coffin and lower it back into the grave. The priest said prayers for this reburial and Will replaced the soil. Everyone watched to see it decently done.

But even before the grave was refilled, Will suddenly threw his spade down. "Hark," he cried. "Someone's here who shouldn't be."

"What do you mean, man?" demanded Simon of Chichester.

"If anyone strays into my graveyard who shouldn't be there, I *know*," said Will. "Someone's here now, watching us." He paused, listened and then said, "Whoever it is has just run out through the gate."

"Some drunk roaming the city after curfew," said Giles Worsdell.

"Drunks wouldn't care who knows they're around," said Will. "This one was skulking secretly. But he couldn't cheat my sharp ears."

Simon of Chichester took this seriously. "Go and see," he said to the constables. "Catch any intruder you find and bring him here."

While they were gone, Will said, "I'm right. I *always* know. I've charge over this place same as the priest has over the church and I won't have it interfered with by those who shouldn't. I'll wager that whoever it was was the same as stalked this young fellow yesterday."

"Stalked me?" cried Joslin.

"Who was it? Describe him," said Simon of Chichester.

"A man. I don't remember his face, but he wore grey with brown hose and he ran like a hare before the dogs as soon as I called out."

A cold feeling which had nothing to do with the frost crept over Joslin. So he had been right about yesterday's stranger. "I saw him myself," he said. "In grey with brown stockings, like you said, watching me by London Bridge. I wondered if he was following me – but then he disappeared. So I thought he was just a passing stranger."

"And so perhaps he was," said Simon of Chichester. "A chancer, a hanger-on; a frequenter of graveyards and follower of strangers."

Joslin knew that Simon of Chichester was wrong. There *was* someone watching them, laughing, who knew their business, who knew they would be in the graveyard tonight, who knew Joslin even before he had been in London for twenty-four hours. Just as at Stovenham, the dreadful feeling came that everything about him was known and his fate was being worked out by a silent, murderous watcher in the dark.

Simon of Chichester carried on speaking as if what had happened was of no consequence. "Our melancholy business here is finished. We know the truth. Two brothers are dead and their deaths are not rightful. I shall call a jury of all those who have inform- ation to give on these sad matters to meet before the sheriffs at the Guildhall the day after tomorrow, after Hugh has also found his resting place in the ground."

The constables came back. They had seen no one. They plainly believed that Will of Essex was drunk him- self – or driven daft by being with dead people all his life.

So the silent procession left the graveyard and started its journey through a London deserted because of the curfew, carrying lanterns, wary of footpads, pleased when they had reached their destinations. Meanwhile, Will of Essex closed his graveyard gates and went back to his hovel, hoping that he would not be called upon again for such terrible tasks as he had twice now performed.

*The watcher Joslin so feared looked on as the exhuma- tion party unknowingly passed within a few short yards of him. Fleetingly, he wondered if he had miscalculated. Perhaps things weren't going quite as he intended.*

*No, that was impossible.* He *was master of events, nobody else.*

Simon of Chichester climbed into bed beside his sleep- ing wife. Before he slept he thought. *That was a strange time in the graveyard. Real evil was afoot. Could the Frenchman have anything to do with it?*

As he asked himself this question, a thought came into his mind which made him gasp with its signifi- cance. Suddenly he was sure he was close to unravelling this riddle.

When Joslin slipped into his bed, the apprentices were soundly sleeping, too tired even to hear the night's result. For a moment he lay awake, looking back over the eerie experience in the graveyard, expecting at any moment a knife at his throat and the whispered threats of the last two nights.

But nothing came. Soon he slept, deeply and soundly because he was tired out. When he woke at daybreak John and Alexander were already dressed and on their way downstairs. He sniffed. No smell of fish glue. But of course not. Randolf would not be going into any church to work this morning because Hugh would be laid to rest today. Besides, William was not back yet. That meant neither was Wulfrum – and glue-making seemed to be his job and nobody else's.

Fish glue. Why did his mind keep coming back to it, as if he was just out of sight of something important?

William and Wulfrum made good speed through the beechwoods, down to the river and across Hounslow Heath. With such news to bring back, William never thought of robbers. He kept his horse going at a good trot and Wulfrum, who seemed happier on his beast, kept up. They stopped again at Heath Row to eat Dame Cicely's pies and drink Jacob's ale, then carried on to Westminster, Ludgate and the city itself. Even when they were eating, the two hardly spoke. Wulfrum, William noticed, seemed preoccupied, as if dreams in the night had made him far more stirred by these two deaths than he had appeared the evening before.

As they clattered under Ludgate, the new cares in Randolf's house came back and filled William's mind. By the time they were in Silver Street he had half forgotten what happened yesterday. Soon he had joined the melancholy band bound for St Olave's to the tolling of the passing bell, to see that all was done fitly and fairly for Hugh. Yesterday might as well never have been, especially when he heard about last night at All Hallows. But by the graveside he remembered the day with new force and couldn't wait to tell Randolf. He looked for Wulfrum to back him up – and then realized he had not seen him since they had entered the gates of Randolf's courtyard.

Joslin, like the rest, listened to the Latin phrases of the funeral rite in the old priest's reedy voice and wished that for the time they had known each other he and Hugh had been on better terms. What had poor Hugh and his brother done to deserve such dreadful fates? What were they but apprentices to their crafts, with lives ahead as, at worst, journeymen who would turn their hands for anybody, at best, masters as rich and influential as Randolf and Walter? They'd never want for anything because they had good trades at their fingertips – and a goodly home in the country as well. Not only that, but solid inheritances were held in trust for them until they came of age. Why, they were almost rich already. The lives they should have had were so much more fortunate than those of most people in this benighted, fallen world.

Yet now they were gone, never to enjoy their good fortune.

He caught his breath. *Was that why they had died?* Was someone so jealous that he – or she – would kill out of envy? Might Wulfrum or Perkin or Herry or the ostlers have said, "Why should you have so much and me so little?" and slit their throats in anger at the unfairness?

But the more he thought, the more unlikely that was. Anyway there was that terrible fact, beyond understanding, that Hugh and Thomas died in the grip of the plague. Wulfrum and the rest certainly weren't. They were healthy and as well fed as Randolf could make them. There was no plague in this house.

He looked at William, soil-spattered from his journey. He was shifting from foot to foot, restless, as if respect and sorrow for his workmate was at war with something making him nearly burst with impatience. He wondered where Wulfrum was. Perkin, Herry and the ostlers were standing solemnly with the rest. So why not Wulfrum?

Randolf would not let William say a word about their visit until Hugh was properly laid to rest and everybody had come back from St Olave's. But then Randolf took William into his solar alone to say what he had found. When they emerged, Randolf's face was grim and William's was still as excited and flushed as it had been by the graveside.

"To work, everybody," Randolf roared. "There's too much death in the air today and only hard graft can shake it off us. We'll get ready to go to St Benet's and make the most of the last of the light."

Soon the apprentices and labourers were hard at it in the workshop. The familiar fishy smell wafted over them as Wulfrum, returned from his mysterious errand, started the boiling again. Everything needed on the handcart was brought out, while Randolf watched. Joslin gave a hand – and noticed that Randolf looked preoccupied, as if hard graft didn't apply to him today. "Go to St Benet's on your own," he said to the apprentices. "You know what you're supposed to do and you don't need me. I must talk to Walter. Everything is changed. There's problems beyond our wit to solve."

"What does he mean?" Joslin asked William.

"He means that Hugh's mother and stepfather are dead as well. Mother, guardian and two wards, all gone. There's a tangle to sort out."

"How can they be dead?" Joslin asked.

William described what they had found in Stoke Poges. "Laid out straight like effigies on a tomb. Hands clasped in front of them, coins over their eyes, still warm from the lives they'd been leading till just before we arrived. It was a sight to chill the blood, I'll tell you, especially so soon after seeing Hugh huddled up in the roadway."

"Tell them about the wine," Wulfrum grunted. He was listening to every word, for all he seemed attentive only to his glue.

"I don't like to, for fear of what it means," said William.

"If you won't, I will," said Wulfrum.

"All right," said William. "They were poisoned. Gaylor admitted as much. But not by him. He had some tale about the wine being a gift from far away."

"S-so what d-do you th-think it means?" asked John.

"*I'll* tell you," said Wulfrum. "I'm not frit. That was no gift from a stranger. He killed them, didn't he? He'd poisoned their wine. He's been all over Europe, he has. He knows about things to slip in your drink or sprinkle on your food that make Death creep up before you know it and he's brought them with him. And he used them on those two. But he didn't want William to go the same way." He spat on the floor. "Good of him, wasn't it?"

"Why should he want to kill them?" cried William. "That's his brother who's dead."

"But who is this man?" asked Joslin.

"Edward Gaylor," Wulfrum replied. This affair was making him very talkative. "Brother to Jacob and so uncle to Hugh and Thomas."

"Only a half-uncle," said William.

"That don't matter," said Wulfrum. "He's still—"

"The nearest relation, who'll get everything at Stoke Poges and Hugh's and Thomas's legacies as well," Joslin excitedly finished the sentence for him. "So if that's right, we've found Hugh's killer, too. And Thomas's. It was all to get their inheritances." It suddenly seemed so clear. Find Edward Gaylor and the whole mystery would be solved.

But this clarity lasted no more than a second. "Can't be," William said. "Edward Gaylor couldn't have killed Hugh. He'd been in Stoke Poges for a matter of days and I don't reckon he'd left it in that time. The priest said he'd been there seven days in all. His word's to be trusted if anyone's is. Anyway, the horse isn't born who could get Edward from Stoke Poges into London and back all in one night and let him kill Hugh and drop him in the street while he was here. Besides. . ." He paused.

"What?" said Joslin.

"I reckon he was telling the truth. He didn't know what he'd given Cicely and Jacob to drink. He'd not bothered to hide the flagon of wine but when I picked it up he was frightened. That wasn't like some crafty murderer, to pull it away from me and pour it on the ground outside and make up some story about touching it being impious. No, I reckon he knew what had happened without him realizing what he was doing and it had scared him half silly."

"That's daft. He did it," Wulfrum muttered. "Nobody

else. Find him and everything's sorted."

"All right, where was the plague on him?" retorted William.

Joslin didn't want to join in this argument. But of one thing he was certain. They might not have found out *who* had killed Hugh and Thomas. But he was sure he knew *why*. Now the problem was – what to do about it? If they found Edward, would they find the murderer? Which version of what happened at Stoke Poges was right – William's or Wulfrum's? Would Edward come to London again – if he had ever been there before?

Mid-morning next day. Joslin looked round at new surroundings. They were in the Guildhall, for the jury called by Simon of Chichester to account for the deaths of Thomas and Hugh. Facing them were the city sheriffs, John Turgold and William Dykeman. On John Turgold's right was Simon, the coroner. One by one the jury – everyone with information which could throw light on the brothers' deaths – gave their account.

The day before at Randolf's house had ended quiet and subdued. Supper in the hall had been short commons. Joslin was not called upon to sing and he hardly knew what would have been suitable if he had. He tried to speak to Alys but Dame Lettice kept her close. He had wondered if he, a passing foreign, would be allowed on the jury. "Of course," said Randolf. "You know as much as anyone and have thought about it a lot more." No apprentice spoke in the bedchamber; each had slept quickly and Joslin soon followed them, somehow sure that this night nobody would wake him with a knife. And nobody did.

So now, an hour before midday, here they were in the

Guildhall before the coroner and sheriffs – Randolf, Water Craven, Alfred of Ware from Ludgate, the two lightermen who had found Thomas's body, Will of Essex the gravedigger and Joslin himself, all hoping that what they said would bring them nearer the truth and not further away, as every twist and turn so far seemed to have done.

First, Walter told how Thomas Hockley, a good apprentice with but two years to go, was missing one morning and a search had failed to find him. No, there was nothing in his behaviour to raise any suspicion; he had been the same as ever. Yes, perhaps it was wrong to presume Thomas had just got bored with apprenticeship and gone home to Stoke Poges. Yes, perhaps he should have raised the alarm before. But what else were they to do but hope he would think better of it and come back? Yes, apprentices *could* get killed and often had – he granted that. But surely those deaths were in the open, in drunken brawls and fights over women. Not secretly like this. Yes, it was true – if he had his time over again he'd have raised the alarm sooner.

Next, Randolf. Hugh, too, was a good apprentice and becoming a fair painter. Soon he would be able to complete a wall-painting or altar panel for any church. There were four years to go before his apprenticeship ended. Every week he met his brother; this week Thomas had not been there and Hugh was worried. No, there were no troubles with Hugh that he knew of and his disappearance that morning was a shock to them all. But it was surely reasonable to think he'd gone with his brother to Stoke Poges if Walter was so certain?

Alfred of Ware next – brought in to tell of his strange encounter after Thomas's disappearance. "That man had chilled me to my soul before ever the young Frenchman and his girl came calling," he said.

"And yet," said John Turgold, "it seems strange that a murderer working secretly by night should come up to a guard at the city gate and show himself with his victim."

Sheriff William Dykeman said, "You're lucky that he didn't knife you as well and be done with it."

Alfred of Ware drew himself up straight, like the old soldier he was. "If he had, there'd be no more chilling of my soul," he said. "And there'd be no need for this jury, because the murder would have been known and the murderer got his justice through my own sword."

"But he wouldn't, would he?" said Sheriff John Turgold. "This is a cunning and shifting killer whose ways are inscrutable."

"What befell next?" said Simon of Chichester.

"I listened to his story, told him he couldn't go through the gate at night and watched him walk off down Bowyer's Row away from me, the dead man on his arm for all the world like the paralytic drunkard he said he was. They turned right at the end past Baynard's Castle."

"Where did you think they were going?" said William Dykeman.

"Not the King's Wardrobe, that's for sure," said Alfred of Ware. "They could have been heading for the river. I never saw them again."

Next came the two lightermen. Yes, they were about their lawful business early that morning. And they found a body, drifting down from Oystergate and about to fetch up against the stone piles of London Bridge. If it hadn't, it would have floated out to sea and nobody would ever know what happened to the poor wretch.

Oh yes, your worships, they found it well inside the city boundaries, they'd swear to that.

So why take it to the Tower, outside the city?

"So nobody could say it was anything to do with us. There are no better witnesses to good faith than the soldiers of the King, so they say," said the older lighterman. "Besides, if we'd tarried there another moment, we'd have lost the tide through the bridge. The Tower was the first place we could have landed."

John Turgold looked unconvinced by the first reason, satisfied by the second. "What made you suspicious about the body?" he said.

"Ah, it was a fearful sight. Slit by the throat and swollen with the plague. Two deaths in one body."

"But only the knife wound concerns us," said John Turgold. "If he had died by plague alone then only God would have caused his death. We might have fallen to prayer but we wouldn't have met as a jury. This is strange and must give pause for thought. A murderer who might as well have left his deadly work to God? This doesn't make sense."

"That's what we thought, your worship."

"So you gave him up to the guard at the Tower and told him where you had found him?"

"Yes, your worship."

"Which is why the people in the Tower called the city coroner, to avoid responsibility themselves. How thoughtful of them," said John Turgold drily. But Simon of Chichester was relieved. Nobody would think he had overstepped his authority. He could concentrate entirely on the huge suspicion forming minute by minute in his mind.

"What does the Frenchman have to say?" said William Dykeman. "Your name, I'm told, is Joslin de Lay. Why are you in London?"

Briefly, Joslin told them of his quest and his journey

from Suffolk. When he entered the Guildhall he had vowed to say nothing about this; something, he wasn't sure what, in the atmosphere had subtly changed his mind. Soon he was answering questions from all three. No, he'd not been in London when Thomas disappeared. Where was he then, at that precise time? "I think," he said, "in a tavern in Colchester." He reminded them of his errand with Alys. No, he'd not met Hugh before the night he disappeared. Had he heard of him? Yes, just once. Alys spoke about him as they rode together.

Throughout these questions, Simon of Chichester had not spoken. But now he drew breath. John Turgold quietened him. "Later, Simon," he said. "I want to hear everything from the Frenchman." He turned again to Joslin. "Did you see Hugh the night before he disappeared?"

"Only for a little while."

"Did you speak?"

"A few words."

"Is that all? Only a few words?"

Joslin had not wanted to tell them about Hugh's night threats. But something about these sheriffs facing him, their stern gazes demanding the truth, told him he must. Now he knew what had changed his mind about telling everything. He remembered standing before Roger de Noville, Earl of Stovenham. That was a trial with no truth in it. Joslin had to speak out for himself or die. This was different. All they wanted was the truth, so this city could live at peace with itself. So did he.

"He threatened me with his knife. Now Robin was dead he was jealous of *me*. He called me a French fancy-boy."

Someone laughed. William Dykeman shut whoever it was up with a freezing look.

"But nothing came of these threats? No fight, no wounding?"

"No. You can ask the other apprentices. They'll bear me witness."

"And that was all?"

Should he say this? "Your worship, I was threatened with knives over Alys three times more. Once before Hugh did, walking across the courtyard in the dark, and once waking me up as I slept and then once again the next night. But I didn't know who it was and still don't."

"But it wasn't Hugh?"

"At first I thought so. Then I knew otherwise." He told of noises in the dark, signs of someone hiding on Robin's empty bed. "And there was another time, the next night. That could not have been Hugh."

"The apprentices will bear witness to this?"

"Yes, your worship," Joslin replied, with a slight flicker of doubt.

"I'm not sure this is material," said John Turgold. "We seek a murderer, not a bearer of private threats. London's full of those, without need of juries." Simon of Chichester took breath to speak, but John Turgold quietened him again. "Go on," he said to Joslin.

So Joslin told how he went with Alys to Walter Craven's, how they reasoned that if the brothers had left for Stoke Poges in the night they might have been seen at Ludgate and how they sought out Alfred of Ware, how what the watchman said made Joslin search the waterfront, how he heard about the first body from the boatman at London Bridge. And then – was this relevant? Well, he had resolved to tell these people everything. So it was.

"It was then that I saw someone watching me," he said.

"What do you mean?" said William Dykeman. "London's full of people who watch their neighbours. Why should one more or less catch your eye? Was he a monster that you should remember him?"

"No, your worship. I can remember nothing about him except his grey tunic and brown hose."

"Joslin de Lay," said William Dykeman reprovingly, "half the folk of London might wear grey with brown hose and have faces you could never remember. Why should this one warrant our notice?"

"Because he was watching me," Joslin said stubbornly. "Why should he watch me?"

"Did you see him again?"

"No, your worship."

"Then he was a loiterer with but passing interest in a conversation between the boat and the shore. Go on with your story, Joslin."

So Joslin told how what the boatman said made him go on to the Tower, but the outside of that hostile pile frightened him, so he skirted Tower Ditch and tried the shot in the dark of looking in a churchyard. And how he met Will of Essex who had confirmed all his suspicions.

"And that is your story?" said John Turgold.

"Yes, your worship."

"Then, as nobody's here from the Tower, we'll hear Will of Essex."

Will lumbered to his feet. He confirmed what Joslin said, what Simon of Chichester knew for himself, that the young man's body, throat cut and plague-ridden, had been buried at night. But he added his own extra detail. "Your worship, the Frenchman's right about the stranger watching him. I saw him myself, hiding in the gravestones, listening to us, wearing grey and brown, just like Joslin said. He ran off when I saw him and it seemed to me he had no good intentions towards the Frenchman. And he was there again the night we took young Thomas's body out of the grave to know who he was. Someone lurked secretly, watching us. I'd stake all I have that it was him, even though it was dark. The coroner himself can vouch for that."

"I see," said John Turgold. "So it seems there may be a witness who's not here that we should talk to."

And now, all Joslin's trust, his belief that only truth would prevail here, were blown away like thistledown. For at last Simon of Chichester drew breath to speak and this time nobody stopped him.

All Simon had heard, all that came out that morning, had added shape to last night's sudden blinding flash, which he had been leading up to from the moment he saw Joslin on the day Hugh died. He had worried over it for hours, had put everything said this morning together with what he knew already. Now, surely, he was on the verge of the truth and the identity of the killer. He had been to Cambridge before he took service with the King and he had spent there many hours disputing in logic and dialectic. Remorseless and unanswerable logic that would have pleased his University masters had shown him the way to solve this puzzle.

Perhaps the bones of it had been in his mind ever since he first saw Joslin, with Hugh's body not yet cold in Randolf's courtyard. "New arrivals and new deaths go together," he had said then and now he knew he was right. He had pieced together quite a lot about this Joslin de Lay and was almost prepared to say it aloud. No foreign not four days in the city should know so much about everybody's business. *Ergo* – he *must* have known more about Hugh's disappearance and death than he had said.

Joslin's story was ingenious and hard to fault. But it had one weakness which gave him away. The stranger at London Bridge. A clumsy attempt to divert suspicion. Except that . . . Simon of Chichester exulted inwardly at the perfection of his theory. One other person said he had seen him. Why, he had even claimed this mysterious stranger was hiding in the churchyard that night at the graveside. Well, nobody else saw him. Far from proving Joslin's story, this made it all the weaker. What if it were a lie to make Joslin's story sound true? What would that mean? Two people claimed to have seen this stranger. But this stranger did not exist. *Ergo* – that is a lie concocted by the two claimants. *Ergo* – those two have something to hide.

If Joslin and Will of Essex were in league together, then *ergo* – Joslin must have lured Hugh to his death at the hands of Will. Why? Alys was the prize. What about that story of Robin dying in some town in Suffolk? That sounded like suspicious hocus-pocus. Who was to say that Joslin himself had not killed Robin – because Alys had tired of him and wanted her so-called lover dead? And Thomas and Hugh? Potential rivals. Will of Essex must have killed him on his own, without Joslin's help. But certainly on his orders. And look at Will of Essex. An ugly brute, fit to kill anybody, if not with a knife then with his bare hands. No, this was a dreadful conspiracy with love and jealousy at its core – mainspring of most conspiracies leading to death – and he would bring both of them to justice.

But how to prove that Joslin and Will of Essex had known each other before?

Easy. Will, as his name said, was of *Essex* – to the east of London. It was where he had come from and where he would often return. Just as he himself had left

Chichester to seek a new life. And Joslin had come to London from the east. What had he said? That he was in a tavern in Colchester, in Essex, the very night Thomas disappeared? *Ergo* – Joslin and Will met in Colchester that evening and Joslin gave his orders. Where better to meet? Will would have taken horse at once, galloped hard through the night and been back in London in time to abduct Thomas before sunrise. Or perhaps Joslin detailed someone to take a message to Will. Certainly there would have been contact between them, whether directly or by go-between didn't matter.

Simon of Chichester sighed with satisfaction. He had fed his suspicions and applied the rules of logic until they told him a story which was no castle in the air because it had logical truth. Logic could never be denied.

"Your worships," he said. "I know who did these crimes."

Joslin, back in the apprentices' room over the workshop, was trembling with relief. What a narrow escape! And how wise the sheriffs seemed to be. Joslin listened unable to believe his ears as Simon of Chichester told his great new theory. Will of Essex was thunderstruck, nearly purple with silent anger. Randolf looked at Joslin strangely – but as soon as Simon mentioned Alys he, too, spluttered with wrath and Walter had to quieten him. For a moment angry chaos nearly broke out, which would be bad for them all. There could be a full lock-up that night.

At last, Simon of Chichester finished. "I believe that Joslin de Lay and his accomplice Will of Essex should be taken from here and locked in the Fleet prison until confessions can be extracted from them."

The Fleet? That terrible place he had seen by Ludgate? Would he be in a prison for a murder he hadn't done for the second time in three weeks? No, this *couldn't* happen. He looked round at Randolf for help. But Randolf's pursed lips showed an anger Joslin could not fathom. Was it at him or the coroner?

The sheriffs listened patiently to all the coroner said. Joslin tried to read their faces. When Simon of Chichester had finished, they conferred in whispers for some minutes. At last, they nodded, as if they had reached agreement. Joslin held his breath.

"Simon of Chichester," said John Turgold, "we don't find your account, attractive though it may be, sufficient warrant to commit these two to the Fleet. For our part, we have detected truth in much of what they've said. We don't deny you may be right, but you must find better proof for us. I shall send both Joslin and Will of Essex back to their homes with orders that they may not contact each other, nor leave the city for any reason until this day week. By that time, Simon of Chichester, you should have found stronger evidence to prove what you have alleged. Joslin de Lay, I understand you have a journey to make. It is delayed until no suspicion hangs over you. Will of Essex, you may not visit your home shire, nor receive any visitor from it. Randolf and the priest of All Hallows will stand surety for each of you. Failure to bear this yoke puts you in the Fleet at once. Is that clear?"

"Yes, your worship," said Joslin. Will of Essex's grunt of acknowledgement sounded ungracious but John Turgold did not press him for more. Randolf replied, "Yes, your worship," in a strong, level voice and at last looked straight at Joslin. But his face bore no anger and Joslin sighed with relief. It was clear Randolf didn't believe a word of it.

Randolf had not finished either. "Your worships," he said, "there's another matter which you should know about in connection with this." He explained how William and Wulfrum had gone to Stoke Poges and found the Hockley brothers' mother and stepfather dead.

Walter joined in. "I was their guardian and their legacies from their fathers were held by me in trust. But now there are no living relatives. What happens to these inheritances must be decided."

John Turgold pronounced again. "A court must decide. All people with an interest in the inheritances of Thomas and Hugh Hockley will attend. The matter must be disposed of quickly. We'll hold court here, at the same time tomorrow."

Joslin felt a slight quickening of the pulse. Such a court might ferret out more of the truth than had been uncovered today and remove this new cloud over him. He had found a new enemy; Simon of Chichester's zeal for investigation might serve him badly yet.

But how would he know what would happen at tomorrow's court? Well, Randolf would surely be there. If Randolf had to keep an eye on him, there was a good excuse for him being there as well, party to everything that went on.

Joslin lay awake. In all his time in England, even on his first night at Cry Ashbourne among the dead, he had not felt so alone. Why hope for some new revelation to come out in court as the inheritances were disposed of? Simon of Chichester, a high official with all the weight of the King and the city of London behind him, had made up his mind. The sheriffs wanted more proof and Simon would not rest until he found enough to let people think justice was done and everything could be forgotten. After all, the whole Hockley family was dead now. Who else remained to be murdered? A charge would be trumped up against him and Will of Essex and together they'd pay the penalty. But why was he supposed to have done all these murders? There could only be one reason: the love of Alys. He groaned aloud. Bad enough that attackers in the night thought that; worse beyond belief that the city coroner thought so too. This England was a huge and hostile country. While some people showed warmth and welcome, deep down others hated and wanted an end of him. He almost wished he *had* been flung into the Fleet and forced to confess to what they wanted and get it over with.

The other apprentices were asleep. Under William's direction they had worked hard at St Benet's that day. The altar panel was finished; there would be no more of the morning ritual of boiling up glue. He would almost miss that pungent fishy smell spreading over the house. What would Wulfrum do without his own special task?

Suddenly, he sat up bolt upright in the dark. Fish glue. That stinking substance never far from both his nose and his thoughts. What was it about fish glue, this nagging itch which he kept coming back to? Think. *Think.* Everything seemed hopeless – but if only he could work out what was worrying him it may be a chink of light in his darkness.

Anything about the fish glue was also about Wulfrum. When glue was needed, Wulfrum boiled it up before sunrise ready to take away in the morning. It was Wulfrum's job and nobody else's. So when he had been making the noisome stuff, he stank of it.

What did he know about Wulfrum? A servant, who lived over the stables, who slipped out after curfew with Perkin and the ostlers over the wall and along Babe Lane to the taverns and a night's drinking, leaving poor Herry behind. Gruff, a man of few words, but just once or twice surprisingly forthcoming – as when he described the peculiar incident of Edward Gaylor and the wine at Stoke Poges. Joslin had suspected Wulfrum of being his night assailant, but Alys had put paid to that idea when she said that if he was, he'd have smelt of fish glue. The assailant hadn't, so it couldn't have been Wulfrum. So Wulfrum had slipped to the back of his mind. But the assailant wasn't an apprentice and couldn't be Herry, he was sure it wasn't Perkin and he'd never considered the ostlers. So he had no idea who he was and after the murders, didn't particularly care. But today had made him think again. Sheriff John Turgold had said who it was wasn't material, if it wasn't Hugh. And perhaps he was right. Perhaps none of them believed Joslin anyway, not now, after Simon of Chichester's theory. But perhaps finding out the assailant *was* material. Perhaps it would be the first stage on the trail of proving Simon of Chichester hopelessly wrong.

So what was it about fish glue that nagged away at him so? He screwed his eyes tight shut, willed his brain into action. *What was it?*

And then, like a candle in blackness, he knew. *Of course.*

Randolf and the apprentices weren't due to assemble the altar piece for St Benet's until the day Hugh was found missing. They hadn't even got it all ready – indeed, William had to stay behind next day to paint the panel depicting the Virgin. So no glue was made until before sunrise that morning, a good five hours *after* the night intruder held a knife to Joslin's throat and whispered wicked things about him and Alys.

So Alys was wrong. Wulfrum wouldn't smell of fish glue because he hadn't even started making it yet. So he could well have been the one who threatened him and stuffed rags into his mouth two nights running. But what about the second time? Wouldn't he still smell of the stuff after boiling more up and working with it? Then he remembered a detail which had puzzled him at the time. Before they loaded up the cart on the morning they found Hugh dead, Wulfrum had looked different. New tunic, face subtly changed. *Of course. He'd dowsed himself in water and put on different clothes to rid himself of the giveaway smell. And it was Wulfrum he'd seen the previous night, after he'd spoken to Alys, wet*

*and clean because he was straight from that dowsing.*
His first wash, probably, for months. And the reason he
wasn't there on the third night was not because he
thought he had made his point. It was because he was
far away in Stoke Poges.

So Wulfrum did it. Why? Was it connected with the
murders?

His mind was too weary to deal with these questions.
They merged into a wordless jumble and he drifted into
a dreamless sleep.


Dawn was not yet streaking the sky when he and everybody else were suddenly woken.

"What was that?" cried Alexander.

They listened. Frenzied, desperate shouting.
"Murder! Help!"

"It's in the courtyard," said William. "Let's go."

They sprang out of their beds. William lit a lantern
and they followed him down the stairs. Already, Randolf
in gown and nightcap, Lettice, Alys, servants and the
two ostlers were there. By the shifting light of four
lanterns and the faint gleams in the eastern sky, Joslin
saw, coming into the courtyard, grinning vacantly,
Herry.

But Perkin was the centre of the disturbance. He
babbled incoherently to Randolf. "Wulfrum . . . we went
out . . . orchard . . . curfew. . ."

"Calm down, man," said Randolf. "*Show* us what you
mean."

Perkin turned away. Joslin knew where he would lead
them – through the orchard to the gap in the fence. There,
half in, half out, Wulfrum slumped forward on the
ground. A ragged, bloodsoaked tear in his tunic between
his shoulders showed where he had been stabbed.

Randolf bent down. "Careful," he said. "Drag him through."

John held up the board in the fence. William and Alexander bent down to Wulfrum's shoulders and pulled. "Gently," roared Randolf.

They laid him on the ground. "He's not dead," said Alys.

He was still breathing. He tried to talk. Randolf bent to listen. Joslin, sure this was important, pushed close enough to hear these snatched, indistinct words. "He found me here . . . ran away . . . never safe . . . he knew . . . made me . . . Hugh . . . and. . ." he gasped for breath and Joslin waited for the next. When it came, he felt dizzy. "Joslin. . ." That was Wulfrum's last word in life.

"Call the priest," said Randolf. "By God, he'll know this house well."

"And Giles Worsdell?" said Lettice.

"In good time," said Randolf. "If he comes we can't keep Simon of Chichester away. There's a face I could do without seeing again."

They looked down on Wulfrum's body, face grey, blood seeping under him on the thin grass.

"There's no more to be done," said Randolf. He looked round the appalled faces. "This is too much to bear," he muttered. Then, louder: "Alexander, go to St Olave's. Fetch the priest." At once, Alexander was gone. Randolf turned to Perkin, standing over his dead friend, weeping uncontrollably. *Unexpected*, thought Joslin, *for so ox-like a person.*

"Pull yourself together," said Randolf. "Tell us what happened."

Perkin calmed down. He spoke, haltingly, between gulps and occasional sobs. "Master Randolf," he said. "You never knew this. Me and Wulfrum, we went out most nights through this hole in the fence."

"Did you now?" said Randolf grimly. "Well, not any more. That gap will be sealed up *now*. I'm not risking servants of mine being locked in the Tun and worse."

He looked through the gap and up and down the alley. "No sign of life now," he said. "Your attacker's made himself scarce. Go on, Perkin."

"We went up the alley into Babe Lane and there before Cripplegate there's a little tavern set in the wall. They don't think much about the curfew there. Why, even men on the watch come in and have a drink."

"Not any more," Randolf repeated.

"Anyway, Wulfrum, tonight he was worried. He kept on about these two he'd found dead when he went off in the country with William. He couldn't seem to get them out of his mind. I said, 'What have they got to do with you?' but he wouldn't have that. 'It's catching up with me, Perkin. I know Edward Gaylor never did that to his own brother,' he said. 'I shouldn't have done what I did'."

"What did he mean?" said Randolf.

"He was talking about when he ran away when he was just a lad. He came from Thame in Oxfordshire. His people were all serfs. They had a hard master. So he got out."

"I know," said Randolf. "It's why I took him in when he was wandering around London. There must be more than that. But what's it got to do with his visit to Stoke Poges?"

"I didn't understand what he was saying half the time," said Perkin. "But he always feared his master would find him and take him back and that would be the end of him. He was really scared it might happen. Nothing in this world frightened Wulfrum like the thought of his old master."

"It stays in my mind that there was something shameful about his old master," said Randolf thoughtfully. "I can't recall what it was. I can't even recall his name. He was a knight, I know. And like many, careless of his bondmen. Wulfrum would do well to be afraid. Except that. . ." Randolf thought a moment, then, "Yes, I'm sure of it. I may not remember his master's name, but I'm quite sure he's been dead these many years. In foreign parts, too."

"Wulfrum said his master had come back and it would have been better for him if he'd stayed where he was in Oxfordshire," said Perkin.

"But why should he regret running away?" asked Randolf. "It was the best thing he ever did. He found a good home here."

"He knew that, Master Randolf," said Perkin earnestly. "So do I. I reckon he thought that now he'd been caught up with he had to play canny-like to stay alive."

"Did he say so?"

"He didn't have to. While we were drinking, this man came in the tavern. I didn't know him. Wulfrum was really scared. 'Let's get out,' he said. But the man came over, as if he knew we'd be there. 'Well, Wulfrum,' he said. 'Here I am again. There's one more task for you. The one I told you about.' 'No,' says Wulfrum. 'I've done enough. You can ask all you like. I won't do that.' 'Then I'll have to do it myself,' said the man. 'Don't think I can't. I never really needed your help.' "

"What did they mean?" asked Randolf.

"I don't know," Perkin replied. "But Wulfrum, he said, 'I'll tell my friend Perkin here all about it. Then he'll tell the sergeant,' and the man said, 'I don't think Perkin would want to know. Those who know too much have to die. Nobody will think twice about two servants dead in a tavern brawl.' Then he went out into the street. I said to Wulfrum, 'That was never your old master, was it? He didn't look like a lord.' But Wulfrum, he didn't answer. He was white as a sheet. He could hardly stand. He said, 'Come on, Perkin. We're going home.' He grabbed me by the arm and pulled me outside. We ran down Babe Lane and into the alley. But as soon as we turned the corner we heard the footsteps behind us. Oh, Master Randolf, he could go faster than us and I knew we'd be getting knives in our backs. But we made it to the fence and I scrambled through but poor Wulfrum, he was a bit too late."

When Perkin finished there was silence. Then Randolf shook his head. "Wulfrum's old master's dead. Someone told me. I'm sure of it."

"He's come back," Perkin repeated stubbornly.

The sun was showing over the rooftops to the east; the day would be clear and cold.

"Where's that priest?" Randolf muttered irritably.

Joslin had to ask his question now. "Perkin, why was my name Wulfrum's very last word?"

Perkin looked him wonderingly in the face as if he'd never seen him before. "I don't know," he said.

"But he was your friend."

"I didn't know everything he did. These last weeks he had been. . ." His words tailed off.

"Doing bad things at the behest of his master and killer," Randolf finished the sentence grimly.

"Perkin," asked Joslin, "what did this man look like?"

"I couldn't tell you," said Perkin. "I'd never know him again."

"You will when the grief of the night is over," said Randolf.

Perkin repeated firmly, "I would never know him again."

"What did he wear?" Joslin asked.

"A cloak for the night air," Perkin replied. "In the torches of the tavern I could see he had a grey tunic and brown hose."

*I knew it*, thought Joslin.

At last, Alexander came through the orchard with the old priest, who at once dropped to his knees by the body. Everybody withdrew respectfully. When he had finished, the priest stood. "Another one for St Olave's," he said. Even Randolf looked uneasily away. The priest might as well have said, "This house is cursed."

Giles Worsdell had to come and then Simon of Chichester. The stories were repeated to the coroner. Joslin, he had to admit, could not have done this. The apprentices were too certain that he had never left their room – so unless the whole household was in league in some grotesque plot. . . What about Will of Essex? The priest of All Hallows knew his duty and it was easy to find out if Will had broken his bond, broken curfew, crossed the city, found Wulfrum drinking, chased him and knifed him. *But let's suppose*, thought Simon of Chichester, *that he hadn't. What then? My theory falls to the ground.*

*Or does it? Who says the death of a mere servant in a brawl has anything to do with the greater events I'm following? I know I'm right about Joslin and Will. This latest death may be but a casual knifing in a tavern by a footpad we'll never trace. If so, I'm not interested in it.*

He told Randolf as much before he returned to the Guildhall.

Randolf watched him go. "Good riddance," he said. Then – "Fool!"

"It *must* have been Wulfrum each night. Don't you see?" Joslin said.

He was talking to Alys. It seemed as though he hadn't seen her for half a lifetime until this snatched conversation in the courtyard.

"So I was wrong about the fish glue," said Alys. "But why? Nobody knew you. Why would Wulfrum obey a stranger's orders?"

"It might have worked two ways," Joslin answered. "What if Wulfrum was doing what this man told him, and telling him everything that happened here? But why would he be so interested?"

"Because of Hugh?" Alys asked.

"It must be more than that. The man would know you were away, who with and what for. When you came back, Wulfrum must have told him – and also that you were alone except for a strange Frenchman who'd escorted you home. This worried the man so much that he ordered Wulfrum to do all he could to warn me off you. But why? Not to leave the way open for Hugh. He was going to kill Hugh."

"I wish I knew." Alys shivered. There was, Joslin realized with horror, fear in her eyes. She went on, in a low, frightened voice. "You said that everything which happens seems to lead back to *me*. I know that now. I have to believe it. How do you think it makes me feel?"

"There's got to be more to it," Joslin replied.

"I hope you're right," Alys said.

"Why was Wulfrum told to make all those threats?" said Joslin.

"To warn you off, of course," Alys answered.

"But even if I needed the warnings, why should a complete stranger want them made?"

"Perhaps he's not a complete stranger."

"Who is he, then? He was strange to Perkin but not strange to Wulfrum. If he was Wulfrum's old master, who'd seen Wulfrum in London, knew he'd be scared stiff of him and so made him do anything he wanted in return for staying free, how could he know you?"

"Perhaps he was doing it for someone else." Alys shuddered. "I don't want to meet the person who'd cause all that to be done."

Joslin didn't answer. Perhaps Alys was right. But he couldn't begin to imagine why. Especially now those orders had led to three deaths, including the poor wretch who had to carry them out.

And what had Perkin said? *"One more task."* A task which Wulfrum, even after all he'd done already, wouldn't carry out – a refusal which had killed him. What could it be?

And would it still happen even though Wulfrum was dead?

Not even the need to keep an eye on him would make Randolf consent to take Joslin to the court set up to dispose of the legacies of Thomas and Hugh. Randolf had left soon after Simon of Chichester, bound first for Walter Craven's goldsmith's shop in Cheapside. There would be nobody else at the court, now Jacob Gaylor and his wife were no more. Walter as guardian to both brothers and Randolf as owner of Hugh's apprenticeship were the only two left with any connections and they had no claims. The legacies would be held in trust by the city.

The apprentices and Perkin, not allowed even a day to

get over his shock, loaded up the handcart and made a belated journey to St Benet's. Alys disappeared again with Dame Lettice. An uneasy peace descended over the house. Joslin, alone, paced impatiently up and down. This was a frustrating time, when he could do nothing at all.

It was late afternoon and the first signs of an autumn dusk were showing before Randolf and Walter returned. Randolf was furiously angry.

"I never thought to see that man again," he growled as they crossed the courtyard. "I thought I'd closed my doors to him for ever."

Walter laid his hand on his friend's shoulder. "There's much happened lately you never thought to see. Nor me, neither. It seems our friend has made good his promise. He's a rich man with his own estate and he's come to make a claim for the brothers' goods which nobody can deny. You can't stop him making his other claim, especially now there's no other man promised who can come before him."

"How do you know? There are plenty of good men in the world."

"Then you'd better find one quickly."

"If that man comes here, I'll throw him out," Randolf roared.

"I wouldn't if I were you. You must hear what he has to say."

They disappeared into the hall. Joslin watched after them, trying to piece together what he had heard. Something important had happened from which he was excluded.

Darkness was well on its way before William, John, Alexander, Perkin and Herry came home from St Benet's.

As they trundled the handcart through the gate, some-one followed them in. By the light of William's lantern, they saw a heavily-built, dark-jowled man.

"Hello," said William. "What's Edward Gaylor doing here?"

Edward Gaylor took no notice of the crowd by the gate watching him. He crossed straight to the hall as if in search of Randolf.

He was still there when they ate, sitting only one place lower than Dame Lettice herself, opposite Alys, who kept her eyes averted and ate little. Randolf said nothing throughout the meal. His face wore an odd expression; Joslin could not decide if it was anger, sadness, concern – perhaps all three at once. Edward Gaylor ate heartily. His huge pleasure seemed all the greater because of the black pall which had settled over the rest of the table.

Not until the meal was over did Randolf speak. Then he rose from his place. "Our guest will be staying the night," he said. Joslin waited for more. It didn't come. Instead: "Joslin, will you play for us?"

Tonight, because that was how he felt, Joslin played sad songs of exile and misfortune in love. Edward Gaylor seemed to like them immensely.

At last Randolf spoke again. "Enough, Joslin," he said. "We'll retire now. I have to show our guest to his room."

Joslin looked at Alys. She looked back – and before she left the hall herself, slipped to his side for a snatched message. "Remember I told you how once a man came to ask Randolf for me in marriage? Well, this is him. He's now rich like he said he would be and won't take no for an answer."

**S**imon of Chichester had left Randolf's house feeling discontented. He had hoped to connect Joslin directly with Wulfrum's death but the witness of Perkin was too strong – and so was the word of those three apprentices. But he was not downhearted. Was the whole household of Randolf Waygoode engaged in some elaborate plot? Very unlikely. But his theory stood. The killer, if not Joslin, was his accomplice, Will of Essex. By afternoon Simon was in All Hallows graveyard with the ward sergeant and constables, questioning the gravedigger.

It was just as bad. There was no way he could shake Will's insistence that he'd had his first untroubled night's sleep for some nights. The parish priest, standing surety for him, was just as certain.

So he came to the only conclusion left. It was a casual killing. Servants drinking after curfew. A sudden flare-up, a chase, a knife in the dark. One servant less and a killer escaped. Both of no account.

And yet – there was something in the garbled story of that great lump of a labourer who survived. Such a man

161

was of use in the world only because of the strength in his arms, but something he had said disturbed Simon of Chichester and made him reach far into his own memory. Buried deep down in it was a very similar little nugget.

*"No, I wouldn't remember him again," this Perkin had said. Simon of Chichester had snorted with impatience. But then Perkin said more. "I could look deep into his face for a week and I'd not remember it."*

That worried Simon of Chichester. Years before he had said exactly the same of somebody. Who was it? Did it matter? This man had looked so insignificant that his name had disappeared as well. All this was when he had first come to Westminster from Cambridge anxious for work in the King's service. But he'd forgotten when he'd met the man whose memory struck such a strange chord when Perkin spoke. What this man had done, Simon of Chichester uneasily thought, had not been insignificant – which was why he so badly wanted to recall him.

Not that it would have anything to do with this new killing. But he'd like to know, all the same.

Before the apprentices had turned in for the night, William spoke to Joslin. "Randolf wants you to work at St Benet's tomorrow now we're a labourer short. We're so close to finishing that it would be silly to stay there a day longer than we have to." Joslin merely nodded. His thoughts were far away.

*Find who gains from the brothers' deaths and you find the murderer.* That's what he'd once believed. Edward Gaylor had their legacies as sole surviving relative. He was there when Dame Cecily and Jacob Gaylor died. Were they poisoned? Had Edward done it?

William thought not. And – he suddenly remembered with a slight shock – neither did Wulfrum, after all he had said when they returned. Among his last words was almost a recantation of the opinion he held then. Why bother about Gaylor as he lay dying? But whether Gaylor had killed them or not, he was now master of large domains – a man of substance. And he wanted Alys as wife. Truly, he wanted everything.

But how could he have murdered Thomas and Hugh? And if he had, who was it who killed Wulfrum and nearly did for Perkin as well?

Most important of all: Alys was on the point of being married against her will unless Randolf could – and was willing to – find a reason why not.

No, Edward Gaylor might not be the murderer they sought. But in his own way he was just as dangerous.

Next day dawned dark and foggy. Edward Gaylor left before Randolf set off for St Benet's. He would return, he said, on the evening of the following day for his answer. Celebration of a betrothal would follow. Joslin thought it would be a hollow one indeed – an unwilling bride and the shadow of strange deaths. Edward Gaylor was lodging at the tavern of the Broken Seld in Cheapside. Now he was a rich man he had business to transact in the city. But it would be, he said, well finished before he came to claim his last prize.

Randolf had bitten back an angry retort. When Edward Gaylor was gone, he roared at nobody in particular, "How I wish I could say he had killed our Hugh and be done with it. But I know nothing against the man, I can't accuse him of foul play towards his brother and he's made a fair offer. I have to listen and button my lip." Joslin could see the decision was left to Alys.

So now they were wheeling the handcart along damp

streets, their skin cold from clammy mists rising from the river. As he helped push, Joslin cast looks behind at Randolf, striding grim and silent, and wondered what went on in his mind.

Despite the day's greyness, St Benet's seemed light and full of colour. Joslin gasped at the intricate new wall-paintings of Jesus and his disciples, of saints and angels, ordinary folk about their work. If he looked for long enough he would find stories and meanings in them all. At the east end, the altar was just finished. Randolf's first job was to inspect William's work over the past two days. He looked long and hard, pointed tiny things out to the apprentices, then spoke. "You've done well, my lads. We all have. St Benet's is all but done now and that's another commission well fulfilled."

There was really very little for Joslin to do. Most of the day he ground up powders with pestle and mortar for Alexander to mix with oils to make pigments for his painting of Herod and the Innocents. *Had Alexander meant to give Herod such a grotesquely large head*? Joslin wondered. Herod looked oddly terrifying, a scourge whose baleful eyes seemed to follow Joslin round the church. Not even here could he forget that evil presences stalked him through London and England. Sometimes it seemed that more than Herod's painted eyes watched him – even here in God's house where he expected sanctuary.

At noon, they stopped to eat, sitting on the flagstoned floor of the west porch, apprentices and labourers together. Joslin sat with them, until Randolf touched him on the shoulder. When he looked up Randolf beckoned him silently away. They walked towards the altar. Then Randolf led him into a little side chapel, still not speaking. Joslin waited curiously.

164

At last he spoke. "You've seen the man Gaylor? You know why he's here?"

"Alys told me," Joslin answered.

"And what do you think Alys should do?"

Joslin thought wildly, *what answer am I supposed to give?* Aloud he said, "She's in grief for Robin. She should do nothing."

"She has no parents. I'm her guardian," Randolf replied heavily. "Should I order her to marry this newly-rich man who promises a life of ease and comfort?"

Joslin felt even more at a loss. "You should advise her in what you think is best," he said lamely.

"And what *is* best?"

"I don't know." Then, more firmly, "She should not be given such a choice before her grief for Robin has gone. I know how deep it runs."

"And so do I," Randolf sighed. "But here's a man who wants answers now, who'll be happy if he's told that all will be well in time but who wants to go away with a positive reply."

Joslin felt suddenly as if he was choking. "I don't know what to say," he managed.

"There's one way I could send him off empty-handed with no chance of a return," said Randolf. "Do you know what it is?"

"No."

"If I could tell him I've received an offer from another man which I'm minded to smile on more readily, a better, more fitting and seemly man for a girl so young and beautiful, then he'd have nothing to say."

Joslin did not understand the strange shock those words gave him.

"Joslin," Randolf went on, "I asked you once to stay and be my minstrel. You said you wouldn't and I had to be content with that. But now, I beg you, please think again."

"I'm sorry, Randolf. I've given you my answer. If Alys is married to this good and seemly man then Robin's place will be taken and there's no need for me there."

"Please hear me out, Joslin," said Randolf. "If all goes well for me, in time you'd be minstrel to the mayor himself, who'd rank in the land as an earl. You'd be a great man in this city. Your fame would spread to Westminster and Windsor. As I'm a painter to the King, you'd be a minstrel to the King. I can lead you to a great life."

"But Randolf, why are you asking me now?"

Randolf stared at him. "Isn't it obvious? I'd never suggest any such thing if *you* were not her husband. With a wife like Alys at your side, your life would be sweet indeed."

Joslin was speechless. He saw visions of such a life. It would indeed be sweet. An assured place in a respected house, connections with the royal court, perhaps one of the foremost minstrels in the land – and maybe more: a composer, a poet, not in one language but two, not afraid to put his own name to what he wrote, with fame lasting long after he was dead. And above all, a wife who was beautiful, true, capable of such love, with whom he had already shared so much and whose mettle he knew so well.

What prospect could he set against it? A long, dangerous, lonely journey. At the end, for all he knew, failure. A mother long-disappeared, dead – or not the gentle, wise creature of his dreams but a vindictive crone still angry about being deserted by a passing Frenchman. Misery, poverty, death in wild hills in a far-away land at the hands of hostile people. Besides, would not Guillaume be proud of the destiny Randolf offered? He saw his dead father looking down from heaven, thinking, *my son has done all I could ever want for him*.

Put like that, there was no choice. Besides, he would save Alys from a marriage hateful to her. On its own, that would be reason enough.

And still he had not thought of the most important reason of all. He had been asked to do this by a good man whom he admired and whose hospitality he had accepted. He could not refuse; it would be a blot on his honour and leave a stain which would never fade. Besides, in marriage he and Alys would surely come to love each other. The foundations were there already. He made up his mind.

"Randolf," he said, "I will. "Providence brought me here to you and to Alys. I see that now. This moment was cast as soon as I set eyes on Alys in St Joseph's church in Stovenham. Though I grieve that so good a friend as Robin had to die to bring it about."

Randolf stood square in front of him, placed his hands on his shoulders and kissed him on both cheeks. "That's the French way of sealing a bargain, I'm told," he said. "And I'm right glad to make it."

Joslin was too full to answer.

"Say nothing," said Randolf. "Work on till dusk as if we'd not spoken. Alys will not be at supper this evening. I'll keep her apart with Dame Lettice. She'll tell her everything and let her be used to the idea. But Alys will agree; I can tell it in her eyes. I know she still grieves for Robin, but she seeks security as well."

Joslin still could not answer.

"Wait till tomorrow," said Randolf, "then go at noon to the orchard. You'll find Alys waiting under an apple tree. She'll have her answer ready for you, whether yes or no. But you must ask her first, so that all is done with due ceremony."

*Yes, I'll ask her,* thought Joslin. *And then I'll sing to her, the first song of many in the years to come.* He still did not speak. But in the silence, he heard a noise. So did Randolf. "What was that?" he said.

"A latch closing?" Joslin answered.

"Was one of my apprentices listening?" Randolf exclaimed angrily. He marched out of the chapel, down the nave and into the porch. Apprentices and servants sat together, drinking ale, the remnants of their food littering the flagstones.

"Did one of you follow us and eavesdrop?" Randolf demanded.

"Why should we leave good food, Master Randolf?" said William. "If you're not here, there's all the more for us."

"Don't be cheeky," Randolf answered. But he looked at them narrowly. "Somebody was there," he said. Then he changed his mind. "We imagined it," he said to Joslin.

But Joslin felt a tinge of worry. He knew they hadn't.

That afternoon he ground pigments for Alexander in a dream. Towards the end of the day, to save time, Alexander let him mix oils into them. "See, you'd earn a living here if you stayed," he said. But Joslin was far away and for a moment could not share Alexander's triumph as he exclaimed "Finished!" and surveyed his work.

As dusk fell, the work in St Benet's was finally completed – "Until it turns to ash or dust in God's own time and at His will," Randolf said as he led prayers to mark the end of the commission. As they trundled the handcart back home by the light of William's lantern, Joslin felt that one chapter had come to a close and another was beginning.

Joslin knew what he would sing and play that night, even if Alys wasn't there to hear it. Something to fit the occasion, matching his own happiness snatched from looming misery – the wonderful story told in the ballad of Sir Orfeo. Orfeo, the finest harpist ever known, lost his wife Heurodys when the Faery King came to her as she lay under a tree in the orchard and spirited her away to Faeryland. The stricken Orfeo took his harp, left his kingdom and went to the wild lands. Here he lived with the beasts and charmed them with his music. One day he saw the Faery hunt pass by, Heurodys with them. He followed, found the entrance to Faeryland. He slipped in, sought the Faery King and played music such as never heard even in Faeryland. "I've not heard the like. Take any reward," said the Faery King. "I'll take Heurodys," Orfeo replied. However much the Faery King regretted his offer, he was a king and had his honour to keep. So together they returned home and lived wisely for the rest of their days.

Joslin loved this ballad. It was a tale of love and music both. When he thought of Heurodys under the apple tree, he thought of how tomorrow he would meet his own Heurodys under the apple tree with no Faery King to spirit her away.

Randolf was as good as his word. The crowd round the table that night was entirely male. When Randolf asked him to play, Joslin knew from suppressed laughter and expectant looks that they wanted songs of bawdy. Well, he knew some all right. But no, he wouldn't oblige. Tonight was too serious for that. They'd get "Sir Orfeo" and like it.

As soon as he started, he knew they would. Nobody could fail to be bewitched, just as Heurodys was bewitched by the Faery King. When he came to those lines about Heurodys in the orchard –

> This lovely Queen, Dame Heurodys
> Took two maidens of great price
> Out with her one fair noontide
> Into the shady orchardside
> To see the flowers spread and spring
> And listen to the sweet birds sing.
> Together they sat down, all three,
> Under the fairest apple tree
> And very soon this comely Queen
> Fell asleep upon the green. . .

He saw in his mind's eye the scene that would be his tomorrow. Then, in those terrible words –

> And yet, amid them all that day
> The Queen was cruelly snatched away
> By magic, strong and strange and weird
> And no one knew what had occurred. . .

he felt Orfeo's misery with him. But inwardly he rejoiced, because this was just a magic tale and he was living in the real, solid London city.

Joslin slept untroubled. Next morning there was no journey to St Benet's; the apprentices busied themselves with tidying the workshop while Randolf worked at an easel on a single commission for a knight of John O'Gaunt's Savoy palace in the Strand. Joslin helped the

170

apprentices – but his heart wasn't in it. Even John was impatient and said, "G-get out of my w-way, you useless article."

"Go outside and wait in the courtyard," said Randolf.

Yesterday's fogs were gone. As if in answer to Joslin's happiness, the sun had appeared. Surely noon could not be now far away.

When the sun was at its highest and bells pealed all over London, Dame Lettice came from the orchard. She crossed to where Joslin sat on the steps to the apprentices' chamber, harp on his lap, dressed not as a minstrel but in tunic and jerkin. She laid her hand on his.

"Alys is waiting," she said. "Give her a moment to compose herself. She's alone. There's no need today for any chaperone."

Slowly, Joslin rose. "Thank you, Dame Lettice," he said.

Now was the moment. He walked into the orchard and looked for Alys under branches weighed down with apples. . .

"Alys," he called softly.

There was no answer. *She's making me wait*, he thought.

Methodically, he visited each tree. No Alys at the first or second. Or the third or the fourth. "Alys," he called again. The fifth, the sixth.

No, something was wrong. He called out wildly now and searched desperately round every other tree. There was no Alys anywhere.

"*Alys!*" he cried. He hooked his fingers into his harp strings and pulled them upwards in a violent, dissonant, echoing rasp of sound like a word in an unknown and terrible language.

Truly the Faery King had entered the orchard and stolen her away.

> Then there was crying, weeping, woe:
> To a private room the King must go
> And swoon his grief and rage alone
> And sob and weep and howl and moan
> That now his life was nearly spent
> With no consoling comfort sent. . .

Nobody rushed into the orchard to answer his cries or his harp. Why should they? Perhaps they thought this was how French minstrels greeted moments of joy?

He ran to the stables and stopped in the semi-darkness which smelled of fresh straw. Could she be hiding here, too shy to face him? "Alys?" he called, softly. The only answer was horses champing and shifting hooves. Had the ostlers gone, to give the couple privacy?

He stalked into the courtyard. Bitter tears coursed down his face. Was she so revolted by the thought of him that she had fled disgusted?

He burst into the hall. Randolf and Lettice stood at the far end.

"Where is she?" Joslin cried. "Why won't she face me?"

Disbelief crossed Randolf's face. "You mean she doesn't want you?"

"*No*," Joslin howled.

"Joslin," said Dame Lettice softly, "what's happened?"

"She's gone," he groaned.

Randolf did not speak softly. He seized Joslin's shoulders and looked him full in the face. "What are you talking about?" he roared.

"She's gone," he repeated. "The Faery King stole her away."

Randolf looked at him sternly. "Don't live inside your own ballads," he said. "If she's gone, then we must search for her."

He called for servants. Soon he strode at the head of a procession into the courtyard. Here, he shouted for apprentices, labourers and ostlers. A sizeable band, they followed him to the orchard.

Dame Lettice pointed to the largest apple tree. "I left Alys here," she said. "She was happy. I think she saw light again in her life at last."

"There was nobody there," said Joslin. "I looked under every tree."

"I shall do the searching myself," said Randolf.

He slowly walked round each tree, until at last he had to concede there was no Alys. He rounded on the ostlers. "What did you hear?" he demanded. "What did you see?"

"We saw nothing, Master Randolf," said one.

"We kept busy in the stables, like you told us to," said the other.

"Search the house," Randolf commanded. "If she's playing some joke, she'll be punished for it. I'll not have a good man trifled with. Stay here, Joslin. We'll bring her back to you."

Suddenly, everyone was gone. Joslin was alone with one thought. *You needn't bother. She's not there.*

Besides, Randolf was wrong. He didn't live inside his ballads. Only a fool would do that. It was the other way round. Sometimes the ballads lived round him. They might be tales of magic, but they were about true things. They could come to life at any time. Now one had.

What should he do? Sir Orfeo had taken his harp, gone into the wild lands and searched until he found Faeryland. Then he had played to the King and brought Heurodys out. London was not the wild lands, though for Joslin it might as well be. Wherever Alys was, he'd bring her back. His harp was slung over his back; he'd play it for Alys yet.

If she wasn't spirited away, then she was outside the orchard. She didn't come into the courtyard because the only way was past the stables. So she went – or was forced – over the wall. But Randolf had barred Wulfrum's way through. So she went *over* it. But would she? Never. Now his stomach went cold. She was pushed, pulled over. Or *thrown* over. She must be found and brought back. He had to follow. Randolf would understand.

He eyed the wall. He reached for the top. He could hook his hands over, hardly needing to jump. So he pulled himself up, scrabbled with his feet for a hold, swung up to the top, then dropped down.

The alleyway was deserted. To join the passing folk, he had to go to either end, to the streets. Well, one way took him back to Silver Street and Adel Lane where it crossed Wood Street, the other to Babe Lane, the London wall and Cripplegate. Which was it to be? Now his heart sank. Once outside the protection of Randolf's house, he felt again what a huge warren of a place London was and just how little he knew of it. Which way? To the city's edge or its heart? He took three paces.

Then he stopped. Who could have done this thing? Who could have known that Alys was there alone, waiting for him? Nobody in the house; Randolf had seen to that. None of the apprentices. Certainly not Herry and Perkin. They were all in the porch at St Benet's when Randolf spoke to him in the quiet of the chapel.

But then he remembered something. When Randolf had finished talking – did a latch lift, a door close? Not the faraway west door where the apprentices ate. No, one nearby. The sacristy door, perhaps.

*So had someone been listening?*

But who? Edward Gaylor? Why should he? He was sure of himself. Tonight he'd claim Alys. He thought nobody was in his way.

He shivered. Could it be someone he'd seen once, Will of Essex had seen twice and perhaps Perkin once – fatally for Wulfrum? An unmemorable man in grey and brown? Did *he* take Alys away?

But in God's name *why*? What did he have to do with Alys? What cruel game was he playing?

And if Perkin was the last to see him in the tavern by Cripplegate, wasn't that the place to look? He stopped and turned.

But just a minute. *He'd* seen him by London Bridge. Will of Essex had seen him at All Hallows. This man roamed the whole city. Joslin turned back the other way.

Then he stopped again and leant against the wall. He had a square mile thick with people, riven by criss-crossing streets he hardly knew, to search for a man he couldn't remember – but who always seemed to know where *he* was. Well, now they were searching for each other. Joslin had one hope – if he found that man, he'd find Alys. And when he did, he'd bring her home to a lifetime of joy, wealth and love. And he had to do it on his own.

So the hunter would now be the hunted, and with God's help and Joslin's wits he'd be found. His mind made up, he half-walked, half-ran towards the busy streets and the city's living heart.

Randolf stood at the head of the table. The food was prepared; he'd resolved on a great feast even if Edward Gaylor would not take no for an answer. "If he won't believe me when I tell him Alys is another's, let him see for himself," he'd said to Dame Lettice. "Who cares if my food chokes in his gullet? *I'll* still enjoy it."

But now all was confusion. The search had been useless. Alys was not there. *Gaylor has taken her,* Randolf thought. *He guessed what was in our minds and took Alys to make sure of her.*

Would a man be so desperate? Why not? The stakes were high. But where would he take her? To Stoke Poges, of course, where he reigned as lord of his own domains, far from London. Ah, but not from the law. Guardians had the rights of parents *and he would get her back.* The marriage could be annulled. Difficult, but it had been done before.

Happier because he had sorted it out and knew what to do, he looked for Joslin – and received a new shock. Joslin wasn't there, either.

"What's happening?" he roared. "Is our house bewitched?"

"Randolf Waygoode, age is addling your brain," said Lettice. "Can't you see that Alys disappearing is of a piece with our other calamities? That poor lad's out of his mind and he's gone to look for her."

"Then I must follow," said Randolf.

"You'll do no such thing," Lettice replied. "You'll send for Giles Worsdell and the constables. They'll do the looking as they're supposed to. And you'll tell Simon of Chichester that through no fault of your own the bond of surety for Joslin is broken. That will certainly start a search. Meanwhile, you'll stay here and meet Edward Gaylor over the feast and tell him the news. How he takes it is up to him, not you."

Randolf took his wife by her chubby hand. "Dame Lettice," he said, "thank you. If ever I'm mayor it's you who'll have made me so."

Now he waited at the head of his table while cooks busied themselves and delicious smells spread from the kitchens. But he took no pleasure in it. The questions just churned round and round until his head nearly burst. *Where have they gone? Will Edward Gaylor come? What shall I do if he doesn't? When will there be news from Worsdell and the constables? What will Simon of Chichester do?*

Joslin's feet were sore. His limbs ached, his stomach roared through lack of food. This London was a huge anthill full of scurrying figures who knew what they were about, while he had wandered from high noon until dusk, not knowing what he sought. Being a be-wildered stranger was no use. The city was different from the last time he had walked it. Then, he knew what he was looking for.

But where should he look now? Would he see Alys waiting on a street corner? Of course not. But that didn't stop him seeing her, dozens of times, standing with her back to him. How delightedly he'd bounded up to her. How horror-struck he had been as he recoiled from the scab-covered, pox-eaten face that turned to look at him, so often that now he feared to go near anyone.

He had no money. But his stomach could not roar unfilled all night. Yet he daren't steal; ending up in the pillory would ruin everything. But he couldn't starve. He came to a stall laid out with hot pies. The smell was overpowering and. . .

Dare he? Yes, he did. The pie seller was shouting his wares, "Good pies, greasy and salty, pig and goose." Joslin slid a hand out, removed the nearest, shoved it in his tunic so the pastry's heat seemed to pierce his skin and hot fat ran down it. Without moving his eyes or changing his tone of voice the pie seller added to his cries. "There's a thief at the end of my stall. Don't let him get away."

Joslin didn't panic. He was away, running for his life, dodging past people still trying to sort out what went on, out of Eastcheap, down Walbrook Street, south towards the river, across Thames Street, down Grantham Lane past Dowgate, where the Walbrook joined the Thames. The river gleamed blackly in the thickening light. The hue and cry grew fainter. He was gasping for breath. He had to stop. He could imagine the pursuers grumbling, "Let him find his own pies. If he charged a bit less they wouldn't be stolen." Some would wish him luck. Besides, it was nearly dark now and nobody would know him again.

He was at the end of Grantham Lane, looking over the river. There were few people around. Curfew was sounding. Already the nets for catching salmon at night were being laid. He sat on the stones, got his breath back and pulled the crumbling pie from inside his tunic. It was soggy with fat and getting cooler. Even so, he took a ravenous bite and it was good. He savoured a few mouthfuls – then stopped. What had he done? Put himself in danger from the law by his thieving and made his search even more hopeless. Was it worth it?

The constables would be looking for him. Simon of Chichester would hear and be even surer that he was right. Besides, he had broken Randolf's bond of surety. Randolf would be in trouble as well.

What should he do? Go back?

How could he? Always in England, he seemed to have been on the run for something he hadn't done. But now, for the first time, he really had done something wrong. He couldn't go back.

Besides, he wouldn't go back without finding Alys.

And if he didn't find her – well, he'd never want to go back. What then? Go on his journey to Wales? How could he? His minstrel's tunic and cloak and his cache of money were still by his bed. Randolf had Guillaume's dagger; how could he travel across England without it? Most important of all, the locket Guillaume gave him as he lay dying on *The Merchant of Orwell* was wrapped up with his clothes. He was suddenly glad he wasn't wearing it: to have it smothered in grease would have been an insult both to his father and his unknown mother.

So that was it. He couldn't go back unless he found Alys. He wouldn't be going to Wales if he did find her because they'd marry and he'd stay. But if he never found her – or found her married to Gaylor after all – he could *never, ever* go to Wales.

His life seemed reduced to a pinpoint, the merest chance. He was standing, like the clowns and tumblers he saw in the castle when he was still a child, on a swaying tightrope. To lose his balance either way would send him crashing not on a stone floor but down into Hell itself.

Edward Gaylor had taken it badly, as Randolf knew he would. He turned up before supper, dressed in finery which meant good profits that day to drapers and haberdashers all over London. He was loaded with gifts for Randolf and Lettice and betrothal offerings for Alys. He strode into the hall, his face split by a smile which sat oddly on his dark, jowly face, and went straight to Randolf.

"So my soon-to-be-betrothed is shy and cannot see me straight away," he said. "Well, such demureness is pleasing. But tell Alys I'm here and that I'm impatient to be with her again."

Randolf cleared his throat. "We have grave news," he said.

The night would be cold. The river was deserted. Joslin shivered. He had no lantern. If the watch found him, he'd be in the lock-up and that would be the end of everything.

The sky was cloudy. Stars and moon had disappeared. At least there would be no frost. But a vicious breeze was blowing up from the river. He left this open place and found a doorway in Grantham Street which gave some shelter. His tunic was thin and though his jerkin was heavy, it gave no warmth and he sighed for his cloak. He took his harp off his back and laid it carefully beside him. Then he curled into a ball, pulled his knees up to his chin and tried to will warmth into himself. He would pass the whole dark, cold night like this, alone with desperate thoughts and sure that when daybreak came he would be too cold to move.

"You've played me false," Gaylor raged. "You've gone back on a bargain."

"We made no bargain," Randolf replied. "I only said I'd find out her answer. But I'll be frank with you. I didn't like this marriage because I thought I knew who I

181

wanted Alys to wed. I thought I'd arranged it and that you couldn't argue with a better offer, however angry you were. But it seems I was wrong. Things have happened which I don't understand."

"I'm listening," Edward Gaylor growled.

"We've both been cheated. It looks as though they've laughed at my offer. You can think what you like about that – just be sure it was none of my doing."

Edward Gaylor grunted. "If you'd kept to my plan, this would not have happened." He picked up his parcels and turned on his heel. At the end of the hall he paused and spoke again. "If you can't find her, I'll have to find her myself. I bid you goodnight."

Randolf watched him go. "I wish I could say good riddance, he said. "But I'd almost rather her marry Gaylor than what's happened." He waved his hand towards the food. "Take this away," he said to the servants. "Eat it yourselves. I've no stomach for it."

He left the hall bound for his solar and the rooms beyond, and Dame Lettice sorrowfully followed him.

Against all the odds, Joslin did sleep. No matter that he had wild, disturbed dreams in which his father died again and again before his eyes, Alys lay bleeding on the deck with him and twisted, pock-marked faces and grey, unmemorable faces hovered over them – he at least lost consciousness.

Amazingly, as dawn touched his eyes open, he found he had kept a little warmth in his body and no night watchman had discovered him. And more than that – he had thought of something he could do.

**15**

$e$ dward Gaylor, with lantern shining and papers to show who he was, strode angrily to his lodging at the Broken Seld. No watchman had cause to stop him even though it was hours before curfew would be lifted. Tonight he should be happy: this was the last act in the strange drama which had unfolded since that wonderful night of deliverance in Cologne when his life nearly ended so miserably. See what had happened. His fortune was here in full measure. Step by unlooked for step it had come. Though the nights spent wracked with nameless fears about how it came – and why – dampened the joy of his days, nothing should have stopped him reaching this pinnacle he'd coveted for so long.

Until this slap in the face from Providence. Had Fortune's Wheel turned to its highest point and then toppled him off so his fall was all the more awesome? What else would spring from that strange encounter in Cologne? He'd known at once what caused his brother's death. The wine given to him by his deliverer. Had Jacob and Cicely been poisoned deliberately? But how could his deliverer know them? If he did, what could he have had against them? Yet because of that his fortunes rode high. And yet – no, he dampened down the terrible thoughts which sometimes rose like an inexorable tide. Was he somehow guilty of murder by proxy?

Then came the news of Thomas and Hugh. How strange that the one should come so soon after the other. But that was God's way of doing things. Nobody but he would question the deaths of Jacob and Cicely. The priest himself thought them no more than sudden misfortune. Nobody, now the boys were dead, could question his right to the estate as nearest blood relative. So he *would* follow his ambition, even if he was not the agent of it. But now here was an unlooked-for barrier. Was Fate saying, "Nothing comes easy. You must do without the most delectable of your wishes. . ."

His *wishes*? This was the one part of his ambition that made the rest worthwhile. Ever since he'd seen Alys when she was no more than thirteen, when he'd visited his brother's stepson Hugh in his new apprenticeship, he'd *known* that everything would be dust and ashes without her. He had no fortune to offer, so there was no chance of marriage. He should have been rewarded by a grateful King for the service he and others had performed all those years ago. But no such luck. That's why he'd left England and wandered the world until he'd made the sort of fortune he'd hoped might prove enough.

Lost in these thoughts, he reached the tavern of the Broken Seld. He stepped up to the door. And then, without warning, like a breath of warm wind in the cold dark, a voice sounded in his ear. His stomach twisted inside him. He *knew* that voice, whisper though it was.

"Don't worry, Edward. You haven't lost your bride. Come with me and meet her again."

* * *

Simon of Chichester was certain now. He had doubted his own logic when he saw that Joslin had nothing to do with Wulfrum's death. But the news the sergeant brought changed all that. The Frenchman was gone. He'd broken the surety. Randolf had broken his word by letting him go. Well, one thing was clear. Randolf Waygoode could bid farewell to civic dignity. Waygoode for mayor? Whistle for it, Randolf.

But that wasn't the point. This flight and the girl's disappearance showed he'd been right all along. He must find the runaways, bring the Frenchman to justice for his murders and see the girl punished for breaking her guardian's trust. How should he set about it?

Simon of Chichester decided to sleep on it. When he woke up next morning, he'd know.

Joslin rose stiffly, stretched and rubbed sleep from his eyes. He ached horribly in every numbed limb. But now he knew what to do.

There was someone in London who had helped him and asked nothing in return, had offered friendship with nothing to gain. The gravedigger, Will of Essex. Will had helped him three times now – at their first meeting, when Thomas's grave was disturbed and at the jury. Will was to be trusted. He would give good advice. He might offer shelter, a hiding place while Joslin thought out what to do.

He'd certainly give him some breakfast.

After the whisper in his ear, Edward Gaylor knew little. His nose and mouth were smothered with a sweet-smelling cloth. Drowsy and weak, he was half-pulled along streets by ways he would never remember. Then, when he was all but unconscious, his journey ended – in a hot, smoky, suffocating place where his legs could not hold him upright. Did he sink or was he pushed on to a dirty, prickly surface which stank? Did he stay sprawled on it because he wanted to, or because tight bonds held him there? What were those rustling, scratching sounds all around him? These questions passed through his fuddled mind before he sank into oblivion which – he was aware enough to realize – might be his last.

But how was he to get to All Hallows? There were dangers to wandering round London in broad daylight that he hadn't thought of yesterday. Randolf would want him back. The pie seller would still be looking. Every constable in London might be watching out for a young man with a thin foreign face and black hair only just growing again after Alys – dear, lost Alys – had cut it off to make him look like a daft girl called Geraldine. How many years ago did that seem? And, to make it easier, this young man had a harp on his back.

He shivered. Being caught seemed too likely. He couldn't get from the Walbrook to All Hallows in broad daylight along busy streets, that was for sure. He looked out over the river. It was low tide.

For the moment there was a strip of mud between water and wall. Could he walk along this narrow causeway? What if the tide turned? He'd better make his mind up quickly. Perhaps besting the Thames like that would be an omen of success. He hesitated – then: *yes, he'd do it.*

London Bridge was to his left, about four hundred paces away. Below him was Dowgate, where the Walbrook joined the Thames. There was only one way he could go and stay unseen. He'd have to let himself down into the water, wade across Dowgate, then trust to mud and tide to keep him out of sight. Then there was London Bridge, with its vast stone piles, to get round.

He looked down into Dowgate's dark, cold, dirty water. Horrible. But no one would see him. If he wanted help it would have to be done.

Gingerly, he climbed over the edge and let himself down.


Randolf did not sleep that night. Nor did Lettice, nor the apprentices, nor Perkin, Herry or the ostlers. Such woe had befallen the house and everyone felt it.

In the apprentices' chamber, they talked long into the night.

"Hugh was right all along," said Alexander. "That Joslin *did* want to get his nasty foreign hands on Alys. He's gone off with her."

"We sh-should have kn-known," stuttered John. "W-we should never have l-laughed at Hugh the way we d-did. We should have known J-Joslin for what he w-w-was."

William answered them firmly. "I won't hear a word against Joslin. I liked him. I don't believe he thought like that about Alys. It wasn't his idea they should wed."

So the argument went on until, an hour before dawn, fatigue drove them to sleep.

Above the stables, discussion did not rage. Perkin lay remembering dead Wulfrum, vanished Alys and fleeing Joslin and wondering what was to come next. Herry, meanwhile, had one thought. *My only friend has gone away and everyone has turned against him. If only I knew where he was. Then I could help him.*

* * *

Simon of Chichester knew the answer as soon as he woke. If Joslin and Will of Essex were in this together, then All Hallows and the gravedigger's hovel was where he should look.

Even as the weak sun rose, he was walking the streets eastward. Soon he was giving instructions to the sergeant of Tower ward, ending with, "You know where to go and who to look for. Report to me as soon as you see or hear anything. Do not apprehend them yourself. I alone should do that."

Then he left for the Guildhall, well pleased with his preparations.

Dowgate was deep, up to his shoulders. To save his harp he held it high over his head. From the shore he must have looked like a stag with curiously deformed antlers. He struggled shivering on, hugging the wall, cloying mud gripping at his ankles, until he emerged with only a narrow ribbon of mud to negotiate. Ebbgate, Fishwharf at la Hole and Oystergate stood before him. After Dowgate, these were nothing.

But soon the huge stone pile which held up the first massive arch of London Bridge stood before him. Should he climb over, visible against the grey stone? Or wade round it? How deep was the water? It might come over his head. Then what would happen to his harp, let alone him? Besides, he knew how boatmen feared the tide racing through these arches. Perhaps there were currents which would sweep him right away? He nearly climbed out of the river and took his chance in the crowds. But that would be stupid now he'd come so far. No, there was only one course.

He gritted his teeth, held his harp up high and waded in.

* * *

Sometimes Edward Gaylor came to a weird half-consciousness, then he drifted away. But in those brief snatches one thing sank into his fuddled mind. Someone lay close by even more helpless than he was.

Over many years, tides had scoured a deep channel between the stone of the piles and the river bottom. Without warning Joslin stepped right in it. He somehow stayed on his feet, but water came up to his mouth. Just in time he shot his right hand carrying the harp into the air, so it cleared the water as if held by a musical water-sprite. With his left hand he grabbed and scrabbled with his fingers, searching for handholds in the slimy stones of London Bridge.

He inched his way along. His teeth chattered uncontrollably. And all this to ask breakfast from Will of Essex.

Ah, but more than that. He'd get sanctuary and counsel. *Stick at it, Joslin.* He forced himself round the pile, though water chilled, current pulled and mud dragged him down. At last he climbed out of the water, his dripping clothes sticking to his skin.

After that, nothing seemed too much, not the treacherous muddy rim above the water, not the wharfs to climb over or clamber under, not the cold water at Billingsgate or Watergate to wade through. Soon the Tower loomed close and he thought: *once I'm out of this river and on dry land again, I can face anything.* The elements had tested him and he'd come through. What was there left to fear?

The ward sergeant sent his constables to All Hallows. "Simon of Chichester gets the sergeant to do his work for him, then puts it on to us," said one.

189

"That's the way of the world," said the other.

Yes, it was, and they knew they'd never change it. So they went to All Hallows, looked in the graveyard, saw smoke rising from Will's hovel – but saw neither him nor a harp-playing visitor.

"We'll come back and see Will when he's digging," said the first.

The others agreed. They had better things to do. There was nobody here who shouldn't be.

But they were wrong. There was one who was watching Will of Essex's hovel closely but secretly.

*I know you're out, looking for Alys. Does nothing scare you off? In the end you'll come here. You've nowhere else to go. Your hellish curiosity has made things hard for me but fatal for you. To leave you on earth with a puzzle to solve might cost me dear, so I must play this through to the very end, further than I wanted to.*

Will of Essex had lit his fire. The smoke went straight up through the roof and he gratefully warmed himself. The morning was chill. This winter would be harsh – but at least with the cold there would be no more of *those* deaths. The pestilence would go away – perhaps to come back with the heat of the sun, perhaps not.

This year it had come back, not enough for the great and terrible plague pits of his childhood, but enough to keep him digging long and deep and not just in this churchyard, either. Perhaps that poor lad he'd had to dig up again would be the last. So though winter brought hunger, cold and misery, yet it brought some blessings as well.

He looked outside. A dark morning with a pale sun

rising without warmth. Two graves to dig today, their plots already marked out. Plenty of time – there'd be no leaving this place all the while the fool of a coroner had placed that ridiculous ban on him.

He sniffed the air. Once – and then again, this time suspiciously. Someone was here – or had been – who shouldn't be.

*Keep out, Will. Don't go looking. Strange things are happening and you want nothing more to do with them. . .*

When Will heard Simon of Chichester accuse him of being a murderer in league with the young minstrel he felt contempt for a man not worth his job. No different, in Will's view, from anyone put in charge over better people. Well, two things could happen. The coroner would be made to stare his stupidity in the face, or justice would play one of its strange tricks and this false accusation would stick. God would decide – and God, Will knew well, was not above playing weird pranks of His own now and again. However it ended, Will could do nothing about it. He'd have to wait and see what Fate offered.

He surveyed his graveyard. Another day with just his spade, the wet earth and the long-dead for company.

But not just yet. Time enough for bread, cheese and beer to give his stomach a lining against the cold. He went back inside to the warm.

Randolf's sleepless night ended. He had paced muttering up and down for hours; Dame Lettice had listened to him. As day broke, she repeated for the hundredth time the only thing she could say: "There's nothing you can do, Randolf. It's in God's hands."

But now day was here, Randolf's answer was different. "I *shall* do something. I can't wait for God."

"Where are you going, Randolf?"

"Where I should have gone to start with. I'm not living like this."

Then he was gone, clumping through chamber, hall and courtyard, shooting the bolts of the gate and then out into Silver Street, leaving Lettice open-mouthed and deeply worried.

Joslin climbed out of the river at Petty Wales. Wet, bedraggled and covered in mud, he looked nothing like a minstrel on the run – except for his harp which had suffered little and which he kept low by his side. So, reasoning that people who had fallen in the River Thames might not be uncommon here, he risked walking the last stretch.

To his right, the Tower rose and Tower Ditch dropped. Soon he was at the end of Tower Street and All Hallows was in front of him.

He entered the graveyard. In the far corner was Will's hovel. Twice before he had been watched here. He crouched to the ground and dashed from grave to grave like a small, scuttling animal.

But before he could reach the hovel, the door opened; Will of Essex looked out and called, "Who's there?"

Will looked at the muddy, woebegone figure in front of him, puzzled.

"It's me, Joslin."

Will's first thought was to shout, "Go away. You're trouble." But then he thought: *he's God's creature like me and everything's in God's hands. I'll welcome him whatever the cost.* "Come in, Joslin," he said. "Warm yourself and then eat with me."

* * *

Light touched Edward Gaylor's eyes as it touched every-body else's. Still that suffocating heat, still that human presence lying close to him. And still that chattering, scrabbling, rustling was everywhere in this place of Hell. There were pains on his shoulders, in his armpits, near his groin, whose source he wanted to touch – except that he could not move. The worst terror of all struck into his soul and he cried aloud to God to stop mocking him and take his soul there and then.

Will of Essex's bread was dry and heavy, his cheese mouldy and his ale sour. But to Joslin, famished and shivering, it was food that God's elect would eat, while the smoky fire was the heat that warmed Heaven.

"What about those clothes?" asked Will.

"They're drying on me," Joslin replied.

Will considered for a moment. Then, "Are you running away?"

"Yes."

"Then you can't go on wearing them. Wait there."

The hovel was tiny. The fire was in the middle of the floor, a straw mattress lay to one side, a bench and stool to the other. On another wall were shelves with rough earthenware jugs and pots. Opposite was a wooden chest. Will opened it and rummaged inside.

"Try these," he said and threw out a worn leather jerkin, a faded and patched brown smock and hose which had once been green.

"I can't take your clothes," Joslin protested.

"They're not mine."

"Then whose. . .?"

"Their owners aren't going to want them now."

Joslin hesitated. Did he want what the dead once wore?

Yes, why not? He peeled his old clothes off and pulled Will's offerings on. Then he hoisted his harp on his back.

Will surveyed the result. "You still look like a French minstrel." He pointed to the harp. "Take that off. I'll look after it until you're safe." Without protest, Joslin did so. Will still looked at him critically.

"You may not be a minstrel now, but you're still French."

He burrowed in the chest again. This time he brought out a large, fur-lined hat. "Once this belonged to a sheriff of the city," he said. "It will sit so large on your head that nobody will guess what's underneath."

Joslin put it on. It was huge; it came over his eyes so he could hardly see. But it hid his tell-tale hair.

"There," said Will. "Now you're just a churl with a rich man's cast-off on his head."

Joslin felt created anew. "Now I can escape any hunter," he said.

"Not yet," replied Will. "I think there's someone outside."

*I'm as near to the miserable hut of this miserable man as I dare be. And the two are talking. But I can hear nothing. Even the walls of a pig-sty like this keep searching eyes out and muttered words in.*

*But what can they say that's worth my hearing? The minstrel can't stay here for ever. When he emerges I'll be in the street waiting. And then I'll shepherd him like the meanest sheep on a Cotswold hillside to where he'll meet his love at last.*

"Wait here," Will whispered. He pushed open the door and looked outside. "Who's there?" he called.

No answer.

"I know you're there and I'm coming to look for you," he shouted.

He strode through his graveyard, looking methodically behind each headstone. Suddenly, a figure sprang from behind one not ten paces away from the hovel. Will gave chase but the figure was too fast.

"What's the point?" he said. "Let him go."

Even so, as it dwindled away at frenzied speed, Joslin knew it, not just by the grey with brown hose but by the face he saw for a mere instant – that face whose sheer forgettability made it memorable.

Randolf was in the Guildhall arguing fiercely with Simon of Chichester.

"You let a suspected murderer get away," screamed Simon. "You've ruined the course of justice; you've broken a promise to the sheriffs. I'll make sure you'll *never* hold any civic position in this city."

"Suspected murderer? Joslin is as likely a murderer as my easel is to chant plainsong. What promise to the sheriffs? They believed your daft theories as much as they think the Devil lives in a vat of cheese."

Simon of Chichester was so angry he could not speak.

"And *when* I'm mayor," Randolf went on, "the first thing I'll do is ask the King for a new coroner."

They glared at each other for a few moments. Then, suddenly, Randolf burst out laughing. He clapped the coroner on the shoulder and said, "Simon, we've known each other for years. We've always got on."

"You broke a bond," Simon of Chichester muttered.

"All right, so I did. But hear me out and you'll know why. I should have come to you yesterday myself and not trusted Giles Worsdell to get the story right. I think you'll agree any promise was broken for me, whether I wanted it or not. And believe me, I did *not*."

"Go on," said Simon stiffly.

Randolf told the story of Edward Gaylor, Alys and Joslin. When he had finished, Simon said, "Well, at least we're looking for the same person. So what are we going to do now?"

*That was close. The gravedigger seems to have the Devil's own eyes when it comes to his cursed graveyard. But who will he think I am? Just a grave-robber, a pick-harness, a picker-up of trifles from the dead. The carrion crow settles where the dead lie and so do they. So now I'll wait outside this place of death, where nobody will look twice at me.*

Will came back in. "Wherever you are, so is that man. Who is he?"

Joslin considered his answer. "I don't know who he is but I know that my fate and his are bound together. He watched me by London Bridge as I searched for Thomas Hockley. Seeing him filled me with dread, but I didn't know why. Then you saw him after I met you – and someone hid here the night we opened Thomas's grave."

"We can't be completely sure that was him," Will said.

"But it's likely, isn't it?"

Will nodded. "Go on," he said.

"Then again, Perkin met a stranger in the tavern by

Cripplegate, who killed Wulfrum as he tried to run away. I believe he was the same man. Who knows how many more times he's watched me from afar?" Suddenly, like a candle lit in the dark, a tiny memory flared. "God help me, he was watching outside Randolf's when I first came to London with Alys. He's dogged me ever since I've been here."

"Then that's your man," said Will.

Joslin continued as though Will had not spoken. "So he took Alys away. But why? What did Alys do to deserve that?"

"Likely, nothing. He took her away from *you*."

"Or from Edward Gaylor. Or both of us. Who is he?"

"More to the point for you," said Will, "*where* is he?"

"Here, near the graveyard. We've just seen him."

"I don't mean that. I mean, where does he live in London? Where does he sleep at nights? He may roam the city but he's no vagabond."

"But. . ."

"Find out where and you might find your Alys."

Joslin's heart sank at the prospect. As if he were a soaring bird, he saw in his mind all the criss-crossing streets of London at once, and the scores of thousands of people who trod them. "*How?*" he cried.

"I don't know," said Will, "but we'll try. Follow me outside."

"So," said Randolf, "Joslin's no murderer but he's broken a trust. And my ward has disappeared. Find one and I reckon you'll find both."

"But they may be miles away," Simon objected.

"I know," said Randolf heavily. "But we can only search the city."

* * *

198

By mid-morning the apprentices in the workshop were tired of doing nothing. William found some tidying up, but there was nothing else.

"We must wait till Randolf comes and gives some orders," William said. Alexander and John muttered mutinously but could not disagree.

Perkin, though, was very agitated. He whispered to Herry, "I can't stay here. I've got to go looking."

"What for?" asked Herry.

"For the man who killed Wulfrum."

"Wait for me," said Herry. "I'm coming too."

Will led Joslin to a far corner of the graveyard, behind a clump of bushes to a large plot of loose earth about four paces square. Close by was a yew tree. Its evergreen leaves gave this corner a sombre hue making the long morning shadows seem even darker.

"A mother, father and four children lie here," he said. "I buried the last yesterday."

Joslin wondered why he had been brought here.

Will raked the top to a fine tilth and then with his spade scored a wavy channel in the earth along the side nearest to them.

"That's the River Thames," he said.

He broke a stick off a bush and stepped into the middle of the plot. He traced a line with the stick starting at the bank of the river to the far corner, then from one side of the plot almost towards the other and back to the river, making an irregular square.

"Those are the boundaries of the city."

"Should you be doing this on a new grave?" Joslin asked timidly.

"It may be their resting place but the grave is the labour of my hands," Will replied. He broke off another, smaller stick and laid it across the first channel. "That's London Bridge," he said. He searched for a large stone and placed it at the join between river and boundary. "That's the Tower." He took six smaller stones and placed them at intervals round the boundary. "The city gates," he said. "Ludgate, Newgate, Aldersgate, Cripplegate, Bishopsgate and Aldgate." He took a larger, long stone and placed it a little way in from Ludgate. He broke off another stick and stuck it in the soil next to the stone so it pointed upwards like a little spire. "St Paul's," he said. With his first stick he scored lines across the square, from top to bottom and side to side. "These are streets," he said and pointed them out. "Thames Street, Tower Street, Cheapside, Fenchurch Street, Lombard Street, Bread Street, Wood Street, Milk Street, Aldermanbury. . ."

Joslin stared. It was like his vision of the city from above. And Will had created it so quickly. He looked at him with new respect.

Will now broke off some small branches from the yew tree and laid them out neatly by the grave.

"You're quite sure you saw him when you first arrived at Randolf Waygoode's?" he asked.

"Yes. Now I am."

"Very well."

He picked up a yew branch and stuck it in the soil at the stone representing Ludgate, so it stood like a tiny tree on the edge of a tiny city. "That's the first time of all that he was seen," he said. "By Alfred of Ware with the man you say was Thomas."

Then, with his first stick, he scored in a short street near Cripplegate, close to the city wall. "That's Silver Street," he said. He took a small stone and placed it halfway along the north side. "That's Waygoode's."

Opposite, he placed another yew branch. "That's your first sighting. The next was at London Bridge, you say?"

"Yes."

Another branch was placed close to the channel next to the stick which crossed it. "Then I saw him at this graveyard," said Will. Another stone to represent All Hallows, then another branch. "And we'll say it was him that night when the grave was opened." Two branches close together now, like a grove of young saplings.

"Where was the tavern where the labourers met him?" Will asked.

"Close to Cripplegate."

In went another branch by the stone representing the gate, right next to the city boundary.

"And the death of one labourer?"

"Behind Randolf's." Another branch. "And also that's where Alys must have been taken," cried Joslin excitedly. In went a further branch, close up to the last one.

"And again this morning," said Will. The last branch now waved by the church. London looked like a series of small spinneys.

They looked over the result. "What does it tell us?" said Will.

"We've seen him a lot," Joslin replied.

"But does it help us know where he hides?" asked Will.

Joslin looked at the map uncomprehendingly. Then his mind cleared. "I see," he said. There was a method in this. "There are two main groups of branches. One over to the north by Cripplegate and one over here to the east. So he'll hide somewhere in the middle."

"Why should he?" Will asked. "As I remember, Alfred of Ware said that he told him he lived in Westcheap. Did you believe that?"

"Well – he wouldn't have so far to go to each place he's been seen."

"Why does he come here?" asked Will patiently, like Guillaume when Joslin was small and could not master something very simple.

"To watch for me," said Joslin.

"Did he know you were coming here this morning?"

"How could he?"

"So let's look at the clump round Cripplegate. Why was he there?"

"First, watching me when I arrived in London with Alys."

"Did he know you were coming?"

"No."

"Then how could he be watching for you?"

"You're right. He couldn't be."

"So was he watching for Alys? What else has he done there?"

"Met Perkin and Wulfrum and then murdered Wulfrum."

"Why?"

"Nobody knows. But Perkin said he was Wulfrum's old master."

"Who was that?"

"A knight with lands round Thame near Oxford. Wulfrum broke his bonds and ran away when he was young. That was many years ago."

"Why should Wulfrum run away?"

"He was a serf with a bad master."

"Why should that master kill Wulfrum now?"

"Because he saw him and wanted to punish him for escaping?"

"Is it likely?" asked Will. "What does one serf matter to a knight?"

Joslin was thinking furiously. "No, there was something else. Perkin said the stranger asked Wulfrum to do one last service for him but Wulfrum wouldn't. Perkin thought that's why he killed him."

"So it could," said Will. "Seeing his old master again scared Wulfrum. He must have been forced to do things on pain of his own death. What could they be? What was so awful that when Wulfrum wouldn't the refusal meant death? As if to say, 'If you won't do this your life is of no more use to me'?"

"Perhaps his master ordered him to take Alys?" said Joslin.

"But you say that wasn't the first task. What else could he have asked Wulfrum to do?"

"I don't know."

"Had Wulfrum done anything to *you*?"

"Yes – if it *was* Wulfrum." He told Will about the strange night visits, knives at his throat, cloth stuffed in his mouth, a whispering voice threatening him to leave Alys alone.

"Could Wulfrum ever win Alys for himself?"

"Never."

"So why should he do it?"

"As you said. It must be because he was ordered to do it."

"Why?"

Joslin didn't answer. *Why* was too hard a question.

"There's only one possible reason," said Will. "You came from nowhere, out of the blue. This made difficulties for our stranger."

"Robin should have come back," said Joslin. "Perhaps Robin would have been warned off, like me." Now his thoughts ran on. "But it would have been no use warning Robin off. He and Alys were already betrothed.

So. . ." A terrible possibility dawned. Robin could have been murdered. If he hadn't died in Stovenham he might have died in London. The thought struck him dumb for a moment.

"There was nothing between you and Alys then," said Will. "But for all he knew there could have been. Evidently Alys had to be kept free and available. But for who?"

"Edward Gaylor?" asked Joslin. "But Alys disappeared before he was to come back to Randolf's. Gaylor didn't know that. He must have thought everything was going his way. So was Alys taken for our stranger himself?"

"Whoever it was, it was not for you," said Will. "Joslin, you've been getting hints for your own good to stay out. Because you haven't, because you've gone on worrying away finding out more and more, you're in the gravest danger possible for mortal man. You're in the way of someone who's so used to killing that he thinks nothing of it."

When Joslin spoke his voice was small and subdued. "So when it came to seizing Alys, Wulfrum wouldn't do it and so he was murdered."

"I think he had already done something as terrible," said Will.

"What?"

"Joslin, do you think that scaring you was all he did that night?"

Joslin remembered the footsteps in the dark, the shape left in Robin's bed by someone's body. "Of course not," he said. "Wulfrum was lying low until the time was right. Then he rose and took Hugh away as we all slept deeply." He remembered the strange, foul taste of the cloth in his mouth. "Perhaps we slept too deeply," he said.

Then, as if it had been lying at the back of his mind like a trap covered with leaves, another fact came into his mind. "Thomas and Hugh didn't just have their throats slit. They were locked into plague. The swellings were well advanced. They'd have died anyway."

"I know," said Will. "We seek a double-dealer in death. This makes me pause."

"Yet our stranger walks the streets a well man."

"There are mysteries to do with the pestilence beyond learned doctors, let alone a simple gravedigger. I only bury the results."

Joslin didn't answer. He stared at Will. Simple gravedigger? With a few well-placed questions he had pierced to the heart of things.

Will seemed to know what he was thinking. "I spend long days alone," he said. "Digging sends me into far countries in my mind. I have time to ponder on many things and come to many conclusions. I'd rather think alone than dispute with those learned doctors."

"So what have we found?" asked Joslin.

"We begin to know how all this was done. We may have an inkling of who by. But we don't know *why*."

"I thought it might be for inheritances," said Joslin. "Find out who profited by Hugh's and Thomas's deaths and you find the murderer. When Edward Gaylor came, I thought it must be him. Except that he wasn't in London when they were killed."

"And is now cheated of his new wife," said Will.

Joslin looked again at Will's map of London. "But where does our man hide?" he said.

"Close to Silver Street, somewhere near Cripplegate. He had to be nearby so Wulfrum could slip out and back unmissed to see him, but not so near that he would be seen keeping watch. He told Alfred of Ware he lived in

Westcheap. That's near to Walter Craven's place in Eastcheap. When Thomas was taken he probably did his own abducting." He picked up another yew branch and stuck it halfway along Eastcheap. "But he dared not be seen dragging Alys through the city, so that's another reason why he's close by. If there's plague where he is, then it's only in a very small space. You must look for a house set apart from its neighbours. Whatever flies through the air and settles on us to give us these black boils gets weaker as winter comes, so this plague is trapped where it won't spread. Even at its worst, some people were left alone while all those round them died. So when you look, don't fear the pestilence, Joslin.

"A house set apart from its neighbours, somewhere near Cripplegate," Joslin repeated. He grasped Will by the hand. "Will," he said, "for the first time I feel like a knight wearing full armour. But my armour is the armour of knowledge, because now I know what I'm doing and where I'm going."

"Then it's time for you to leave," said Will. "Your harp's safe with me until you come back triumphant."

They returned to the hovel. Joslin picked up his new hat and placed it firmly on his head.

"Don't go through the gate," said Will. "If he's watching, that's where he'll be. I'll show you where to climb over the wall."

At the opposite side of the graveyard, they briefly stood together.

"Goodbye," said Will. "And may God be with you."

Joslin grasped the top of the wall, and vaulted over.

When he had gone, Will picked up the branches, sticks and stones from his map of London and raked the soil over so the family underneath could sleep on undisturbed.

* * *

The watcher outside had been patient. Nobody had been in or out. But the minstrel could not stay there for ever. An hour passed. Two constables arrived. The watcher fumed. *I've waited too long. They'll take him away.* But they emerged with nobody.

Then the watcher beat his forehead with frustration. He was losing his grip. For the first time since – well, since he could remember – he'd made a mistake. Even an addle-brained gravedigger and a meddling minstrel might not be complete fools. Half an hour before, a figure in brown with a leather jerkin and a rich man's cast-off hat had walked down Tower Street from All Hallows.

*That was the minstrel.* He had been taken in by the oldest trick in the world. A whole half-hour lost. What could he do? Just one possibility. Run hard to the one place the Frenchman knew, hope he too went there to work out where to go next, then follow.

**R**andolf and Simon of Chichester stood outside the tavern of the Broken Seld, preparing to talk to Edward Gaylor.

"It may be," Randolf said, "that where he is, Alys will be. Perhaps last night he was playing his own cunning game."

"Or he's the latest victim of Joslin de Lay and the gravedigger," said Simon. "The end of Joslin's hated rival."

They looked at each other with pity for two such ludicrous ideas. Then Simon said, "At least we may have found a helper in our search."

But the landlord told them that Edward Gaylor had not come back the night before. He showed them his room, cluttered with the purchases of a rich man excited at the thought of his young bride-to-be. They knew something was very wrong.

"He's not fled," said Simon. "This man was set on returning."

"I have another bad feeling at my heart," said Randolf.

* * *

Perkin led Herry over the wall through which he and Wulfrum had so often pushed, up the alley and into Babe Lane. Herry was not happy.

"William's going to be angry when he sees we've gone. He'll tell Randolf and we'll be thrown out on the street."

"I don't care," said Perkin. "I want to hear Wulfrum's murderer's neck crack under my two thumbs."

Herry shivered. "I don't think I want to come with you after all."

"Then go back. But if you tell, I'll make *your* neck crack."

Herry thought again. Perkin would, too.

"It's all right, Perkin. I'll come," he said.

Perkin grunted. He'd rather be on his own. "There's the tavern," he said.

In borrowed clothes and hat, Joslin felt safe and walked free.

But where to? They had reasoned where the stranger's lair might be and Alys as well, but Joslin could never walk straight to it. On the basis that to walk from All Hallows to Cripplegate he'd better start from somewhere else, he headed for somewhere he did know – Randolf's.

But then he had a problem. Should he go to Randolf's, say, "I'm back again and I'm looking for a stranger's house?" Would Randolf understand? No, best stay alone. Finding Alys was *his* quest – just as finding Heurodys was Sir Orfeo's and Sir Orfeo's alone.

Now he was in Silver Street. From thirty paces away he surveyed that familiar gateway into the courtyard, the workshop windows, the windows of the apprentices' chamber in the overhanging second storey. He felt a lump in his throat. For a few days this had been a real home. Now he was cast out. He could not enter again, not until this search was ended one way or another.

*I was right. You came to Randolf's and I cut you off. Joslin de Lay, you've not practised staying unrecognized, as I have for so many years. You should never have put that hat on. There's not its fellow in London. Once I know your head's underneath, it stands in the crowds like a beacon, still on your head as you wait outside Waygoode's, your only foothold in the city.*

*Now, are you here just to get your bearings or to go inside? I will you to go away again so I can follow you to the end.*

"Edward Gaylor was full of his own importance," the landlord of the Broken Seld had told them. "He seemed to think he ranked with a knight. I don't think he was used to wealth."

"You're right there," Randolf answered.

"Before he went out he insisted I drink with him. He made a strange toast. 'To the Wheel of Fortune and the Devil's powers which make it turn.' He drank long and deep, then fell quiet. As I stood not knowing what to say, he made another. 'To the will of God which alone stops the wheel turning.'" The landlord suddenly grasped Simon by the arm. "I know you – the city coroner doesn't call unless he's on dire errands. When I knew my guest wasn't coming back and setting the whole tavern about the ears preparing his journey to his fine manor at Stoke Poges I remembered the toast – 'the Devil's powers'."

"Where did he go while he lodged here?" Simon asked.

"The Guildhall to claim his inheritances. Silver Street

to claim a bride. To every draper, haberdasher and gold-smith in London. Nobody came to meet him; he walked alone."

"He's roaming the streets distracted because his longed-for wife is gone," said Simon.

"He was angry," said Randolf. "But he wasn't the sort to go distracted. He'd come back here and plot what to do next. And he'd *never* simply leave all this." He waved his hands round the rich, brightly-coloured, fur-lined clothes which bedecked the room. "No, I reckon he met foul play on the way home."

"Remember Alfred of Ware's testimony – a man supporting a dead body as if it was a drunkard," said Simon. "We seek one who could take Gaylor through the streets unnoticed."

"But which way?" said Randolf. "West or east? To river or wall?"

"That's the big question," Simon replied.

Herry looked at the old tavern set under the shadow of the huge wall. It seemed a broken-down sort of place – and so noisy so early in the day that it made him flinch.

"I don't want to go in," he said. "Besides, I en't got no money."

"Me, neither," said Perkin. "But we en't here to drink. We're here to watch, in case he comes back."

"What do you want him to come back for?" cried Herry in alarm.

"Because then we can see where he goes," said Perkin.

"But I've come to look for Joslin."

"Then look on your own. I'm after *him*."

"But if he comes back, he'll want to kill you, too."

"That's all right. I'm ready for him."

"But what if he don't?"

This did not seem to have occurred to Perkin.

"He *has* to. In the end," he said uncertainly.

Now Joslin was outside Randolf's, where could he go? There were so many directions. How could he choose?

Yesterday he'd stood in the alleyway where Alys must have been dragged. He'd chosen to go south into the city's heart. What if he'd gone the other way? He could have found what he was looking for. But he wouldn't have spoken to Will of Essex. So perhaps everything worked out for the best. Even so, why not stand in that same place and think again?

Two minutes later he was there. He imagined through Alys's eyes what had happened: the sudden awful figure scrambling over the wall like a wild beast, a split second of shock, perhaps a noxious cloth pushed in her mouth, then she was swept off her feet by hideous strength, shoved over the other side and bundled off – which way?

Well, he must have chosen wrong yesterday. He set off up the rutted alley, towards Babe Lane and the wall.

The watcher observed Joslin disappear up the alley.

*You make it so easy. I can cut you off at the other end by going up Wood Street. I'll watch where you go from there. But I begin to see what you think you're doing. Well, I'll let you believe you've found the object of your search yourself. But I'll be leading you there.*

Outside the Broken Seld, Randolf and Simon were completely at a loss.

"Now where?" asked Randolf.

Simon racked his brain for an answer.

"We should start from the beginning again," he said. "We're here because first Alys, then Joslin disappeared. Where from?"

"My orchard," said Randolf patiently.

"And that was where your servant was found murdered?"

"You know it was."

"Then we must go there again. This time we stay outside, in the alley where they must have gone. Nobody thought to look there yesterday. That was a mistake."

Randolf followed him unenthusiastically.

When they reached the point where Randolf had repaired the wall, they stopped. Simon looked down at the ground. There was a mass of footprints, most so recent they obscured anything done the day before.

"There's no point in going back the way we've come," said Randolf. "The tavern where Wulfrum met his killer is at the end of the alley. If that man took Alys, that's where we should go because he might have been there again."

Simon agreed, because he could think of nothing else.

Joslin emerged from the alleyway. In front of him were shops, houses and taverns; behind them the city wall itself rose, high and forbidding.

Familiar bustling London was all round him. Overhanging upper storeys cut out the sun in the narrow street. Shop and tavern signs projected low over his head. He felt he had plunged from dry land into raging sea. For a moment he felt as overwhelmed as when he entered the city with Alys. This was hopeless. Without some sign to tell him this was not in vain, his search would be over.

Then, as if God was indeed smiling on him, a sign came. To his right, where Wood Street ended, he saw that familiar sight – the grey, the brown, the unmemorable smooth face – come as if to be his guide.

Herry was unhappy. Perkin was slurping at a tankard of ale. Herry wondered how he'd managed to get it if he had no money. Perkin seemed to have forgotten about Wulfrum's murderer. So why should Herry keep looking? Nevertheless, he watched on, hoping that something inside him would know when their quarry came.

Once he nearly nudged Perkin to say, "Look over there." Just for a moment he thought he knew the person standing opposite, in green with a leather jerkin and a huge furry hat on his head. Oh, how Herry would love a hat like that. Fit for a duke, it was. But he daren't distract Perkin – and when he looked again the man in the hat had gone.

"I haven't seen any murderers," he said as Perkin came back with another full tankard. Perkin did not answer.

Several minutes went by. Then Herry nearly dropped to the floor with shock. "*Look!*" he squealed, shaking Perkin by the shoulder.

"Watch what you're at!" Perkin spluttered.

"No, but *look!*" He was pointing across the street. There stood Randolf and Simon of Chichester.

"They're coming here," Herry stuttered.

Perkin took a long final draught and put his tankard on the ground. "Come on," he said. "It's time to go."

He sidled along close to the houses, hidden from the other side of the street by hurrying people, away from Cripplegate and along Babe Lane. "If they're going to have a drink, they'll never know we were there. The landlord won't tell them, that's for sure."

"Where are we going?" asked Herry.

"Anywhere. So long as Randolf doesn't see us."

It was hard, keeping the stranger in view. Several times Joslin nearly lost him – but each time the figure appeared again, leading him ever onwards. The further they went, the faster Joslin felt his heart beating. The search was nearly over. Surely soon he would see Alys again. This man would never harm her – not if he wanted her for himself. Surely the plague was gone now. Will had said so. So there would be no more weeping black boils on a fair skin and a slit throat to go with them. He and Alys would be reunited and then they would use their wits as they had before, to gain her freedom.

Randolf and Simon found the fatal tavern full of tipsy apprentices and labourers who should have been about their work. Randolf was relieved to see nobody from his household there. But when they tried to question the lumpish landlord, they got no sense at all.

"Hopeless," said Randolf.

"I shall go back to the Guildhall," said Simon. "Perhaps those constables have news of whether Joslin hid with the gravedigger."

"I'll walk with you," said Randolf. "I've a mind to see Walter Craven. By the Guildhall's as good a way as any to Cheapside."

So they walked on together, each with his own thoughts about how huge and various a rabbit warren London was and how easily people could disappear in it without trace.

* * *

Where was he going? Joslin felt like a traveller at night chasing the flickering light of a will-o'-the-wisp across treacherous moors and swamps. Now he seemed to leave his own body. He really was Sir Orfeo following the Faery horde to the secret entrance to Faeryland. Or Sir Gawain seeking the green Chapel where his fate lay waiting. Or Sir Galahad, closer and closer to the Grail itself. The press of people in the noisome streets vanished; he struggled alone across a desert wasteland, towards the lair where the dragon guarded its hoard, the cave to which the worm returned after ravaging the country round about, the Dark Tower in which lay his heart's desire or baleful death. And like Orfeo, Gawain, Galahad, St George himself, his destiny was very near.

"I can't see Master Randolf now," said Herry. "Where shall we go?"

"I don't care," said Perkin. "I en't going back in that tavern because he'll go there to check on us. We can't go back home for fear he'll see us going in. We'll walk on till we're tired."

"We en't found nobody, then," said Herry.

"I know," said Perkin. He sounded very depressed, as if sorting out the world's troubles was way beyond a labourer's capabilities.

Well, Perkin might not have any idea what to do, but Herry had. That man with the big hat – Herry *did* know him though he couldn't for the life of him place who he was. But he'd seen him again. They'd follow him instead. Perkin needn't know. Besides, he didn't seem to care where they went.

Joslin stopped. Burningly, it came on him all at once.

This was the place. Why so sure? He did not know. Except that he had seen his quarry again, looking back, quickly, furtively, as if to check he was not followed.

Joslin was in a little street which led from the end of Adel Lane into Aldermanbury. Just ahead was a turn left into the alley. Beyond that was where the Walbrook flowed to the city wall and out into the country beyond. Houses here were less close-packed. There were little plots behind them, where trees grew, vegetables were tended, chickens ran and hogs foraged. One house was cut off even from those by scrubby, dead land. It stared, squat and blank, back at him, its shutters closed even in daylight, somehow unmemorable like the face of his quarry. From its roof came smoke, a steady stream upwards. So a fire was lit inside; Joslin could see piles of split firewood to make sure it stayed that way. Joslin remembered the gravedigger's words – "*You must look for a house set apart from its neighbours.*"

*I am here*, he thought.

Now what? He looked round. Nobody watched him. Perhaps his quarry was inside. Well, he had to meet him sooner or later. God would be with him – and Alys as well. Together they would prevail.

There was a door at the front, barred and immovable. He crept round the side, then the back. Another door. It swung on its hinges, inviting him inside.

Again he looked round. Just piles of logs and the backs of other houses. He slipped inside. There was nothing wrong with the door. The latch was in perfect order; it was just not clicked shut. A tremor of doubt crossed his mind. Was he expected? Then he noticed there was a bolt on the outside of the door as well as two inside. What was it for? To shut people in? A warning voice sounded in his mind. Could *he* be shut in?

Did it matter? As long as Alys was here.

Sweaty heat hit him as he entered. In front was the fire, well stoked up. An instant later, smell hit him as well. Rotting food. And what else? *Rotting people?*

Above the crackle and roar of the fire were other sounds. Scrabbling, scratching. Small black rats in droves scuttled across the room. The floor was littered with scraps of vegetables, fruit and meat. Food for the rats. He recalled Will of Essex's words. *"Whatever flies through the air and settles on us to give us these black boils gets weaker as winter comes, so this plague is trapped where it won't spread."* So was that it? Food for the rats and *heat for the pestilence?*

But the rats were not the most important features of the place. Near the fire were two pallets, straw flung untidily across them. On each pallet was a body, tied down with rope.

Horrified, Joslin stepped back. He nearly ran screaming from the house, out into the blessed air. But he steeled himself to look.

He approached the nearest. Its face was swollen and there were more swellings at its neck. He knew it by the clothes which he had seen at Randolf's just two nights before. Edward Gaylor.

He loosened the ropes holding Gaylor down. Gaylor tried to sit up, failed and began tearing at his gold-brocaded tunic. When his shoulders were exposed, Joslin saw – there without doubt, staring him in the face – more black swellings of the plague. *Heat for the pestilence?*

He started away in horror. Edward Gaylor tried again to sit up. Joslin bent down and supported him. Gaylor tried to speak.

"Go away. The Devil lives here." His voice dissolved

218

into gasps. Then he tried again. "He's followed me since
. . . I should have died in Cologne. That's what God
meant for me."

He collapsed back into the straw on the pallet. His
eyes closed.

Joslin looked towards the other body, smaller, slighter
and. . .

A shock of sheerest terror and hopeless inevitability
convulsed him. At last he had found Alys. She still
breathed, but she was not conscious. He looked at her
face. No swellings on it. But what terrible boils might
there be on her body, where he could not see?

Behind him the door closed. He heard the latch click
and then the bolt outside shoot across. His stomach
lurched with even greater terror. He was trapped. Now
he was in hot, suffocating, stinking darkness lit by glow-
ing wood and leaping flames.

Like Hell itself.

He took Alys's limp hand and held it. It was warm; he
felt a weak pulse. But there was no sign that she knew
he was there.

Bitter tears flooded his eyes. It was finished. What a
fool he was – so sure he had been following a quarry
when all the time it was he who was the quarry, lured
into this place like the most wide-eyed of little animals.

Everything was finished. There was no way out. All he
could do now was wait for the pestilence to take him, so
he and Alys would die together.

erry had not seen the man with the wonderful hat for some time. When he stopped to look round for him, Perkin became impatient. "What are you doing?" he demanded.

"I'm looking for the man who killed Wulfrum, just like you," Herry answered. He'd say nothing about the hat.

"Don't be daft. You've never seen him," Perkin muttered. "Keep up or I'll leave you behind. You'll be lost on your own, you know you will."

Herry could not deny that. Without Perkin he wouldn't last five minutes. No wonder Perkin and Wulfrum never took him to the tavern. When the ostlers went too, he spent many lonely nights above the stables with only the champing horses below to keep him company.

The loneliness because he was a bit simple, his lot ever since he could remember, dropped on him in the street like a blanket. Loneliness and being laughed at. Only three people of his age had ever tried to be kind.

Alys, Robin and – suddenly Herry's heart expanded with joy. *That's* who the man with the big hat was. *Joslin*. His friend, who'd listened and hadn't laughed. Perkin had come to look for Wulfrum's killer, but *he'd* come to find Joslin. But he'd expected him to carry a harp. Why shouldn't Joslin have found himself a lovely big hat?

Well, he was going to say it. "Perkin, I've just seen Joslin."

Perkin stopped. "Where?"

"Walking along just in front of us."

Perkin peered ahead.

"I can't see him."

"He looks different. He's got a big hat on."

"But he en't got a big hat."

"He has now. It hides his face."

"How do you know it's him then?"

"I just do."

Perkin sniffed and carried on walking. Herry miserably followed, hoping desperately for another, clearer sighting.

"I don't mind admitting I was wrong," said Simon of Chichester. "I was so certain Joslin would go to the gravedigger."

"I wish he had," Randolf replied. "Then we might see some light." His heart, now he was going home with nothing sorted and his time wasted, was heavy. He saw an empty, quiet house and – sudden miserable prospect – years of *not knowing*. Only Lettice would be left and he could never take joy in his painting again.

Joslin let Alys's hand drop and, trembling and swallowing back sharp vomit, felt his way to the bolted door. There was no way it would open. The window shutters also were stuck, sealed from outside. He stumbled round the room, found a stairway and blindly climbed. Not three steps up his head hit the trapdoor which barred it.

He came down and sat on the floor. This was a trap holding every fear he'd ever had. The panic was the same that he'd felt in the tunnel leading into the castle at Stovenham. Then he'd conquered it. Ah, but Alys had been behind him, goading him on. So later, when he was alone, her strength had got him through.

He took a deep breath and forced his shaking to stop. There must be *something* he could do. He had to try, for Alys's sake. The thought of her terror over these last hours flooded in like the sea through a split in a boat's side. She'd been in the dark, in stinking, suffocating heat; tied down, hardly able to breathe, knowing that deadly swellings beyond human power to quell might be taking her body over. But quick – he had to caulk that crack. Such terror did not bear thinking about.

Yet he had to think it – and feel it, too. There was an invisible, silent winged beast which flew about this room. Where it touched, the plague remained. How could he keep out of its way? Anything he did would be puny. But he could at least move and he could shout.

He did, instinctively in his native French. "*M'aidez!*" It fell dead, without echo. Such a little yelp could never pierce these walls.

Well, failing anything else, he would do what he could for these two. He loosed Edward Gaylor's bonds further and undid Alys's altogether. Then he sat back on his heels and wondered.

How long before that flying beast touched him? The pestilence could strike in hours, minutes even. Or days, weeks. Or never. There was no knowing. He'd heard stories of fit, well physicians come to visit the plague-ridden. Even as they watched by their patients, boils had swelled on their own bodies. Before they could leave for the next afflicted house, they had sickened and died. If that were so, he wanted it for himself, quickly, without fear.

With bitterness he remembered yesterday's joyous time, when he went trembling into the orchard. He had his harp, he had words and music in his mind – English lyrics which Guillaume had taught him. "I have sung these," his father once said, a slight smile on his lips. "And, my son, the day will come when you will sing them, too." Yesterday he had known what Guillaume meant.

Now all was changed. This would surely be the only time he would have with Alys, in a house full of Death, to which God brought us all. He remembered his first sight of her, in St Joseph's church in Stovenham, when she roused him from his own terror. At what? At the sight of Death and the Devil on the Doom she and Robin were painting. So his first terror was true after all, because here they both were for real in front of him.

But he would *not* give in to terror, fear, all the things the Devil – and whoever had locked that door – wanted him to feel. No, *this* was his time with Alys. He would try to savour it none the less because plague hovered in the air. He *would* sing, what he had intended to yesterday. It didn't matter that he had no harp. He had the voice God gave him; it would bring beauty to this awful place. It might – if she could hear – bring a little joy to Alys. And for Edward Gaylor – well, he had desired Alys and Joslin did not blame him for that. Perhaps, if he heard, he might say, "Thank you, Joslin. You're singing for me, too."

So he raised his head and sang:

*Between March and April*
*When the spray begins to spring*
*And the little bird opens her heart*
*And boldly starts to sing,*
*For the fairest of all women*
*I live in love-longing*
*For all the joy she'll bring.*

*I am in thrall: I am her own.*
*And in such joy my time is spent*
*That I know from Heaven it has been lent*
*And for no other woman has it been sent*
*But sweet Alys, and her alone.*

Strange. When he had shouted before, his voice was dead, with no echo. But singing, he felt it reverberate round the room, through the walls, shutters and door, so it must sound outside, over London, into the skies above, so the whole world would know of their anguish.

The song was finished. Tears filled his eyes. He wiped them on his sleeve. He wished he could see Alys, know if her eyes were open. He bent down and, daringly, because by now the plague might be well advanced, kissed her on the forehead.

He heard breathing – and he was sure her breath formed faint words. "Thank you, Joslin." In the darkness he saw a glitter. Yes, her eyes *were* open. He felt something on his cheek, like the merest feather. She had lifted her hand and touched him as he knelt.

He rocked back on his haunches. Was this moment in dreadful hot darkness the end of his marriage with Alys – that wondrous, talented, strong, faithful girl whose presence had made his time in England shine?

But then something happened to take his mind even from that. The bolt on the door shot back, the latch clicked and light entered the room as the door was opened.

Herry could never forget that terrible day when they brought the dead Hugh into the house. Everybody had something to do except him. And Joslin. But Joslin had gone up to the apprentices' chamber, and soon Herry heard sounds such as he had never heard before, as if Heaven itself was speaking to him. How could someone with just a voice and that contraption of wood and strings make such beauty as to put Herry nearly in a trance? Fascinated, he came to the stairs. Daringly, he took two steps upwards. Then, abruptly, the wonderful music stopped. Herry dashed down as Joslin descended. There he waited, hoping to hear more. But, no. Instead, they talked together and became friends. But Herry was too shy to ask Joslin to sing again. So he tried hopelessly to recall it, hour after hour.

Yet now, as he walked with Perkin, he seemed faintly to hear Joslin's voice, just the same as before. Now he could remember the music. No, not *remember*. *Hear.* How could this be?

He stopped. "Perkin," he said. "Listen."

"What to?" Perkin growled.

"Joslin singing."

Perkin looked at him with pity. Twopence short of a full shilling? God had short-changed him elevenpence.

And yet – Perkin heard no voice climbing over the street's hubbub. But the figure in front, disappearing into the squat, blank-eyed house on the corner – if you put a cloak over its grey tunic and brown hose and. . .

"*Hey!*" Perkin shouted.

Joslin turned. He knew who it was. He saw the stranger's bright knife; sickeningly he thought of Guillaume's dagger hidden uselessly in Randolf's chamber.

"Face to face at last, eh, Joslin de Lay?" the stranger said.

"Who are you? What do you want with me?"

"Who am I? You'll never know. *What* am I? Perhaps I'll tell you."

He paused. Joslin waited. The stranger looked past him at Alys and Edward Gaylor.

"If not dead yet, then little time more," he said. "And you're doomed as well, Joslin. Now you've been in here, nothing can stop the swellings, the fevers, the agonies, smothering Death coming to you."

Joslin did not reply.

"Why not ask about *me*? Why does the plague leave *me* alone?"

Joslin still refused to speak.

The stranger continued. "Well, you should know that at least. The plague is my friend. I, Joslin, am immortal."

He waited to see the effect of this revelation. Joslin tried not even to blink, whatever inhuman smile on that blank face.

"And why? Because I am a child of the Devil. No more, no less. Nothing that afflicts mortal man can ever touch me. I go wherever and do whatever I want because my master is always with me."

Again, no reply from Joslin. The smile intensified.

"I've walked this world from Barbary to Brittany, Scotland to Spain for many, many years. I've seen such sights, learned such things – strange, terrible knowledge which I've stored up and used when it suited me. I've walked untouched through the plague while it killed everyone round me because I have the Devil's special protection."

No answer. Joslin would not be drawn. He breathed deeply. He needed all his control now.

"And I'll tell you how it came about, Joslin. Once, far away from here, in the very toe of Italy at the height of a long, hot summer, I found a place where the plague returned and took hold again. The folk died in their hundreds round me. I saw the swellings on my body, too. Death was very close. I prayed to God to take the boils away. But then – why pray to *God*? What had *God* done for me? Why was I walking a far country instead of living a peaceful, happy life in England? Because of *God*. Because He let me down, played me false, infected contemptible little men against me. *No*, I thought. *I'll pray to the Devil*. 'Satan,' I cried. 'Release me from this and I'm your faithful servant for ever.' Then in my sleep the Devil with his horns and stings came to me and said, 'You'll survive. From now on nothing can touch you. You'll live for ever. You'll live in peace, rich again in your own country because sooner or later I'll show you the way back. But you must take the chances I give you and do what you must to help yourself. And never forget that the powers of Hell are behind you.' Well, I woke. And see – the swellings were gone. My skin was fair and smooth, my fever abated. The plague had magically left me while others died. The Devil had kept his word. So I waited until my chance came. One day I saw a fellow countryman about to be done to death by thieves. I knew him, Joslin. My master had brought him to me. He *was* showing me the way back. I knew the chance was here. So everything else followed."

"But what did Alys do to you?" Joslin cried. "Or

Thomas or Hugh? Why Wulfrum? Why kill them? Why take away Alys, who had such grief of her own and who harmed nobody? Why me?"

The stranger smiled. "Why not?"

Joslin lost his control. His stomach knotted inside him. He made a sudden blind rush. The stranger merely raised a hard hand and a strong arm to stop him.

"Why you, Joslin? You should first ask why Edward, why Jacob. Because they among many others were the reasons for my exile. What sort of world is it when great men can be brought low by wretches who are little better than serfs?" The stranger's voice had risen to an angry scream. *I am on the edge of knowing everything,* Joslin thought. But then the voice changed; he had collected himself again. "Edward didn't recognize me. *But I knew him.* Fate knows who deserves its favours." He laughed. "But this isn't helping you, is it? Oh, my poor boy. There was no need for you to be even touched. Except that you scratched and scratched at an itching sore not even on your own body. You had nothing to do with this or me until you made it your business. We tried to warn you, Wulfrum and I. Wulfrum did his best to scare you away. So did I; leaving Hugh dead in the street for all to see would have made anyone else run for miles. But not you. In a sort of way, I admire you."

Joslin remembered what Herry said about Hugh. "*He was put there for us to find him.*" How right he'd been. And how strange that the effect had been the opposite. Instead of running away, Joslin had stayed. But there was more to find out.

"So Edward was your first target. But what about the others? Why Alys? I *must* know *why.* I know *how.* I see what happened to Hugh. After Wulfrum threatened me in the night, on your orders, he hid on Robin's bed and then when we were all asleep. . ."

The stranger sniggered again. "A very *deep* sleep, Joslin," he said.

". . .he brought him out to this place. The plague came to Hugh, but still you slit his throat and left him as a warning to me. But what about Thomas? Wulfrum never took him out of Walter Craven's, did he?"

"No, I did. He slept the night out in this house where the plague came in summer and where I kept it going with heat as the weather turned cold. Has nobody but me noticed that when black rats and heat are together, there the plague is also? And I slit his throat to get his dying body out of here. Whether Father Thames threw it out afterwards did not matter. But when you squirrelled away until you'd found it, I knew you'd have to die, too."

"But why slit the throats of men dying of plague already?"

"Joslin, I am master of many ways of Death. I can kill quietly with strange potions I have learnt of in far-away lands, as I did with Gaylor's brother and his wife. I can stripe a sharp blade through throat and between ribs as gently as any surgeon. And, best of all, I can murder people using the very plague that God Himself sent. Is that not power enough? He who kills with works reserved to God as well as weapons of men is in very truth a Devil incarnate. And yet my blade releases my victims as well. Is that not Godlike, Joslin? Am I not indeed merciful?"

Joslin did not want to hear this. He asked a different question. "Was Wulfrum once a serf on your lands?"

"I knew him. A surly oaf, from a line of surly oafish bondmen. Yes, he ran away, just before Edward and his like meddled in my affairs. It wasn't luck that I saw him in the street when I came back to London. My master Satan brought him to me as well – the perfect watchman. Until he wouldn't do the last and most important service. Taking Alys. Then he had to die himself."

"But *why* was taking Alys so important?"

"I'm sorry, Joslin. That's what you'll go to the grave not knowing."

The stranger's voice was insistent. It surged towards Joslin and then died away, surged and died, like sea waves. Joslin was dizzy; sweat broke out on his forehead and soaked his body. Was he coming out in a fever? He swayed, reached out to the wall for support – and the awful fear struck like a sea wave, that the invisible winged beast in the chamber had touched him and the plague was in his body.

Edward Gaylor opened his eyes. He heard voices dimly, far away. He saw his scourge standing near him. He heard that well-remembered, once looked-for voice – and in his extremity he remembered. The voice, the face with features you never remember again – *of course*. Years before, he, Jacob and other minor gentlemen of the Thames Valley got wind of unrest and rebellion among certain great noblemen in their midst. Oh, there was treason afoot – but the rewards could have been great. "Shall we risk all and join in with them?" That was the question.

"No," Jacob had said, "I'd rather keep a head on my shoulders and avoid seeing my insides torn out while I'm still living to give the London mobs an afternoon's entertainment."

And they all agreed, though Edward had felt a whiff of regret. So they got word to the King himself – and his revenge was swift and terrible. Executions and exiles had followed. And this man had been among them. Shortly afterwards, Jacob inherited his own estate and Edward left, because the King did not seem grateful to his informers and there was little enough for him in England.

Now could it be that his actions of years before had caught up with him? How? Why? Then he drifted into a vision clear as day, as complete as living. He was back in Cologne in the lodging house – and into his mind at last came that fateful night he had never managed to remember.

*The wheaten beer was going to Edward Gaylor's head. And something else as well – he had drunk too much many times before and not felt like this. He blinked. His rescuer on the other side of the table seemed now clear, now indistinct, now huge like a bloated fish, now tiny like a perfectly-formed midget. Edward Gaylor fought to keep mind and voice clear.*

*"Tell me your story," said his rescuer.*

*His voice thickening, Edward Gaylor commenced. "I left England because there was nothing for me. My brother had an estate – and a trade as well, while I could never settle to one. Then he married a rich widow with another fine estate left to her and he became twice the gentleman he was before." He laughed in contempt. "The easy way out. Why marry a widow-woman who's past her best and borne her children when there's younger and fairer flesh in the world?"*

*"So you married a fair young wench and she proved too hot for you so you fled?" smiled the rescuer.*

*"Never," said Edward. "I'd seen who I wanted. The ward of a master craftsman and Gild man of London. What a girl. Too young for marriage – but give her a few years and then what a prize! A prize for me. She will be.*

*I* know it." He thumped the table in his passion.

The rescuer smiled. "You're very sure of yourself," he said. "And yet you say there's nothing for you in England."

"Oh, but there could be," Edward Gaylor groaned. "If only my smug brother and his dumpy wife were gone, and then the widow's two sons – why, I'd be the only one left with a claim. I'd gain the smartest estate in England bar what a baron might have. And the widow's sons – why, they've come into their father's good legacies; I'd have their portions as well."

The rescuer surveyed his new friend, eyes narrowed. "And perhaps you could. I know what it is to be landless and fortuneless through a trick of Providence, to be thrown on nothing but your own wits. I could help you."

Edward Gaylor looked at him, his eyes dimmed by sharp-tasting beer – and that strange something else beyond it. "How?" his slurred voice managed.

"Leave it to me. Everything will fall into your lap. I promise you: soon after you're in England all you want will be yours. You'll be a rich gentleman; soon after, a knight, I shouldn't wonder. I'll make it so."

"You? How can you?"

The rescuer smiled. "I can do anything I want. If I say it will happen, it will happen."

Edward peered at this miracle-worker through hazy eyes. "And will I marry the girl?"

"That's for you to manage. But I've yet to meet the woman who'll say no to wealth."

Edward cried a self-pitying tear. "If I can't have her, I don't want my wealth."

"Don't worry," said the rescuer.

Edward breathed a deep sigh of satisfaction.

"But I think you'll agree that if I do all this for you, I

deserve something in return."

"Yes, you do," Edward cried.

"Then I'll put this to you. Do you promise that you'll leave all your possessions, all your lands after you're dead, to me?"

"To you?" Edward tried to get his mind round this idea.

"Yes. To me. It's the least I deserve for securing them for you in the first place. Besides, what use will they be to you when you're dead?"

Edward had to agree. "None," he said.

"Then that's settled," said the rescuer.

Through the fogs of Edward's brain, something awkward tried to pierce. "Wait a minute," he cried. "What about my wife and all the children I will have? The law says my goods must pass to them."

"Not if you make a will saying otherwise."

"But why should I?"

"Because if you do not, you will never be a rich man."

Even in his stupor, Edward knew the threat in that. But his fuddled mind made him silly. "I could make a will leaving it all to you. And then, afterwards, I could make another one leaving it to them."

The rescuer looked at him thoughtfully.

"In fact," Edward recklessly continued, "I could make a will leaving it to my wife-to-be when we are betrothed. In fact, I could will it to her before we are betrothed."

"Yes," said his rescuer. "You could, couldn't you!"

In his last moments, Edward Gaylor had a moment of complete, awful clarity. He saw the whole game. Black arts culled from strange places as well as wheaten beer had blanked his mind. He had already consigned Jacob, Cicely, Thomas and Hugh to murder. With that last stupid remark, he had signed Alys's death warrant as

233

well as his own. He cried aloud in anguish. And then he was back in the lodging house.

He had come to a huge decision. "I want to write," he cried.

"No," said his rescuer. "You're not well enough. I'll write for you."

He called for pen, ink and parchment and wrote busily in a clear, neat hand for a long time. Then he looked up. "Finished," he said. He passed it over to Edward.

The words meant nothing. "You have no Latin?" smiled his rescuer. "Don't worry. Every lawyer in Christendom has it. Let me read aloud in English what I have written."

So he did, and it sounded good to Edward Gaylor.

"Tomorrow," said his rescuer, "we'll go to the notary for this to be witnessed and sealed, to make it legal all over Christendom. And then all you desire will come to pass. Do nothing – just watch and wait. But first I must know names and places, because without them your ambitions can't happen."

So Edward blabbed out all his business and the rescuer listened carefully. And then he said, "You're lucky. You're being served by a man who is immortal. So what can go wrong for you except the death which comes in time to everyone but me?"

Then Edward's head hit the table in a dead swoon. The next he knew, he woke, head splitting, the night lost, no memory of what he'd done, to a new day. England and fortune called.

And now, with so bitter a memory to leave this earth with, Edward Gaylor died, his body destroyed by plague as much as his mind was ravaged by foolishness, regret and greed.

* * *

Joslin had collapsed; he half-sat, half-leant against the wall. The stranger stood over him, laughing. This was the end. So often it had loomed close these last weeks; now it was really here. Nothing could take it away.

Through the open door Herry could see Joslin. He looked near dead.

Perkin was behind Herry. "Come here," he shouted and tried to pull him back by the shoulders. But then he saw who else was there – and Perkin was back in the dim-lit tavern with Wulfrum.

With a howl of rage he sprang on the creature who had murdered his friend. But Herry was in the way, screaming, "You've hurt Joslin." He clawed hopelessly at this stranger, and then there was a blade's bright flash, Herry gasped in a quiet, surprised way and fell to the ground. Blood seeped through his tunic from his chest.

Now Perkin was beside himself, with the strength of three. "You've killed *both* my friends," he roared. With his left hand he seized the stranger's wrist. The knife clattered to the floor. Perkin's thumbs were on the stranger's throat and squeezing. Yet the stranger just smiled, as if all Perkin's strength was of no account. Then, with a heave upwards which even Perkin could not counter, he sent him staggering backwards. As the man picked up his knife, that smile turned into a shrill laugh of triumph which made Perkin think he was fighting with the Devil himself.

Something in Joslin's mind said "No!" He would not let his eyes close. He would not give in. Not in Stovenham, not here, not anywhere. Besides, something strange was happening. Figures grappled and writhed in front of

235

him. One fell: Joslin saw a knife thrusting and then the brightness of blood. Two still struggled. Shouts, grunts and sudden weird laughter filled the air.

Had fortune magically changed? He couldn't leave this to others, whoever they were. He lunged forward as one figure rose up and the other staggered backwards. He hooked a weakening arm round the rising figure's neck. The face turned – and his tormentor's fierce eyes stared and made him blink with their force.

Joslin wilted. That shining blade was in front of his eyes. The voice spoke. "You will never leave things well alone, will you, Joslin de Lay? So now the time has come to pay."

The stranger drew his blade back to slide it between Joslin's ribs. Vainly, Joslin clawed with failing hands. *This is my last living action*, he thought as his fingers hooked into the grey tunic and pulled it away.

The cloth was rough but it was loose on the man's body. It came away enough to expose shoulder and armpit. And, though Joslin's eyes were dimming fast, he knew exactly what he was seeing. Like a sparrow's tiny egg, though black, a boil was rising. Round it, blotches like bruises were spreading.

His tormentor stared down as well, at his own skin. Disbelief nearly blinded him. The knife clattered on the ground.

Randolf and Simon had not yet parted. Passing a small house on a corner, they were dimly aware of a scuffle round the back. *None of our business*, they thought.

Then Randolf heard angry voices. "You've hurt Joslin!"

Then, "You've killed *both* my friends."

How many times had he heard those voices wherever

there was work to be done? Before Simon could stop him he bounded round to where they came from.

Herry lay on the ground. Someone indistinct in the shadows sprawled against the wall. Behind, in near darkness, lay two bodies. In front, Perkin seemed to be killing somebody. Then he staggered backwards, the figure he was killing stood up, then the shadow by the wall stood as well and the first figure turned away to it.

Randolf seized Perkin. He panted, then struggled to be free. "You should let me finish the rat," he shouted.

But Randolf saw no menacing killer in front of him; rather, a shivering creature almost unable to stand and a deathly pale, sweating face. The man tore desperately at his grey tunic. *Rip, rip, rip* – the rough cloth came away from shoulders and chest. What his skin showed was clear to everyone. He turned his face upwards and howled like a dog. "*Why do you forsake me? You gave me your word.*"

Before they could stop him he had burst past, running away along Adel Lane and then down Wood Street towards the river. Within a minute he was lost in the press of people.

Randolf and Simon surveyed the sight. Two bodies lay on pallets. One lay dead of the plague – Gaylor. Another seemed dead – Alys. Tears rushed to Randolf's eyes. He turned to Simon and the coroner supported him for long minutes while grief ran its course. Herry lay dead, freshly stabbed. Perkin's grief was for him. Joslin was propped against the wall. His fever was growing.

Simon spoke to Perkin. "Go to St Olave's church. Fetch priest and gravedigger, then find the constables. These bodies must be buried. And then this dreadful house must be burned to the ground."

Without a word, Perkin left.

Randolf stooped again to Alys. He folded her arms across her chest and stood back. He was in a pit of despair.

Then a weak voice spoke. "Randolf, I'm not dead." Alys tried to sit up, failed and sank back on the pallet.

Randolf cried aloud, "*God, don't mock me!*"

Alys spoke again. "Randolf, I have a fever. I've no memory of anything since I sat in the orchard. *But I'm not dead.*"

Randolf brought himself to look. Alys was deathly pale and too weak to rise – but it was true. She was not dead – yet.

Simon's mind was in turmoil. What had he just seen? *A face so unmemorable he could not forget it* – his thought when he first heard of this stranger. Now he saw for himself – and yes, he did remember.

It was twelve years ago now. The wars in France were taxing the people grievously. More than one group of knights and nobles grumbled in secret. Some plotted against the King – until the victory at Poitiers made the whole land happy. But many were tired of feeding Edward's ambition to be King of France as well as England. Well, Simon was fresh down from Peterhouse in Cambridge then, a young man with a way to make in the world. He had come to London to the Inns of Court to study the law and then take Government service. And he'd seen a group of angry, tax-ridden barons and knights brought to London to be tried in Westminster Hall for treason and conspiracy against the King. Men he thought that England would be foolish to discard. But how should he know the rights and wrongs of the case? Well, some were beheaded, others exiled, their lands confiscated by the King. Now he remembered that one face – bearded then but, he was certain, the very same. A face so featureless, so – what was the word? – *neutral*, that one should never remember it again. Yet its sheer lack of expression burst through the bounds of forgetta-bility so it was the one face which stayed in his mind. Never seen again – until today, in an evil house of Death. Sir Guy Spufford, of Thame in Oxfordshire. Dispossessed, exiled, thrown out of the land of his birth, never to return on pain of immediate execution.

Yet here he was, back again. Why? Did he think that with that face nobody would recognize him? Well, *he* had. But Simon of Chichester could never understand people's minds, especially when his job decreed he should only take interest in them when they were dead.

"*This cannot be*. Why have you brought me to this when you said you would not?" Thus the stranger cried aloud as he pushed through the crowds. He tried to summon up the thought of his master. But no, his mind stayed blank. No comforting vision of the Devil's grinning face appeared. Not even a glimpse of hell. Just a great white nothing.

The heat and itch of swelling skin were too great to bear. Streets passed under his faltering feet – Milk Street, Bread Street, Salt Wharf. At last he stood over Queenhithe and saw the Thames itself, dark and bitter cold but infinitely welcoming.

Only then, in its depths, did he see the Devil's face.

Alys and Joslin were brought gently back to Randolf's. Alys was left in her chamber while Joslin was placed alone in a small room on a specially made up bed. A physician was called to both and said gravely to Lettice, "I've seen this too often. The stars in their conjunctions

239

are against them. The boils will come, be sure of that, and then all's lost."

Lettice said nothing. There was too much grief in this place.

For two nights and days, fever raged. Joslin moaned and cried out grievously while Lettice watched. On the third morning, he woke.

He sat up. His brow was dry, the heat gone from his body. He felt no pain. Gingerly, he felt the skin round his neck and armpits. All was smooth. There were no swellings.

The stars were wrong. The plague seemed to have looked and decided not to take him. Lettice saw he was near to himself again, and brought him news from Alys's chamber. "Her fever's gone, too. It's not God's will that either of you die yet."

When Randolf knew this and after he had given thanks, he said, "Physicians know nothing. Plague and fever don't go together. I believe Spufford gave Alys a deadly unction of his own when he took her and Joslin was too highly wrought with all that's happened to him over the last weeks to avoid a fever in that dreadful place."

There was nobody to say he was wrong.

Joslin was at least able to see Wulfrum, Edward Gaylor and Herry buried, all in the churchyard of St Olave's by the old priest who had done the same for Hugh. He stood behind Randolf and Lettice and next to Alys. He knew that he would soon have much to say to her.

Three days after Guy Spufford's name had occurred to Simon of Chichester, the same boatmen who found Thomas were, as then, about their business in the early morning. The river was cold, the sky overcast and a fine drizzle chilled their faces.

"Look over there," said the steersman.

A body floated face down. They hauled it aboard, laid it face upward on the planking and gasped at the staring eyes and gaping mouth. "He was seeing the torments of Hell," the steersman whispered.

The other was looking at where the dead man had pulled the grey tunic away in his agony and exposed his shoulders and upper arms.

"Look," he said. "Another with the pestilence on him."

"He drowned himself rather than suffer such an end," said the steersman. "No one's slit his throat."

"And who can blame him?" said the other. "Surely God won't."

They were through London Bridge by now. "Another for the Tower," said the steersman.

"What's this?" said the other.

Something poked out of a pocket inside the tunic. He pulled it out.

"Parchment," he said and peered closely at it. "I think there was writing on it once."

"Well, there isn't now," said the steersman. "Let's be rid of this freight as soon as we can."

So their boat came to the Tower, leaving the Latin words, two signatures, the notary's seal and the seal of the city of Cologne dissolved somewhere in the great maw of Father Thames himself.

# EPILOGUE

Two days later Joslin asked Alys his much-delayed question. She was quiet for some time before she answered. Joslin's heart beat fast.

At last she spoke. "Joslin, if you'd asked me when Randolf wanted you to, I would have said yes joyfully. Ever since Robin died, you've meant more to me than I could ever tell you. But now. . ."

"What?" Joslin asked, knowing what she was going to say.

"Now, all's changed. We've come through the plague. We could have died together in that dreadful house. But we didn't. Why not? God wanted us here. There's more for us to do yet."

Joslin remembered Will of Essex. "*The plague left some people alone while all those round them died.*" This must have been God's will.

"Of course," he replied. "He wants us to marry."

"No," Alys answered. "He wants you to go to Wales to find your mother. That's why you came to England. It's your destiny."

"What about you?"

"He has a purpose for me. I don't know what it is. Perhaps another man will come with a marriage offer. Perhaps I'll love him as I loved Robin – and might have loved you. Perhaps no man will. Perhaps I'll live as a spinster and run Randolf's business when he's gone."

"And paint, as Robin taught you?" said Joslin.

"Yes. Nobody would dare stop me then. Or perhaps I'll go to a nunnery. That's a good life for a woman tired of the ways of men."

Joslin heard all this and grief rose in him. He grasped her hands and cried aloud, "*No*, Alys. We were spared the plague to marry."

"Maybe, but not each other. All your life, you'd chafe and in the end you'd resent me. You'd wonder what might have been. You'd never rest. I'd see that and be sad for you. I couldn't bear it."

She was smiling slightly. "Joslin," she said. "I release you."

"But I don't want to be released," Joslin cried.

"Yes, you do. And one day you'll know it."

Joslin went to bed that night more miserable and empty than he could remember. But when he woke up, he knew she was right. He vowed he would never mention it again.

A workshop with but three apprentices and one labourer was a poor place. Randolf seemed a broken man. Within the space of a fortnight he had lost Robin and seen Hugh, Wulfrum and Herry placed in the ground. Work was neglected and the apprentices kicked their heels in the workshop. Joslin visited Will of Essex and brought back his clothes and harp – but his joy in the visit was tempered by the thought *Alys doesn't want me.* Meals in the hall were sombre affairs; Joslin was only called to play when Randolf wanted songs of quiet and comfort.

The weather worsened. October passed and foggy November, then frosty December. The winter struck deep; the roads from London were hard and the land hostile. He could not move until the seasons changed.

Perkin and the ostlers came into the hall to eat at the Christmas feast for company's sake and sat awkward and silent. There was an honoured guest, though – Will of Essex joined them and Randolf saw a firm friend in the thoughtful gravedigger. Joslin played and sang to take them out of themselves and feel some of the season's joy. But he kept thinking that he could have been married to Alys by now and this Christmas would have been the first of many.

Yet in his heart he knew this was wrong. It should have been Robin's Christmas. Besides, however he might have loved Alys, she was right. He would have chafed here. His horizons were not in London.

Christmas came, and the new year. In January the snows were deep. February brought more snow and bitter winds, wild March came with harsh rains. But spring started at last. Joslin watched the sun sink in the west and remembered John Hammond on the quay at Ipswich. "*Follow the sun and sing your way to Wales.*" Yes, now he must leave.

But he hesitated. How could he tell them?

Randolf made it easy. "I shall go on a pilgrimage," he said.

Where to? Canterbury? Walsingham? The Holy Land?

"A short one, but necessary," he continued. "To Stovenham, to Robin's grave. I shall raise a great tomb and pay for masses to be sung for him for thirty years.

Lettice and Alys will come with me. Come to Stovenham as well, Joslin."

*Yes, I will,* Joslin thought. *I'd see Gyll again.* Then: *no, I can't go back. I have to go onwards. Alys is right. My destiny's not come yet.*

"I'm sorry, Randolf. It's time I was on my own way," he said.

"Ah, well, lad, I knew you'd go in the end," said Randolf. "Don't worry about us. We'll start afresh. I'm looking for a new apprentice and two labourers. New commissions will come with the warmer weather. I want to paint again, just as you want to sing." He laughed. "So does Alys. She and Robin could never keep a secret from me. I'll let her loose in the workshop."

That night they gave him a farewell feast; he sang with a light heart. Next morning, clothes roll packed, harp on his back, locket round his neck, body-belt round his waist – lighter by three shillings that he gave towards the cost of Robin's tomb – and with Guillaume's dagger returned, he was ready.

"One last gift," said Randolf. One of the ostlers led out the piebald horse that Robin had ridden to Stovenham and Joslin had ridden back. "You'll need more than shoe leather for the miles you're going."

Joslin stammered out his thanks – then: "I shall call him Herry, in memory of a good, faithful friend," he said.

Randolf and Lettice, Alys, William, John and Alexander, Perkin and the two ostlers smiled. Seeing them there, he nearly stayed after all. But his possessions went into two panniers, Perkin pushed him up on the horse, Randolf gave it a slap on the flanks and it walked out of the courtyard into Silver Street. Joslin turned for a final look – and knew he was seeing Alys's face for the last time and that he'd never forget it.

245

So he left Silver Street, to head along Bowyer's Row, through Ludgate, across Fleet Bridge and away from the city walls past the King's city of Westminster. A strange delight filled his heart. He thought of Wales, land of legend and heroes, music and mountains. Yet also he remembered Gyll, alone in a castle many miles behind him.

Then he urged the piebald horse called Herry into a trot and looked forward to what fortune might bring him.

*Another horseman watched from a vantage point a little way off as Joslin crossed Fleet Bridge.*

*"I thought I'd lost you," he said to himself. "Well, there are long roads to travel and many miles to pass before you and I finally meet."*

*And, lest Joslin should see him and remember, he held his cloak in front of his sallow face to hide the pock-marks and twisted mouth.*

**Here ends the second story concerning
Joslin de Lay's journey to Wales.**

# AUTHOR'S NOTE

The London Joslin came to was much different from the London of today. The cities of London and Westminster were separate, with green fields between them. Peasants tilled the broad acres round the little villages of Hackney, Islington and Tottenham. Inside London's walls, less than fifty thousand people lived – though as the total space was no more than a square mile it was very crowded. Many of the old street names still remain, others have long disappeared. St Paul's had a tall spire then, not a dome. The Thames was full of salmon and shellfish. The city walls stretched almost intact since Roman times and the great city gates guarded the people from the perils outside.

So where have they all gone? Medieval London disappeared one terrible night in 1666 – the night of the Great Fire. So all the tall wooden houses, the taverns and workshops, the churches, St Paul's cathedral itself and even the paintings like those Randolf and his apprentices were so proud to finish would indeed have turned to ash along with everything else. So what it was really like in the fourteenth century is something that we can only imagine.

One thing I must make clear before people dismiss me as an ignoramus. Yes, I know it looks as though the ballad Joslin sings on his first night in London should be called *Lay la Freine*. But medieval French was as different from modern French as Middle English was from modern English and the edition I possess of the medieval text is quite clear that the title is *Lay le Freine*. So please don't write to me about it!

DENNIS HAMLEY